COMING HOME TO ROSEFORD VILLAS

FAY KEENAN

B

Boldwood

First published in Great Britain in 2024 by Boldwood Books Ltd.

Copyright © Fay Keenan, 2024

Cover Design by Alice Moore Design

Cover Photography: Shutterstock

A CIP catalogue record for this book is available from the British Library.

Paperback ISBN 978-1-80280-591-8

Large Print ISBN 978-1-80280-592-5

Hardback ISBN 978-1-80280-590-1

Ebook ISBN 978-1-80280-594-9

Kindle ISBN 978-1-80280-593-2

Audio CD ISBN 978-1-80280-585-7

MP3 CD ISBN 978-1-80280-586-4

Digital audio download ISBN 978-1-80280-589-5

Boldwood Books Ltd
23 Bowerdean Street
London SW6 3TN
www.boldwoodbooks.com

For Nick, who proved that long distances were actually surmountable.

PROLOGUE

He's leaving tonight. I don't know how I'm going to make it through tomorrow, the next day, and after, without him. I know it's for the best, but there's a huge part of me that just wants to beg him to stay. There's so much I wish I could tell him, but I can't. His bloody, bloody parents! Why do they have to do this? Why can't he at least stay with his aunt and uncle? OK, so they're miles away, too, but we'd still have been in the same country! I feel I'm being ripped apart, and nothing will ever make that go away.

We've promised to email and MSM every day. But is that enough? I know he says he'll be back for uni, but that's another two years away, and what if he meets someone else out there? Some fit, surfer type who'll make him forget all about me? I don't think I'll survive if that happens. I'm so scared of losing him...

— FROM THE DIARY OF AURORA
HENDERSON, AGED SIXTEEN

I will come back to you, my darling, darling F. I'll find a way. And we will find a way to spend the rest of our lives forgetting about all this un-pleasantness. The storm is about to break, I can sense it. It won't be much longer until the ship sails and I'm back where I belong, with you. Have faith, dear F, if you can still trust in God, that He will find a way to end this, and end our separation. The thought of returning to your arms sustains me through these long, un-ending nights...

— LETTER FROM EDMUND
TRELOAR, JANUARY 1915 (UNSENT)

1

If Rory Dean had included this scenario in the opening chapter of her yet-to-be-written novel, she would have cut it as being far too convenient. The timing, it had to be admitted, was eerily perfect. The last school bell of the year had chimed its irritating *Peppa Pig*-like tune, which usually for Rory and the rest of the large secondary school where she worked would be the most exhilarating moment of the year. Unfortunately, the chirruping of the bell had coincided with her phone emitting a received message ping – the contents of which had been most unwelcome.

We regret to inform you that we have had to cancel your booking at Hyacinth Cottage. However, Airbnb is delighted to offer an alternative, at a substantial discount to compensate you for the lateness of this cancellation. If you choose to take up this alternative booking, you will be able to check in after 1 p.m. on Saturday.

Lateness! That was putting it mildly, Rory thought. She was due to drive three hundred-odd miles from her flat in York down to Somerset that very evening. She'd packed her bag the night before and now, having tidied the desk in her classroom, picked up a bag of exercise books, washed out her absolutely filthy coffee cup and replaced it in the department office, all she had to do was head home, remind her flatmate that she was going away and head down a succession of motorways until she got to her destination. Now she didn't even know what that destination was.

Slamming the door of her classroom a little harder than she intended and forcing a smile as a large number of students surged past her, wishing her, 'Happy summer holidays, Miss,' she hurried out to her car. This was meant to be six weeks of a complete change of scene – getting away from York to the rolling hills of Somerset and, for the first time in a long time, forgetting that she was a teacher. For six weeks that summer she was going to be Rory Dean, writer. The fact that she hadn't actually written anything since she was in her teens, well, nothing serious, anyway, wasn't going to stop her from spending the summer holiday acting out the fantasy that she was the novelist she'd always aspired to be.

Unfortunately, losing the booking on the Airbnb cottage that she'd secured in the dark cold days of a January winter was a major fly in the ointment. The cottage had been intended to be a total retreat for her, away from the inevitable chaos of her flat share and the frantic workload that being a secondary school teacher entailed. The sleepy Somerset village of Roseford could not be further from her hectic life. And Hyacinth Cottage would have been the perfect place to get started on a project that she'd had in the back of her mind for years. Now, it seemed that wasn't to be.

'Shit!' Rory couldn't help banging the steering wheel in absolute frustration. Then, realising she'd been spotted by one of the assistant heads, also beating a hasty retreat to their own car, she forced another smile and wound down her window.

'How can it be the end of term, and I've still got a bucket load of marking to do before we get back in September?'

The assistant head smiled and offered her condolences before heading briskly to her own car. Gathering what was left of her wits, Rory started the engine and drove swiftly off the premises of the large secondary school where she worked, breathing a sigh of relief as she left. She loved her job as an English teacher, and was happy at her school, but she also felt a sense of relief that she was able to put the day job behind her and focus on something else. She'd worked incredibly hard this year, as always, but with a slightly different goal in mind. And now, despite the last-minute change of accommodation, the anticipation of more than a month of creative freedom was enough to raise her spirits as she drove home.

Later that evening, excitement battled, once again, with disappointment. She'd wanted the perfect retreat, and Hyacinth Cottage, while pricey, had been it. A small, one-bedroom place just off the high street of historic Roseford in Somerset, it had cost a fortune to rent for the summer holiday, but Rory had saved hard all year for that exact purpose. It was now or never, she thought, to write something for herself. It was an indulgence she'd fantasised about for years, and she had been on the verge of achieving. But now, the shine had tarnished. Instead of a pretty cottage to herself, she'd been offered a different option, albeit at a third of the price of Hyacinth Cottage. But it wouldn't be the same.

Rory was inclined to just cancel the booking – after all, she could write anywhere, couldn't she? – but she knew she'd struggle to find anywhere else at such short notice. All of the holiday cottages in the entire South West would have been booked up months ago, or if they hadn't, they'd cost a fortune now. And the thought of slobbing around the flat for the break, staring at the walls and just doing what she'd done every single other summer holiday, cleaning and panicking about her marking, just didn't appeal.

'Everything OK, hon?' The voice of Alex, her flat-mate, coming in from work, broke into her gloom.

Rory gave a brief grin. 'Oh, you know.'

'I thought you'd be long gone by now?' Alex flumped down on the sofa next to Rory and grabbed a slice of the pizza that Rory had been picking at.

Briefly, Rory filled her in on the change of plans.

'The worst of it is that I was really looking for-ward to living in Hyacinth Cottage for the summer and being totally on my own – no offence intended,' she added hurriedly. 'This place I've been offered isn't exactly the same.'

'None taken,' Alex replied. 'Frankly, I was kind of looking forward to getting rid of you, too!'

'Thanks,' Rory said dryly. 'So do you think I should still go?'

Alex paused a fraction too long. 'Of course you should.'

'Were you, er, planning on *company*, when I was away?' Rory asked, sensing Alex's reticence.

'Well, Luca was going to spend some time here,' Alex admitted. 'Since we'd, you know, have the place to ourselves. But I can always go to his place...' Alex trailed off.

Rory felt sympathy for her friend. The prohibitive cost of rent in York, as in all cities of the UK, meant that people in their thirties like them were more often than not sharing accommodation with at least one other person, if not a few. She and Alex had maintained a happy and harmonious flat share for a few years now, but she knew, eventually, if things with Luca worked out, that Alex would want him to move in, and then there would be three of them in a flat that was barely big enough for two. It was another reason why she'd wanted to escape to Somerset and be on her own for the summer holidays: to play house and imagine what it would be like to be in her very own home, even if that was just an illusion. She knew she should have been saving the cash, just in case she needed it as a deposit for another place to live, but the pull to get away was just too strong.

'No, you don't have to do that,' Rory said. She knew how much Alex and Luca wanted an uninterrupted few weeks. 'I mean, how bad can it be? The place they've sent me seems nice, and it's a third of the price of the cottage. That's not a bad deal, really.'

'Well, if you're sure...' Alex replied. 'I don't want you to feel as though you're being chucked out of your own home, hon.'

Rory leaned over and hugged Alex. 'I don't. You enjoy the alone time with Luca. It'll all be fine, I'm sure.' She got off the sofa and bade Alex goodnight. She might have sounded cheery when she'd reassured her friend, but as she got into bed a bit later, she couldn't help wondering what she was going to be getting into the next day.

2

The next morning, Rory checked her packed bags for the fifteenth time and dithered. She'd not slept particularly well but couldn't work out if that was through nerves or disappointment. She'd never been away from home for this long before, except for when she'd been at university, and the thought of being three hundred-odd miles away in a strange place for such an extended period of time was making her anxious all of a sudden. She berated herself for her daftness: people her age, and younger, travelled the world, for goodness' sake! They set off with a backpack and a passport and disappeared for months, years even. She was talking about a few weeks in the

West Country; it was hardly the other side of the world.

'Are you all set?' Alex's voice broke into her reverie.

Rory nodded. 'I think so.' She resisted the urge to check her bags and her backpack, where her newish MacBook Air laptop was securely stashed.

'Well, I'm heading out to the supermarket, so I'll say goodbye now.'

The two friends hugged, and, ridiculously, Rory fought the urge to cry. 'I'll see you soon,' she said rather shakily.

'Not too soon, I hope!' Alex smiled as they released each other. 'I hope you love every minute of your solitude. Make the most of it.'

'I will.' Even though she and Alex were close, Rory hadn't confided her plan to begin her novel during her time away. She wanted to keep it to herself, as her own special, secret thing, at least until she'd made some progress.

As Alex left her room once more, Rory unzipped her backpack again and, almost compulsively, checked to see if the ziplock bag she'd put right at the back of it was still in place. She felt a frisson of excitement as her fingers touched the spines of the four A5 notebooks that were inside. Those were what she'd hoped to seek inspiration from during these next few weeks: they were vital to her plot. She'd shied away from looking at them after she'd uncovered them at her parents' place, for fear of losing her enthusiasm, but she was now itching to crack the spines open and immerse herself in their contents. But not yet. Not until she was in Somerset and away from her 'normal' life.

Zipping up the backpack once more, she began shifting her bags down to her car, and in a little more time she was on the road. The journey, long as it was, would be fairly straightforward, but she needed to get going. She only hoped she wouldn't be too disappointed with the change of accommodation when she arrived.

* * *

After a brief stop halfway, Rory finally reached Roseford mid-afternoon. It was too late for lunch, but too early for dinner, and her stomach growled. She'd had a coffee and a Danish pastry at the services, but that seemed a long time ago now. She suppressed a flare of irritation that she should be cooking her own dinner in the beautifully cosy kitchen she'd been looking forward to at Hyacinth Cottage but decided that she needed to stop dwelling on it. The alternative accommodation did, at least, have cooking facilities, so it wasn't as if she couldn't whip something up.

Roseford was beautiful in any weather, but in the late days of July it looked at its best. The shortbread-coloured stone buildings that lined either side of the main street gave off their own warmth in the strong summer sun, and were a perfect foil for the hanging baskets of petunias that tumbled and showed off their vibrant pinks, purples and reds. The entrance to Roseford Hall, the stately home that had been taken over by the British Heritage Fund a few years back, had its wrought-iron gates open, and a quick glance as she passed told Rory that it was busy. The car park was rammed, and there were tourists ambling both in the village and around the house itself.

As she drove down the main street, eyes peeled for the accommodation that she'd been booked into, Rory noticed a charming café, perfect for sipping on a latte while tapping away at her laptop, she thought, a pub, the Treloar Arms, and various other charming independent stores, including a clothing shop, Roseford Reloved, and a general store. There certainly would be plenty to look at during her stay, and lots of time to experience it all.

But where was this place she was looking for?

Feeling crosser by the second, Rory slowed down, worried that she might have missed it. The annoying ping of Google Maps repeating 'you have reached your destination' grated on her after such a long journey, especially when she was sure she hadn't already passed it. Reaching the end of the main street, she slowed down to take the corner, which would eventually lead out of the village, and a brisk hoot from the car behind her made her jump. Holding up a hand in apology, Rory pulled the car over so they could get past her, and then looked more closely at the sat nav on her phone. Where *was* it?

Just as she was about to give the contact number a ring, she caught sight of a tiny little lane, shooting off to the right of the main street. Could that be where it was? Taking a chance, and hoping against hope, she swung the car out and meandered up the lane, looking left and right as she did so. Then, giving a sigh of relief, she noticed a white sign with black lettering swinging slightly in the summer breeze, right at the top of the lane. That *must* be it.

'At last,' Rory muttered, praying the place had off-street parking. She didn't fancy lugging her cases and bags all the way up the hill if she had to park in the village.

Thankfully, as she drew closer, she saw that the

road widened, and there was indeed a driveway that looked as though she could park on it. And as she turned in, she had to admit, rather reluctantly, that it looked lovely. It might not be Hyacinth Cottage, but Roseford Villas looked friendly and inviting, with its light stone frontage, mullioned windows and well-kept front garden.

Rory tucked her car as close to the front wall as she could, and then decided that she'd get inside before she unpacked. Stretching wearily as she got out of the car, she headed up to the dark blue-painted front door and pushed the bell. She was looking forward to getting to her accommodation and setting herself up, and hopefully having a cup of tea and relaxing for an hour or two before making plans for the next few days.

For a minute or two, no one answered. Feeling slightly impatient, and her need for a cuppa beginning to become more insistent, Rory pushed the bell again, wondering if it wasn't working and she ought to knock instead. She sighed. She just wanted to get in now. Standing on the doorstep like a lemon after travelling for most of the day hadn't been part of the plan. But then Roseford Villas hadn't been part of the plan until late yesterday, either. Despite herself, the exasperation crept up on her again.

Rory pushed the bell a third time. This was getting stupid. She was about to look the contact number back up and give them an assertive phone call when the door finally opened. And there, standing on the other side of it, was someone she'd once have given anything to see in front of her, but now, twenty years later, was the last person in the world she'd ever have expected to see again.

3

To say that Leo McKendrick wasn't having a good day was an understatement. In fairness, this whole year had been a bit of a car crash, and he didn't make that comparison lightly. A warning twinge in his back as he headed towards the front door of Roseford Villas was more than a reminder.

'I'm coming,' Leo muttered. He knew there was a last-minute guest – the Airbnb app had pinged yesterday afternoon to signal the acceptance of alternative accommodation by a Rory Dean, whoever they were, and he'd been working ever since to spruce up what had been offered and accepted. Just when he'd thought he was going to have a few days free, his plans for a quiet time had been thwarted.

He knew it wasn't the guest's fault: cancellations happened all the time, as did last-minute bookings. It was a benefit and also an irritation of the internet, and, while he was in charge of Roseford Villas, he'd had to learn very quickly how it all worked. It wasn't as if custodianship of a guest house in the back end of Somerset had been in the plan, after all. But did they have to keep ringing the bloody doorbell? Rory Dean was probably yet another London tourist, he assumed, coming down to the South West for a change of scene and a so-called 'slower pace'. Swanning around the pretty village of Roseford like they owned it; imagining it all to be some Cath Kidston-decorated rural idyll...

He stopped himself, yet again, from going down that ranting avenue. He was hardly a dyed-in-the-wool local, he reminded himself. He'd been co-opted into Roseford Villas as a favour, and he himself had desperately needed the change of scene after the events of the past year. Maybe he needed to cool his head a bit.

At thirty-seven years old, Leo was, even putting it charitably, in the grip of a mid-life crisis. He'd come to Roseford four months ago after relocating from Melbourne's sunnier climes. But missing the British weather that he'd grown up with wasn't the reason he'd ended up back in the UK. Melbourne had been home for the best part of two decades, but he could quite conclusively say there was nothing to call home about it now. His career was over, and his personal life... well, now he was just back to car crash analogies.

He was also self-aware enough to know that he wasn't a natural B&B host. He'd struggled to adapt to the precision and dedication that running a smart establishment in a tourist village entailed and had often been exasperated by the huge binder of instructions that his aunt and uncle had left him, with tips, tricks and procedures for every last damned thing. But, over time, he'd begun to adapt and get into a routine, and had even played host to a few visitors since his aunt and uncle had departed on their 'pre-retirement recce' of desirable residences in Spain. He'd promised them he'd look after Roseford Villas in their absence, and he was determined to do just that.

With that more positive thought in mind, he clicked the lock on the front door and pulled it open. He'd get this guest settled and then try to get his head around the job offer he'd been sent by the London firm. London was his future, when all was said and done. Roseford was just a convenient stop-gap.

'Hi,' he said, forcing a note of cheer into his voice. 'How was your trip?'

And as the person on the other side of the door raised her eyes from her phone, Leo was knocked sideways by the shock of recognition.

'Aurora?' he said, cursing the note of surprise in his tone. 'Aurora Henderson?'

It was some compensation that the woman on the doorstep seemed as flummoxed as he was. He watched as her eyes widened, and a flash of colour warmed her pale cheeks.

'It's Rory Dean these days, actually,' she replied, and Leo marvelled at how steady her voice seemed. And familiar. The kind of familiar that made something in his chest ache. Or maybe that was just hearing the change of name.

'Come in.' Leo gathered what was left of his wits and gestured through to the hallway. 'What, er, what brings you to Roseford Villas?'

'My Airbnb cottage got cancelled at the last minute,' Aurora – Rory – replied as she walked through the door. 'The company offered me the chalet in the garden here. It was a rate I couldn't refuse.' She paused in the hallway and her direct, green-eyed stare regarded him levelly. 'What are *you* doing here?'

'Looking after this place for my aunt and uncle while they're on a European retirement tour.' Leo, to his surprise, managed a grin. 'Only for the summer, though. I'm taking a job in London in September.'

'Oh. Right. So you're not based in Aus any more then?'

'Nope. I've come back to the UK, for this new job.'

'And is that a permanent move?' Rory asked, then, obviously embarrassed that she was prying, added, 'Sorry, none of my business. It's just a bit of a surprise to see you.'

That was an understatement and a half. 'It's a surprise to see you, too,' Leo replied. At a loss as to what else to say for now, he led Rory through the hall and out into the back garden. 'The chalet is at the bottom. You can get to it via the garden gate at the back of the property if you don't want to keep tramping through the house, or there's a gate at the side of the driveway. Can I help you with your bags?'

'Oh, I should be fine,' Rory replied. 'If you give me the key, I can get my stuff in.'

'Sure.' Leo fumbled in his pocket for the keys to the chalet, which he'd grabbed off the hook on the way through to answering the front door. 'Here you go.' As he passed her the keys, their fingers brushed.

Leo felt the awakenings of something long forgotten in that brief touch. But it was probably just nostalgia.

'Right, well, I'll sort myself out,' Rory said briskly, withdrawing her hand and turning to pick up the suitcase she'd wheeled through with her.

'If you need anything, I'll be in the main house,' Leo said. 'Just, er, holler.'

The ghost of a grin flashed across Rory's face, and she suddenly looked a lot like she had all those years ago. 'I'll be sure to remember that.'

As Rory headed out down the slabbed path to the chalet that nestled at the bottom of Roseford Villa's generous garden, Leo found himself starting to shake, and his breath begin to shorten. Of all the people in all the world to have rocked up at his door... the last person he'd ever expected to see again was Aurora Henderson. Only now, it seemed, it wasn't her. It was, in fact, Rory Dean.

He wondered why she'd changed her name. Had she married? The booking hadn't mentioned another guest, although the chalet slept two comfortably. Maybe a partner or a husband was coming down at a later date. The booking had been for six weeks, and that seemed an awfully long time to be holidaying on one's own. He felt intrigued, but tried to use that fact, that she might not be spending time in the chalet by herself, as a way of grounding himself after the most unexpected meeting. Gradually, as his mind turned over the possibility, his breathing began to return to normal. Twenty years was a long time not to have seen someone, but it didn't mean he couldn't be a mature adult about it. Bumping into your first love on the doorstep of a bed and breakfast was strange, obviously, but they were both adults. He was sure they'd get over the oddness of it and things would be just fine.

4

In the movies, Rory thought, what had just happened would have been the point where the dramatic music kicked in and the slo-mo shots started. Time would stand still, and the camera would catch every single nuance of expression on the protagonists' faces. Having taught Media Studies as well as English for the past few years, Rory knew exactly how the scene *should* go. But this was real. This *had* actually just happened. There, in front of her, had been Leo McKendrick.

Rory had been somewhat reassured to see that Leo was obviously as confused and nervous as she was. He clearly had no idea that it was her on the other end of the booking. But then she'd had no idea that he was going to be here, either. When Leo had confirmed that he was just helping out his aunt and uncle for the summer, somewhere, in the back of her mind, this made sense. She had the vivid recollection of Leo's cunning plan, years ago, after his family had announced they were emigrating to Melbourne in Australia, that he would go to live with his aunt and uncle in the West Country. Back when it had all ended between them. Back when her heart had been smashed in two. Back when they'd hatched all kinds of plans for how they could avoid what was, to them, a world-shattering separation. But in the end, none of it had worked. Teenagers, like they had been then, couldn't call the shots, and they'd realised that, eventually.

Even after Leo had handed her the keys to the chalet, Rory still wasn't sure if she wanted to stay. Being faced with the first person to have broken her heart, a large part of her wanted to grab her bags and run back to her car, hoof it back up the motorway and retreat to the safety of her room in York. But, rather to her own shock, she simply walked through the back door of the house, down the slabbed garden path and made a beeline for the accommodation.

As she walked, Rory tried to get a handle on her emotions. This was unexpected, but not insurmountable, she told herself. She could do this. She might not have come to Roseford to write a book in that genre, but wasn't all of this straight out of a rom-com? For the life of her, though, at this moment, she was struggling to find the comedy.

She headed briskly down the garden path to the chalet, hoping against hope that it was going to be comfortable. She had hazy recollections of staying in such places on family holidays, and prayed that this one would be adequate for her needs. She'd seen some pictures on the phone, late last night, that had made it seem all right, but she'd judge for herself now.

As she unlocked the double-glazed doors and let herself in, she breathed a sigh of relief. It wasn't plush, but it was clean and would be comfortable enough for the duration of her stay. A small kitchen and a space with a banquette bench and a table would be plenty for her, and the bedroom, off to one side, seemed cosy enough. All right, it wasn't the heritage cosiness of Hyacinth Cottage, but it was a fair alternative for the price. Dumping her suitcase in the bedroom, she hurried back out to her car to grab the rest of her stuff. She didn't go back through the house, but scuttled through the side gate. She wasn't quite up to bumping into Leo again before she'd had the chance to get her head around what being this close to him would really mean.

Rory let out a long, slightly shaky breath. How could she get through the next six weeks, knowing that Leo bloody McKendrick was in the big house at the other end of their garden? She'd known all along, from the moment the cancellation on Hyacinth Cottage had come through, that this couldn't be the retreat she needed it to be: seeing Leo had just confirmed what a terrible decision it had been to try to make it work.

She'd come to Roseford to try to get some creative space: to tap into something she hadn't allowed herself to think about in over twenty years. But in the weirdest possible ironic twist, she now found herself sharing ground with one of the people who'd caused her entire perspective to shift. Who'd given her the visceral heartbreak she knew the subject of her novel had suffered as well. She'd been prepared to mine her own experiences, via the materials she'd brought with her, but it was another matter entirely to come face to face with the boy – now a man – who'd broken her heart. That was too much 'inspiration' for her liking.

In an effort to ground herself, she decided to unpack. It didn't take long. The chalet was small, and

Rory got the feeling that if she got everything out, it would just end up looking cluttered. All the same, she couldn't resist grabbing her research folder about the other key figure who had inspired her to begin writing her novel. There was so much to explore about them, and she couldn't wait until Monday, when she was due to get into the Roseford Hall archives to read the diaries and correspondence that was stored there. She opened the folder and flipped the pages until she saw the hi-res image of the portrait that hung in the Long Gallery of Roseford Hall. She was hoping to see some more intimate family photos during her research, but this portrait had been her inspiration, her starting point. A young man in military uniform stared back out of the picture. Painted after his death, his expression had the wistful quality of a life not completely lived. As she studied it for what felt like the umpteenth time, she felt as though she was willing it to give up its secrets. What would she find when she dove into the archives? Would her suspicions be correct? The longer she looked into Edmund Treloar's eyes, the more she hoped she'd be able to discover the story behind the sadness.

5

Rory? As in... short for Aurora? Oh. Shit.

Striding back down the long hallway of the ground floor of Roseford Villas Bed and Breakfast, Leo gave way to the shock that he'd tried so desperately to keep under control since he'd opened the front door. As the memories assailed him from all corners of his mind, his knees started to tremble. Feeling in need of a breather, he took a hasty seat on the settee in the B&B's communal living room, which was too low for him to really sit on comfortably. He leaned back into its squashy embrace, trying to get a handle on things.

Aurora. Rory. Rory Henderson. Well, Rory Dean, now. From the infrequent glances he'd taken at her

Facebook page in the past two decades, there hadn't been any evidence of a marriage, but perhaps she just didn't want to shout about details of her personal life. But then, who used Facebook any more? Maybe it was a recent thing. He hadn't updated his relationship status, or added any photos for that matter, in quite a few years himself.

He sighed. Twenty years ago, they'd meant the world to each other. Two sixteen-year-olds who'd been allies against the whole world, and felt all the pain and ecstasy of first love. They'd spent as much time together as school and their parents would allow, discovered things about each other that only they knew. Then, when circumstances had conspired to part them, he'd eventually broken her heart.

And despite two decades' distance from the last time he'd had any communication with her, it all came flooding back to him. The absolute extremes of what it had been like to be a lovestruck teenager, and to have that love come to an end, hit him with a force he'd not felt in years. That, combined with the frustrations of his current situation, left him gasping for a hard-fought breath.

Calm down, he told himself sternly. This situation shouldn't have been anything, compared to the trials of the past year. So what if Rory was here? They'd been over years ago and they'd been kids when they'd fallen in love. What mattered was the present. They were both adults now, and they'd had whole lives. Rory was his guest for the duration of her stay, nothing more. He'd ensure that he treated her with the professionalism and courtesy that she deserved. And if there was an opportunity for a friendlier catch-up, then it would be light-hearted and focused very much on their adult lives. Their lives after each other.

Although, he thought, light-heartedness had been in quite short supply for him lately. Washed up in Roseford, career on hiatus, relationship over, and in recovery after an accident that left him with potentially life-changing injuries, he had enough to contend with without delving into the past. He'd been used to living day by day since the accident and he had to try to keep doing that. For the moment, that was all that mattered.

Leo stood back up from the sofa, feeling the inevitable twinges in his back as he did so. Thankfully, there were no other paying guests at the B&B until next week, when the three rooms in the house were all booked with guests attending the Roseford Literary and Arts Festival, so, barring any other last-minute bookings, he'd have the main house to him-

self for a bit. It wasn't that he minded sharing the residence – he'd actually quite enjoyed playing host at
the B&B while his uncle and aunt were away – but
seeing Rory had thrown him off balance and he
needed time to regain his equilibrium. What was it
his therapist had said after his life had imploded?
Take each day as it comes, and go minute by minute
if you have to. He'd tried to follow that mantra as
closely as he could, but today he really felt it res-
onate. Today, seeing Rory again, it felt as if living
second by second was too long.

6

The ping from her mobile made Rory stop unpacking. She assumed it was Alex checking in on her. In all the surprise of seeing Leo again, she'd forgotten to text her flatmate to confirm her safe arrival. But when she looked at her phone, she realised it was a message sent to her via Facebook Messenger. From Stella Simpson, of all people.

Stella and Rory had been friends during their university days, and had reconnected on Facebook some years ago, but hadn't kept in regular contact. They'd swapped messages over the years but had rather faded from one another's regular lives. Curious, and still trying not to think about every second of the recent encounter with Leo, Rory tapped the message.

Hi Rory!

Wow – what a surprise to see you're in the West Country! And even more of a surprise to see you're in Roseford. I'm living at Halstead House, Writers and Artists Retreat, which you'll find at the west end of the village. You're probably busy, but if you have time for a catch up, let me know and we can meet for coffee.

Hope to see you soon,

Stella xx

Rory smiled. Of course, Stella must have seen the snap of the notebook she'd put up on Instagram just after she'd got to the chalet. She'd hashtagged #Roseford #amwriting, trying to get herself motivated. She vaguely remembered seeing that Stella was running a retreat these days, but had completely forgotten that it was Roseford she was running it in. These coincidences just kept stacking up, she thought. It was almost as if the universe was conspiring to bring her to Roseford. Or perhaps that was just her own imagination running wild. Whatever it was, she'd be excited and happy to meet up with Stella again. Perhaps

Stella could help with the research Rory needed to do up at Roseford Hall. She'd already got an appointment to see the archives about Edmund Treloar, but it would be great to get the insight of another writer in the village.

Another writer. Rory blushed at her own presumption. She wasn't a writer in Stella's league, having decided to put her English degree to equally good use as a teacher rather than going into the business of writing, as Stella had, in her days as a journalist. But it was better late than never. And even if she and Stella were worlds apart in terms of their output, it would still be great to catch up with her. It had been far too long.

Excitedly, she sent a message back suggesting coffee the next day. She needed reasons to get out of the chalet, and seeing Stella was a great reason. Quickly Stella suggested she come to Halstead House at around two o'clock, and Rory happily agreed. She couldn't wait to see the retreat, and, hopefully, to gain some insight into the kinds of things that Stella was doing to support her own creativity these days.

Well, she thought, as she continued to put her things away. It wasn't quite the start she'd imagined to her six weeks of solitude, but then unexpected things always happened in fiction: perhaps her own life, over the next few weeks, would provide her with ample inspiration to finally get to grips with her own ideas for a novel. Not for the first time since the booking had changed, she thought: you couldn't make it up.

* * *

Later that evening, while the air was still warm but night was beginning to creep around the edges, Rory decided to head out for a bite to eat. Once again, she used the small gate in the garden wall that led back out onto the lane. She was relieved to have that exit route: she had just about settled herself with the idea that Leo was her temporary host, but that didn't mean she wanted to bump into him any more than she had to. If she could get out of Roseford Villas without seeing him, then all the better.

As she ambled down the incline towards the centre of the village, she was better able to take in the sights and sounds around her. The evening sun gave the sandstone buildings a warm, light toffee hue, and the scent of the stocks in the tubs and baskets in several gardens reached her nose. She breathed deeply, feeling some of the stresses of the long drive and unexpected encounter with Leo beginning to dissipate.

From somewhere ahead of her, she could hear the thwack of a cricket ball on willow as an evening game took place, and she looked forward to dinner at the pub with eagerness. She'd forgotten all about food after encountering Leo, but her appetite had returned with a vengeance and her stomach was growling in anticipation of a decent meal.

Rory rounded the corner back onto Roseford's main street and glanced to her right, where she knew, somewhere, Halstead House was. She was excited to meet up with Stella again and looked forward to sharing news with her old friend. But tonight, she just needed a decent meal and a glass or two of something to go with it.

Heading into the Treloar Arms minutes later, Rory appreciated the cool atmosphere of the old stone pub. It was busy, inside and out, with what looked to be a mix of locals and tourists, all enjoying food and drink on a decent summer's evening. The large fireplace, with its oak beam running across the top, was embellished with a large vase of flowers, and alongside them was a prominent advertising card, proudly proclaiming the arrangement to be the creation of Roseford Blooms, the local florist.

A chalk board to the right of the bar area advised Rory to grab a table and order at the bar, so she glanced around and saw an unoccupied one just out-side on the patio. Setting the cardigan she'd grabbed in case of a sudden evening drop in temperature down on the back of one of the chairs, as well as the novel she'd stashed in her bag down on the table, she walked briskly back to the bar to peruse the menu, also all on chalk boards behind the bar, and get a drink.

'Evening,' the landlord, wearing a badge that pro-claimed his name was Dave, greeted her as she ap-proached. 'What can I get you?'

'A white wine and a glass of water, please.'

'Ice with both?'

'That would be great.'

As Dave busied himself with the drinks, he called back over his shoulder, 'Lovely evening. What brings you to Roseford?'

Rory paused. This was her first opportunity to establish herself as a slightly different person to the one who'd finished school yesterday afternoon. Should she do it? The faint prickle of imposter syn-drome cracked at the back of her throat as she replied. 'I'm a writer. I've come to Roseford to work on my, er, new novel.' *My first novel*, she mentally cor-rected herself.

Dave raised an eyebrow. 'A writer, eh? Should I have heard of you?'

Rory grinned and shook her head. 'Not yet, but you never know in a year or two!' She took her drinks and then ordered a delectable-sounding local venison ragu. She'd switch to a glass of red wine to go with that, she thought. Giving Dave her table number, she mooched back outside and took her seat, picking up her book as she did so.

It felt rather lovely to be dining alone, with only a book for company, waiting for a good meal and sipping a decent wine. She took a few minutes before she got really stuck into the novel, to cast an eye around the pub. It was clear who the tourists were, ranging from young families to older couples, all enjoying the food and the ambience of a busy village pub on a Saturday evening. Swivelling her head to glance back into the pub, she could see tables of people who looked to be more local, chatting in a relaxed way, and, from the snatches of conversation she tuned into, talking about some of the village goings-on. The roadworks on the Taunton road seemed to be causing the most controversy.

Whiling away the time before her meal arrived, Rory felt a jolt of recognition when she saw former football manager turned writer Will Sutherland sitting at a table by the fireplace with, presumably, his family. There were three women with him, two much younger than the third. She'd read his recent autobiography, which had come out in the late spring, and knew that he'd settled in the West Country, but hadn't realised that had meant Roseford. Well, she thought, that was another string to add to Roseford's creative bow. Between the film productions and the writers, the place was positively overflowing with talent. Perhaps, she thought, as an attractive older woman came over with her ragu, she'd be able to tap into some of that creativity while she was here.

7

Sitting back in her chair after clearing her plate of the delicious venison ragu, Rory finally felt as though she was relaxing. She'd asked for a glass of red wine, which she was still gently sipping, and it had been a real pleasure, and a rare one, to be eating out alone. She was so used to sitting on the sofa in the flat and either eating with Alex or seeing and hearing her flatmate buzzing around in the background, that although the pub was busy, the relative solitude, where she didn't know anyone else, felt relaxing. She'd read a fair chunk of her book, checked her phone for messages and generally started to unwind.

'Is there anything else I can get you, love?' The

server, who Rory had learned was called Denise, was back to take her plate. 'The specials for dessert are sticky toffee pudding or banana split.'

'Sticky toffee pudding would be great,' Rory replied. She would get back to sensible eating soon enough: she could treat herself to a pudding tonight.

'Coming right up.' Denise scribbled in her pad and bustled back off to the kitchen.

Rory read a few more pages of her book, and then, finding herself a little too drowsy from the food to concentrate on the story, put it back in her bag and just took in the atmosphere. She'd been surreptitiously glancing at Will Sutherland on and off, and it still seemed bizarre that such an eminent sporting personality should be sitting in the village pub. That surprise was compounded further a couple of minutes later when she saw none other than Finn Sanderson, movie star and film director, ducking through the pub's low door and ordering a swift pint. She'd clocked the poster of Finn's comeback movie, *A Countess for Christmas*, in a frame on the wall as she'd walked into the Treloar Arms, and was aware that Roseford had been used as a location for the movie, but that hadn't prepared her for seeing the star of the film in person, a few yards away. This place was certainly providing a lot of inspiration, and she'd barely been here a day!

'Here's your sticky toffee pud, love.' Denise returned, placing a generous portion of the delectable dish down in front of Rory. 'Would you like a coffee with that?'

'No, thanks,' Rory replied. 'I'm pretty shattered and I don't want to be up half the night.'

'Well, enjoy,' Denise replied.

'It's busy tonight,' Rory said. 'Is it always like this?'

'Well, the village is a tourist attraction these days, so we do quite well out of it!' Denise smiled, and cast an eye around the room.

'And, er...' Rory paused. 'You've got your fair share of celebs, too.'

'Oh, Finn, you mean?' Denise laughed. 'Yes, this is his local when he's back in the country. Nice lad. Done well for himself.'

Rory smiled. Denise was understating things. She knew Finn was one of the hottest directors in Hollywood right now, and that was what made seeing him chatting at the bar so incongruous. But then, she figured, even famous film directors had to sup their pints somewhere.

Feeling pleasantly tired after a great meal, Rory decided to call it a night. She paid the bill, thanked the landlord and then headed out into the warm evening air. There were still quite a few people about, and she smiled as she passed a couple coming down the pavement in the opposite direction. The sociable sounds of the pub receded gently into the background as she mooched up the hill back to her chalet.

Getting out for the evening had given her a little breathing space to readjust her perspective on where she'd found herself. OK, so living at the bottom of someone else's garden hadn't quite been the retreat she'd been expecting, but it could have been worse. Imagine if she'd been offered a room at Roseford Villas and had been forced to make small talk with Leo as he served her breakfast every morning! At least this way, although she was in his vicinity, she didn't have to talk to him unless she needed something. And she'd make damned sure she didn't need anything from him, if she could help it.

Pushing open the garden gate, she noticed that a light was on in the chalet. That was odd: she could have sworn she'd switched them all off when she'd gone for dinner. Curious, she ambled over and, as she moved around to the front door, she saw a figure wearing a hoodie backlit in the living area. Her heart began to race. Had someone got in and was burgling her chalet?

Cautiously, Rory edged closer. All the relaxation she'd felt at dinner had vanished, and she now felt the tension coursing back through her. Should she race up to the house and get Leo? Or maybe she should call the police?

Ears listening keenly for any sounds emanating from the chalet, Rory couldn't resist sneaking closer. She heard the clanking of what sounded like cutlery, and then a cupboard door opening and closing. A light went on in the bathroom – was the burglar having a pee? – and then just as swiftly went off again. Finding herself transfixed, she was nearly at the front door now. The door was slightly ajar, and showed no sign of forced entry, from what she could see. Curious, as well as nervous, she gathered her wits and pushed the door open wider.

'Hello?' she called, relieved that her voice sounded strong and authoritative in the evening air. Her teacher voice came in handy sometimes, she thought, smiling slightly despite the nerve-racking situation.

There was a shuffling sound from the direction of the bathroom, and then a bang and an expletive.

'Who's there?' Either this burglar was spectacularly inept, or this was his first job. She reached for her phone, poised to dial 999 if some knife-wielding maniac emerged from the bathroom. Then, thinking better of it, she scurried over to the kitchen area and reached for a frying pan.

Just as she'd raised it, readying herself to swing it at whoever emerged, the bathroom door opened and there was Leo, looking more than a little sheepish and embarrassed.

'Shit! Rory, I'm so sorry. I didn't mean to startle you.' He held up both hands in an 'I surrender' gesture as he caught sight of the frying pan in her hands and took a step back towards the entrance to the bathroom.

'What the hell are you doing in here?' Rory asked. After the initial adrenaline rush, her hands and arms started to shake, and she found herself chucking the frying pan back down on the small counter by her side to relieve herself of the weight of it. The clatter made her jump again.

Leo looked sheepish. 'I couldn't remember if I'd restocked the towels in the bathroom after the last guests left,' he said. 'And, er, the loo roll? I saw you go out earlier and thought I'd nip in and check before you got back. I got caught up with some paperwork, and by the time I'd remembered, it was about five minutes ago.' He shook his head. 'I genuinely didn't mean to frighten you. Please don't think I'm some kind of weird stalker who does this to all his guests!'

Rory, who was still shaking, leaned back against the kitchen cupboards. She didn't know if she'd have rather found a burglar. But, used to thinking on the hop from years in the classroom, she drew a deep breath, let it out, and then put on her best, reassuring smile.

'It's all right,' she said, forcing herself to meet Leo's worried gaze. 'No harm done. Maybe, in future, wait until your guests are home and knock to warn them, rather than doing your best impression of a burglar. I mean, you're wearing a striped T-shirt and everything under that hoodie!' Suddenly over-whelmed by the ridiculousness of the situation, Rory burst out laughing and found it difficult to stop. Especially when Leo glanced down at himself, the penny dropped, and he began to chuckle.

'All you need is the black eye-mask!' Rory added, through her gasps of laughter.

'And maybe a sack?' Leo added.

It was a couple of moments before they both calmed down, and Rory found herself thinking that Leo's invasion of the chalet had broken the ice more effectively than their stilted first greeting on the doorstep of Roseford Villas.

'Well,' Leo said, when the laughter had died down. 'I guess I'd better leave you to it.' He looked at her for a couple of heartbeats. 'Goodnight, Rory.'

'Goodnight, Leo,' Rory replied. 'And thank you for the, er, bathroom accessories. It would have been a bit awkward if I'd got out of the shower tomorrow morning and not had any towels. Or any loo roll, for that matter!' Her face burned. What a subject to bring back up...

'If you need anything else, you know where I am.' Leo brushed a hand through his wavy dark brown hair, and Rory noticed a few threads of grey nestled amongst the generous mop that hadn't receded too much over the years. She also noticed the laughter lines around his eyes, and how they softened his gaze as he looked at her for a little longer.

'I do,' she said softly. 'Take care.'

Leo gave her a nod and then headed out through the chalet's front door. Pushing herself off the counter, where she'd been leaning, Rory couldn't help but track his progress across the lawn as he walked back to Roseford Villas. His long-legged lope, something she'd always loved about him as he'd fallen into step with her on their many walks around the village where they'd lived, seemed a little uneven now. Arthritis? An injury? Curiously, she watched him a little longer. Time had a lot to answer for, she thought, but she was pleased, as she got herself ready for bed, that some of the awkwardness between them had dissipated.

8

The next morning, Rory awoke to a chorus of wild birds living it large in Roseford Villas' grounds. So used to being woken by the traffic in her flat in York, she relished the birdsong for a little while, listening to the many melodies breaking above the roof of the chalet, and basking in the early-morning sunlight that filtered through the curtains of the bedroom as they blew gently in the breeze. Despite her worries about intruders last night, she'd kept the bedroom window open to the night air as she slept, and it promised to be another beautiful Somerset day.

She couldn't help thinking about the encounter with Leo the previous evening. While he'd been a bit of an idiot to choose to check things that late, it had been nice to laugh with him after the awkwardness on the doorstep. It had reminded her of a time when they'd had far fewer responsibilities, when they were just two teenagers who thought their love would last forever. Twenty years of life had intervened to make them different people, but she'd seen a flare of who Leo used to be in his gaze when he'd shared the giggle. It would certainly make their interactions much easier now, she hoped.

All the same, she needed to focus on the reason she was here. She wasn't due to get into the archives at Roseford Hall until Monday, so she had the whole of Sunday to prepare her workspace, get her notes in order and set up the document on her laptop that would, she hoped, be the working draft of her novel.

It was funny how easy it was to shrug off the 'Rory Henderson, teacher' persona and assume the 'Rory Dean, author' one. She already felt different, and excited, liberated by a change of pace and scene. And much as she adored teaching, she felt the pleasurable ripples from a new pool of inspiration lapping around her, and she longed to dive in.

However, she knew well enough that jumping in feet first to anything often wasn't the best approach for her. She'd started and abandoned projects so many times, and she wanted this one to stick. This was why she'd marked out this time alone, after all. It was a scrimped and saved for luxury that she couldn't afford to waste.

After showering and grabbing a quick breakfast (the chalet had included a pint of milk, a loaf of bread, some locally produced strawberry jam, butter and tea bags in its welcome pack), she began the methodical process of arranging her workspace.

It was soon apparent that the small table in the kitchen was going to have to double as a desk as well as an eating space. Feeling a touch frustrated – Hyacinth Cottage had had its own antique mahogany desk under the window, looking out into the small, perfectly formed back garden – Rory swallowed her irritation and made the best of it. If she had to pack things away at the end of each night, so be it. She carefully arranged her laptop, notebooks, pens and blue light glasses and then sat back on the not-very-comfortable bench seat that served the table. Fighting her own sense of disappointment, she glanced around to see where the nearest power socket was to keep her laptop charged, and let out a long, frustrated sigh. It was right over the other side of the countertop, and too far away to have her computer plugged in while she worked at the table. She couldn't even move the table closer since the bench was fixed to the wall.

Trying valiantly to ignore those irritations, she fired up her laptop and opened the novel-writing software she'd spent some time playing with during her last break from school. The document was good to go, she had some preliminary research notes and a bare-bones outline, and now she had the physical space (and the headspace) to begin the first draft.

Nothing happened. For half an hour, she alternated between staring at a blank page and doom scrolling the social networks. Absolutely no words appeared.

Huffing in annoyance with herself, she pushed her laptop away and decided that a coffee and a bit of fresh air was in order. She was just tidying up her makeshift desk space when the topmost notebook from the pile she'd brought with her caught her attention. With its turn-of-the-millennium design, with pastel-coloured flowers printed on the cardboard cover, it contained so much that she'd anticipated would help her bring the idea of her novel to fruition. Flipping over the first page, she felt that awful mixture of fascination and embarrassment when she began reading the impassioned prose of her sixteen-year-old self.

How simple that world now seemed! Musings on friendships, love, things she'd seen on television and read, and all before a time when social media became the equivalent of writing things in longhand. Catching her breath as she saw the familiar, looping 'L' that signified she was going to spend some time writing about Leo, she turned the page, and there he was – longish hair in the same style as Kevin Richardson from the Backstreet Boys, confident smile beaming out from the pages, fashion choices as first-decade-of-the-noughties as they came.

Memories she'd been keeping on the back burner, ready for the very moment when she'd have time to draw on them for inspiration, seemed to bubble to the surface. Perhaps it was coming face to face with Leo again that had done it, but she found herself revelling in the pages of her teenage diaries. Gradually, embarrassment gave way to fascination as she rediscovered the person she'd been in her teens. Yes, a lot of it was self-indulgent nonsense when seen through the eyes of her adult self, but there'd been a spark there, a sense of optimism that *it would be all right*, that seemed irrepressible. The dates, some time before she'd found out that Leo was moving to the other side of the world, bore that out. Their happiness, their desire to be young, have fun, discover things about themselves and each other, reeled out through the pages and pages of looping handwriting. Rory found herself immersed in the raw, undoubtedly naive prose of her adolescence. Surely, she thought as she read further, she'd be able to draw on this for inspiration?

Putting down the diary once again, feeling energised, she tapped the mouse pad on her MacBook Air and once again faced the blank page.

But, to her intense frustration, ideas seemed to flee her brain as fast as the dragonflies flitting across the lawn outside. What was wrong with her? She'd been thinking about this for weeks, months, years, even. Why couldn't she write? What else did she need?

Rory huffed out a breath and, in resignation, closed the laptop. What would she tell a student in this position? How many times had she heard 'I don't know what to write' in response to her peering over a shoulder and seeing nothing but a blank page? She'd take a moment to think and then give them five prompts, straight off the top of her head, and encourage them to write one of them down, make a story out of something they knew. She was well aware that she should take her own advice, but she felt... constipated. If literary constipation was a thing. She smiled at her own self-indulgence. If she'd given herself ten minutes of her lunchtime at school, she'd have jumped in and got on with it. So, what was stopping her now?

Perhaps it was the weight of all that expectation, the fact she'd been planning this for *ages*, and now it was here, she had absolutely no idea how to approach it. The other problem was, she realised with a start, that while she thought she'd be writing a historical time travel novel, known in the business as a timeslip, at the moment, after her encounter with Leo last night, and now having dipped back into her diaries, she felt entirely too much as though she were living in one.

9

Leo had become an early riser when he'd moved to Australia. The bus that would take him from home to his school, some miles away, arrived at 7 a.m., on the dot, and years of having to drag himself out of bed, walk the half mile to the bus stop and then endure the forty-five-minute journey had trained him not to linger in bed. It was a routine that, when he'd started university, he'd maintained, and it came in handy when he'd joined the university rowing team, whose training hours were even earlier.

After the accident, he'd spent months in a hospital bed, which had almost broken him of the habit, but when he'd been discharged, he'd been determined to maintain as much of his prior regimen as he could. This came in particularly handy now he was in charge of the B&B, as many of his guests rose with the dawn and requested breakfast early before heading off on their holiday adventures.

He was showered and dressed by six fifteen most days, and, when the B&B was empty, either cracking on with his physiotherapy or going for a gentle run. When there were guests, he'd be in the kitchen, sorting out the breakfast that his aunt and uncle prided themselves on. This morning, with no guests in the house, and only Rory in the chalet, he went through the stretches that had become part of his morning regime ever since the car accident that had changed his trajectory in so many ways. Raising his arms above his head, he felt the familiar pull in the muscles of his back, the tautness of scarred skin, and imagined, as he always did, the shift of the metal that had been implanted in his spine. There were good days and bad days, but today felt good. Today felt easier.

Which was surprising, given how embarrassed he'd been to be sprung inside the chalet last night. He tried to push the memory to one side, to focus on the stretches through his body as he prepared himself for the day, but the sight of Rory Henderson, Rory *Dean*, he mentally corrected himself, standing there brandishing a frying pan had filled him simultaneously with mortification and laughter. Thankfully, she'd recognised him before she'd clunked him around the head with it.

And push... one, two, three... Leo reached forwards, flattening his back as far as he could, holding himself in place for a few more seconds. Pilates, in addition to the physio, had been a game changer, and he thanked his lucky stars for the excellent medical staff in Melbourne who'd put him back together, many of them expats from the British NHS.

Winding his torso back up to a standing position, Leo took a few more breaths, holding the last one and then letting it out in a long huff. This was almost muscle memory these days, and a long way from his mornings of old, when he'd be grabbing a coffee, kissing his wife goodbye and heading out the door to catch the rail link into town, where he'd spend the next eight to ten hours in the high-pressure world of the corporate lawyer. Contract law had been his speciality, and he'd loved every minute of it. But after the accident, things had needed to change.

There were plenty of times when he'd felt grief at the loss of the life he'd had in Australia, but his counsellor was fond of reminding him that the future, moment to moment, was what mattered now, and for the most part he could remember that. But when he'd seen Rory for the first time in forever yesterday, the past had come rearing up from the depths of his memory to greet him. And now here she was, living in the chalet at the bottom of his garden for a summer, back in his life, but not quite in it, both of them with twenty years of experience since the last time they'd met.

Shaking his head, Leo ran through the list of things he had to do today. Rory was a different person now, just as he was. You couldn't go back. He knew that, from bitter experience. He opened the door to the small office at the back of the ground floor of Roseford Villas and settled into his morning routine – checking the business's emails for any bookings, seeing if there were any invoices that needed paying from suppliers and making sure he hadn't missed anything. He had to steel himself not to keep glancing down the garden. It didn't stop him from wondering what she was up to, though. Why was she here? Of all the places she could have chosen to spend the summer, why Roseford?

Shaking his head, he replied to a few emails and then went to double-check the rooms that had been booked for a couple of days' time. It was quite nice not to have anyone in the house, but it did mean he was rather at a loose end. When the B&B had guests, he'd be in a constant cycle of being host, cook and cleaner, but on the rare occasions when it was empty, he didn't quite know what to do with himself. His aunt and uncle had told him to try to make the most of the quiet periods, as, when the place was occupied, things could be intense, but Leo hadn't quite got used to the solitude. Back in his lawyering days, he'd been accustomed to the high pressure of meetings, phone calls and constant information flow. This lifestyle was different, and although he'd needed different in his life, it still took a bit of getting used to.

As if to highlight this fact, the inbox pinged, and Leo grinned to see the contents of the message. The annual meeting of the Somerset Badger Action Group (SBAG for short) had requested to book three bedrooms at Roseford Villas for some of their members during the annual Big Badger Watch in early September. Roseford was a hotspot for badger activity, much to the excitement of SBAG, and his aunt and uncle had briefed him that these particular visitors would keep rather anti-social hours while they were here. As a result, they often wanted a later breakfast, having been staking out badger sets all night.

Still grinning, Leo confirmed the booking with

Airbnb and entered it onto Roseford Villas' internal system. He wasn't sure if he'd still be around in September, since his aunt and uncle would be returning from their retirement recce to Spain at the end of August, but he wanted to make sure he'd put all the details down so they'd be aware of their visitors.

That job completed, Leo checked the supplies in the kitchen, and the dates on all of the provisions in the fridge. He'd had a crash course in food safety and needed to keep on top of things. Just as he was closing the fridge door, his phone pinged. Picking it up from where he'd slung it on the kitchen island, his heart began to race.

Leo. Am sending the papers via UPS in the next twenty-four hours. Please sign and return by the end of the week. Regards, Corinne.

All of those careful deep breathing exercises he'd completed when he got up might as well not have happened. He'd been expecting the text at some point, but now that it had arrived, it didn't stop the feelings that threatened to overwhelm him. Leo pushed his phone away from him and shook his head. He still wouldn't believe it: not until the papers were in his hands.

10

After a not entirely productive morning, Rory decided that fresh air was what she needed. She'd fiddled around with a snippet of a scene for about an hour, but still wasn't really sure what she was doing. She hoped that spending the day in the Roseford Hall archives tomorrow would help her to get things a little clearer in her head and inspire her to get some more words on the page. She was off to Stella Simpson's house later for an afternoon cuppa. Feeling excited about seeing her friend for the first time in years, Rory packed away her laptop and notebooks, stashed them safely out of sight in one of the chalet's cupboards and set out.

As she wandered down the hill again, instead of

taking a left back to the heart of Roseford, Rory turned right and headed out of the village. Stella had told her that Halstead House Writers' and Artists' Retreat that she and her partner Chris had founded a few years back, was on the outskirts, about three-quarters of a mile away. The buildings began to thin out as she walked, giving way to rolling fields that stretched languorously upwards to meet the foothills of the Quantocks, blurred a calm green in the distance. Having grown up in the Yorkshire countryside, Rory was accustomed to wild and beautiful landscapes, but while the North Yorkshire moors had a kind of untamed beauty, the rolling hills of Somerset seemed softer, more pliant, promising visions of long summer days sipping cider in the rolling curves of its greenness.

Laughing to herself at the purpleness of her own interior monologue, Rory picked up the pace, eager to see her friend, and the place she called home. When Halstead House came into sight, she couldn't help feeling a stab of envy. The tall Victorian house stood stately amongst manicured gardens, with a sweep of driveway from the gatehouse at the bottom of the road to the main house at the top.

The wrought-iron gates were open, so Rory mooched up the driveway. On her way up to Halstead

House she saw there were two other dwellings that shared the drive – a gatehouse at the bottom, and a generously proportioned bungalow with its own well-tended garden a little further up. Rounding the undulating curve of the driveway, she neared the front door of the main house and, as she walked up the tiled pathway to ring the doorbell, the front door opened before she'd got halfway.

'Rory!' Stella exclaimed, a huge smile on her face. Her curly brown hair tumbled carelessly around her shoulders, and the statement tortoiseshell glasses suited her face, giving her an elegant air. For a long moment, Rory regarded her friend, the years rolling back in an instant, before she hurried up the rest of the path and into the welcoming hug that Stella offered.

'It's so lovely to see you,' they both chorused as they let one another go.

'How long has it been?' Stella asked as she let Rory into the cool hallway.

'Entirely too long,' Rory replied. She glanced around her at the subtly decorated hall and gave a gasp as she caught sight of a beautifully proportioned reception room off to the left, adorned with huge bay windows to let in the summer sunshine.

'What a stunning place,' she breathed.

Stella grinned. 'It was a wreck a few years ago, but it's looking pretty good now, I'll admit.'

They walked down the hallway and Stella led Rory through to a large kitchen, which was also bright and airy. 'Shall we grab a coffee and head out to the back garden? I'll give you a tour in a bit if you want one, but it's too nice a day to lurk inside.'

'Sounds good.'

Rory and Stella chatted while Stella made a couple of coffees, and then they wandered through to the slightly more secluded back garden. Stella gestured to a wooden patio set just off to the side of the lawn and Rory took a seat.

'So, what brings you to Roseford?' Stella asked as they sipped their drinks.

Rory paused, but then figured, what the hell. Stella was a writer, a very successful one, and had been a good friend, back in the day. She trusted her.

'I want to write a novel,' she blurted out quickly. 'I've been wanting to write one for years, but this summer I thought it was time to actually do it. So, I've come away to get some headspace to do it while I'm on school holidays.'

Stella smiled. 'Sounds like a good plan. So many people say they want to write but never do. So where are you staying?'

'Well...' Rory filled Stella in on the accommodation complications but left out the part about Leo. Years ago, after a drunken night out, Rory had told Stella all about her heartbreak over Leo, but it seemed daft to dwell on that now, and she really wasn't ready to answer any speculative questions about their most recent encounter. She hardly knew the answers herself, yet.

'Oh, that's such a shame about Hyacinth Cottage,' Stella said as Rory finished. 'I know how lovely it is, and I'm sure the owners wouldn't have meant to cause a problem. But at least you found something else.' She paused. 'I'd have offered you a room here, but we're fully booked right through until the new year, I'm afraid.'

Rory smiled. 'If I'd had the wherewithal to look you up earlier in the year, I'd definitely have booked onto a course.' She glanced around the pretty back garden, which led onto a walled garden behind, and thought again what a beautiful place this was.

'If you want to come back next year, I'll sort you a mates' rates discount,' Stella smiled. 'It would be great to have you to stay.'

'Thanks.' Rory smiled. 'I might take you up on that. By that time, I should have at least a first draft!'

Stella regarded her carefully. 'Don't push yourself,' she said. 'You've carved out this time, which is great, and routine can be a brilliant thing, but you've probably had a busy year at school. Take time to relax as well as write.'

Rory nodded. 'I will.' She must have looked downcast, though, as Stella raised an inquisitive eyebrow. 'I guess I'm still having trouble letting go of Hyacinth Cottage. Especially because...'

'Because...?'

Rory suddenly did have the urge to explain what it was like to come face to face with Leo again. It was as if she and Stella had gone back in time during their coffee and chatter, but it seemed so juvenile to be focusing on him again now, even under the weird circumstances.

'Oh, nothing,' Rory replied hastily. There was no point brooding over it all when she was enjoying spending time with Stella. 'At least Roseford Villas seems like a nice place to stay, and because I'm not in the main house, I do have a lot more freedom to do what I want.'

'You know, it's weird,' Stella mused, taking a last sip of her coffee. 'The guy who's running Roseford Villas B&B... he's had a bit of a tricky time, from what I hear.'

'Really?' Rory tried to keep her tone neutral. 'In what way?'

Stella paused. 'Well, you know what it's like in villages. People tend to talk, but the word is that he came back from Australia to help out his aunt and uncle after a lot of, er, bad luck. Had a God-awful car accident, split from his wife and lost his career, and now he's here, stuck in the back end of beyond, running the family business. Bit of a culture shock, by all accounts.'

Rory's stomach gave a little flip. She couldn't help feeling a stab of sympathy for Leo. What a terrible set of circumstances to have to endure. As teenagers, they'd been so unprepared for the difficulties life might throw at them: it seemed that Leo had suffered more than most.

'Are you all right?' Stella's inquisitive tone brought Rory back to earth with a bump. 'You've gone a bit pale.'

'I'm fine.' Rory smiled quickly, realising that she'd zoned out of the conversation and got lost in her own thoughts. She finished the dregs of her coffee as they continued to chat. Stella filled her in on how she'd come to live with her partner, Chris, and his son, Gabe, and Rory realised that it had taken a lot of work for all three of them to get to this point in their lives. Eventually, as the sun began to fade from the patio where they sat, Rory realised it was time to get back to Roseford Villas and put some of Stella's advice into practise.

'It's been wonderful to catch up with you, Stella,' she said, as they both rose from the garden table. 'Hopefully we can hang out a bit more while I'm here.'

Stella smiled. 'I'd like that. Did you want to see around the house before you go?'

Feeling the sudden need to be alone with her thoughts after everything that Stella had just told her, Rory shook her head. 'I'd love to,' she said, 'but maybe another time? I really do need to get back and crack on with some writing.'

Stella looked quizzically at Rory for a moment, but then smiled. 'Of course. You must pay attention when the muse comes calling.' They walked back out to the front of the house, round the side of the building this time, so that Rory could appreciate the sweeping curve of the countryside that ran in a generous panorama in front of Halstead House. As Rory was about to say goodbye, Stella added, 'I know I said we're fully booked, but if you wanted a hot desk here, just text me – I'm sure I can sort you out one with a better view than the chalet for when you might want a change of scene.'

Rory's heart expanded with gratitude. 'Thank you,' she said, smiling again. 'That would be wonderful. I might just take you up on it if I get too claustrophobic in the shed at the bottom of Roseford Villas!'

'You're welcome any time,' Stella replied. 'Stay in touch, yeah? Let's make the most of your visit here.'

As Rory began the walk down the drive and back to the main road, she felt a confusing mixture of emotions. It had been wonderful to see Stella, and to see how well she was. But she was also mulling over what Stella had told her about Leo, and she couldn't help being curious about what had happened to him in the intervening years since their relationship had ended. It sounded as though he'd really been through it, and Rory found herself aching with compassion for the young man she'd once known, and the horrors he'd experienced since they'd lost touch. Life happened: she knew that, but it seemed as though Leo had had more than his fair share of hard knocks.

11

Mind buzzing with information, Rory pushed open the garden gate of Roseford Villas and breathed in the mixed scents of a garden in full summer bloom. The floral aroma of the honeysuckle, which came into its own at this time of day, was sweet and heady, and mingled with the heavier scent of the lavender that sprung up in the raised beds to one side of the long expanse of lawn. There was a greener, woodier scent of pine balsam in the air, too, and as she rounded the back end of the chalet towards its front door, she realised why. There were piles of hedge trimmings littering the back lawn, from where someone had been giving the garden a summer haircut.

The sound of the hedge trimmer started again, and, as Rory headed towards the chalet, she caught sight of Leo off to the left-hand side of the garden. Leo had his back to her and was trimming slices off the conifers that created the boundary. She could smell their herby aroma, even from here. They'd clearly got a bit out of control in recent years, and Leo's attempt to tame them was long overdue, if the huge pile of foliage that lined the lawn at his feet was anything to go by.

Before she could stop it, her heart had done one of those crazy backflips that she'd read about so many times in fiction. She found herself briefly wondering why the hell Leo had felt the need to remove his T-shirt to do the trimming, before she gave in to the impulse just to stand there, observe and admire until he noticed she was in the garden. After all, she thought, she wouldn't want to startle him into chopping off a limb, would she?

Careful not to disturb him, she settled herself in the nearest garden chair outside her chalet. The late afternoon warmth wrapped itself around her like a shawl as she took breath after breath of the wonderful scents of the garden. Just being here was soothing her in a way she'd never imagined it would when she'd first rocked up at Leo's front door. She'd got past the awkwardness and was finally starting to relax and enjoy being in Roseford.

She also appreciated a few moments to observe Leo and try to get what Stella had told her about him straight in her head. Reconciling the two pictures felt tricky. He seemed to be wielding the hedge trimmer with ease and was clearly recovered from whatever injuries he'd sustained in the car crash, although she'd noticed his slightly uneven gait as he'd walked back from the chalet last night. Lost in these thoughts, it was a few seconds more before Rory realised that the hedge trimmer had stopped. Leo was striding back up the garden towards where she was sitting on the patio, a look of surprise on his face.

'Hi,' he said as he reached her. 'How are you doing today?'

Rory swallowed before she replied, the sight of his bare torso being more than a little distracting up close. 'Well, thanks,' she stammered. 'I, er, went over to Halstead House to see an old friend from university – Stella Simpson. We had a coffee but I'm thinking about dinner now.' *And you, half naked in front of me*, she added to herself.

Leo grinned. 'I'm thinking that way myself. I know you're self-catering, but I can get you a sandwich if you want when I make one for myself.'

'Oh, don't go to any trouble,' Rory replied. 'I can see you're busy. I can do something myself in a bit.'

'It's no trouble, honestly.' Leo's soft accent, that blurred the lines between his native Yorkshire and Australia, made Rory's heart speed up a little more. 'Let me put this away and I'll run you something up.' He glanced back down the garden. 'I can sweep the rest up later.'

'Only if you don't mind,' Rory replied. 'I don't want to put you out.'

'Same old Rory,' Leo said, and Rory noticed the soft tease in his voice. 'You were always so determined not to take up any space, not to be any trouble to anyone. I thought you'd have grown out of that by now.'

Rory's face flushed. So much for forgetting about the past. She shook her head. 'Don't worry on my account,' she said quickly. 'I can do my own sandwich.' She was damned if she was going to give Leo the satisfaction of scoring a point from her about something so trivial. She tried not to let her eyes be drawn to the chiselled, lightly tanned chest and well-defined abs. She remembered just how smooth his skin had felt under her palms when they were excitable teenagers in the throes of first passion. The first time he'd slipped off his T-shirt when they were teens had been a revelation, and she remembered spending a long time just running her hands over his bare flesh. Irritatingly, he'd grown more muscular, and hadn't seemed to have gone to seed in the intervening years.

'I didn't mean to offend you, Rory,' Leo said softly. 'I'm sorry. I had no right to tease you like that.'

'It's fine,' Rory replied speedily. 'And you're right. I'm self-catering so I can sort myself out.' Leo's proximity was making her head spin, and she kept trying not to breathe in the intoxicating scent of his work-warmed body where he stood not two feet away. It was a sensory overload that she wasn't prepared for in the least.

Leo let out a brief sigh. 'As you wish.' The line from *The Princess Bride*, once one of their favourite films, wasn't lost on her. He held her gaze for a moment longer, and then turned towards the garden shed, which was situated to one side of the garden just off the patio. As he did so, Rory couldn't help a sharp intake of breath. Leo's body, the body that she'd become so familiar with when they were sixteen, now had a most unfamiliar addition. There, running almost the length of his spine, was a mostly faded, but nonetheless noticeable, thick, vertical scar. Presumably it was from the car accident that Stella had mentioned. Far from feeling like the teenager she had been, she now felt the weight of time pressing heavily down on her. Eyes fixed to his back as he walked away from her, Rory shook her head. The cross currents between them had just taken a step into even more complicated territory.

12

I only offered to make her a bloody sandwich! Leo's irritable thoughts followed him all the way back to the kitchen. Tired from lack of sleep the night before, and from working in the garden all afternoon, he knew his levels of patience weren't as high as they should be. His back was giving him hell from all of the twisting and bending, too. His physiotherapist would have done her nut to see him pushing himself so hard, but Leo had always craved physical activity to quell his racing thoughts. And having Rory nearby had made them run at the speed of sound. *Funny. She always had the power to calm me down when we were younger!*

Towelling off the sweat with the T-shirt he'd stuffed into the back pocket of his tan-coloured shorts, he chucked it in the vague direction of the enormous washing machine in the utility room. His aunt Violet would have done her nut, as well, if she'd seen him doing that. Before she and Uncle Bryan had left on their overseas trip, she'd drilled him in the importance of order, routine and tidiness if he was to run Roseford Villas successfully.

He thought back over the conversation he'd just had with Rory. She'd seemed flustered, shocked even, to see him in the garden with his top off. *It's not like she hasn't seen it all before*, he thought, but that was a long time ago. He'd noticed the way her eyes had widened when she'd taken in his bare chest, and in his discombobulation, he'd forgotten to feel self-conscious about the state of his body. The saunter back to Roseford Villas had been part annoyance, part defence mechanism, and it wasn't until he'd got through the French windows and into the kitchen that he'd realised his scars had been on full display. Unwittingly, he'd shown her, literally, his most vulnerable side.

Carefully assembling the ingredients for his sandwich, he wasn't surprised when his hands started to shake. It was a combination of PTSD and nervousness, he knew. He was so much better at identifying his own triggers now. Cutting right back on alcohol had seen to that. It didn't mean he was foolproof at avoiding them, but he could at least recognise the signs. He hadn't thought he was going to be disturbed when he'd been sorting out the hedges, and when Rory had returned, she'd caught him on the hop. Added to that his clumsy attempt to reassure her, which had actually done quite the opposite, and he knew he was on the top of an anxiety spiral looking down.

Calm down, he told himself firmly. This wasn't worth getting dragged under for. He took a few deep, steadying breaths and leaned forward, palms flat on the cool surface of the worktop. This wasn't a bad one: he wasn't having flashbacks and his heart, though racing, was beginning to slow down. Simply showing Rory his scars had been a move towards a trigger, but he'd been able to retreat from it. Marta, his counsellor, would have been proud.

A few more breaths and he was back on a more even keel. Swiftly, he assembled his sandwich and gulped it down with a can of Coke from the fridge. There was plenty to do once he'd eaten – he really should bag up the debris from cutting the hedges and take it to the tip. Again, Aunt Vi's voice rang in his ears, urging him not to let things slide or get out of hand. She meant with the business, but he was aware that the advice applied to far more areas of his life than that.

13

After a somewhat less than peaceful night's sleep, Rory was glad of the dawn. She was due at Roseford Hall at nine o'clock, where a curator from the British Heritage Fund would let her into the archives, and supervise and assist her while she researched the life of Edmund Treloar, whose portrait had inspired her. Although her story would be fiction, she'd been intrigued for years by his portrait, which hung in the Long Gallery at the hall, and an idea for a story had been percolating since she'd decided to actually try to write a novel. Months of staring at photographs of the portrait online had eventually given way to wanting to spend some time there, and when she'd written to the British Heritage Fund, they'd been more than happy to support her research endeavours. After coming face to face with Leo yesterday, Rory knew she needed something to take her mind off the confusion of the present.

She wasn't particularly hungry, so as soon as she'd got dressed and got her things together, she headed out of the chalet and through the garden gate. If, by the time she got down to the main street, she felt peckish, she'd pop into Roseford Café for a bite to eat.

It was another gorgeous day, and for a fleeting moment, Rory felt regretful that she was going to be spending most of it closeted away in the archives of Roseford Hall, but nothing could dim her excitement at *finally* getting her hands on some primary sources to help her with her research. Part of her degree had been History, and she'd always adored the research side of the course. There was something particularly satisfying about touching things that previous hands had created, and it brought the subject to life far more than just working from textbooks or photocopies. The Treloar correspondence was a particularly rich seam of information. Edmund Treloar had been a prolific correspondent to friends and family during his time in the army, and many more letters had been returned to his loved ones after his tragic death in April 1915.

The correspondence that had caught Rory's imagination was those unsent letters, in particular. She knew already, from the versions she'd read online at the Roseford Hall website, that they detailed a relationship between Edmund and Francesca Middleton, whom, if sources were to be believed, he was planning to marry upon his return from the Western Front. Francesca was the daughter of a local landowner, and she and her twin brother Frederick were often seen in the grounds of Roseford Hall, as both were friends with Edmund and his sister Maria when they were children. It made perfect sense that Edmund and Francesca should marry upon Edmund's return from war. It was Edmund's death that meant the title of Lord Treloar passed from him to his younger brother Richard and commenced the line of descendants that led to Simon Treloar holding the title today.

Rory had been fascinated by the tragic love story, cut short before it had really had time to blossom, and when she was considering writing a historical novel, it seemed only fitting to use Edmund and Francesca for inspiration. Although she was planning on changing names and details, the opportunity to see Edmund's original correspondence was too good to pass up, and she was itching to get her hands on those final, unsent letters.

Anticipation about what she was going to see that morning was stopping her from thinking too deeply about Leo, for which she was grateful. Although Leo hadn't been lost to her through death, at the age of sixteen the move across the world that had forced them to part had felt close to a bereavement. She could smile in embarrassment now when she thought back, through the somewhat clearer lens of adulthood, to the pain of that separation, but she couldn't altogether dismiss what she'd felt back then. Everything felt that much more intense when you were a teenager, that much she knew, but it had hurt so much at the time. She couldn't help drawing a slight parallel with what poor Francesca must have felt upon learning that Edmund had lost his life. Eventually, of course, she and Leo might have had a future, if they hadn't been sixteen, but for Edmund and Francesca, that option had been cruelly ripped from them by fate and war.

Rory couldn't suppress the shiver of excitement that thrilled through her when the archivist retrieved the box with Edmund's last, unsent letters and diary contained within. With slightly shaky hands, she carefully removed the first of the lovingly preserved letters from the box and set it upon the table. Edmund's handwriting was small, in the copperplate that was classic of the period, and it took Rory a few minutes to acclimatise to the densely written pages. But once she had, what a story they told!

Often, before she'd studied historical letters, she'd assumed there was a kind of reserve in the style and substance of them. A code of manners, or etiquette, that disguised true meanings for the sake of propriety. Looking closely at the first drafts of some of Rupert Brooke's poetry during her degree had rapidly disabused her of that notion. Handwritten documents, especially correspondence to loved ones, had a kind of visceral quality, and whether it was the knowledge that these letters from Edmund Treloar were never sent, that the emotions contained within died when he died, or whether it was just the very fact that they outlined such a doomed relationship, Rory wasn't sure, but there was power in his prose.

A little while later, and Rory was feeling far more affected by what she'd spent the morning reading. *Oh, Edmund.* Her eyes swam with tears she was nervous to shed over the archived documents as she took in the full weight of what had happened before Edmund Treloar's untimely death in the trenches with his comrades of the Somerset fusiliers. To think that, for the sake of a few more days, he'd have returned safely home.

When all of this is over, we'll spend the rest of our lives together, Edmund had written. *I don't know how, or when, but I will not spend my life without you. To me, you are life itself. And, God willing, there will be a place for us.*

How wrong he'd been. Rory shook her head. When she'd first seen Edmund's portrait, she'd never imagined she'd find letters like this. A quaint story of the lives and loves of the inhabitants of the hall, with marriages, births and deaths, all within the grander tapestry of a family who extended back ten generations, was all she expected: a kind of *Middlemarch*-esque epistolary tale. But these final letters from Edmund were intimate, and showed a raw passion that embodied the *carpe diem* spirit of a doomed generation. It was as if somehow he knew he wasn't coming back to Francesca, and he was putting all of his cards on the table, giving her something to cherish, if he never made it back. It felt odd, then, given the intimacy of those letters, that they weren't passed on to Francesca after Edmund's death. Surely the family would have wanted her to have them, rather than keeping them to themselves?

I remember the evenings under the stars, and the way we swore we'd never be parted. The feel of your mouth on mine, and your hands, and everything else... Rory drew in a shorter breath. This man knew how to write a love letter, and no mistake. She wondered if Francesca had been as captivated by her lover's prose as she now was, across the generations.

As she read further, Rory was drawn in by the account of a love affair that seemed so passionate. It was one half of a story: Francesca's letters hadn't been donated to the archive, but it was clear in Edmund's impassioned prose to 'darling, dearest F, whom I desire with every fibre of my being' that one side of the partnership felt torn apart by the separation they suffered during wartime. Rory couldn't help speculating what Francesca's responses would have been: would she have allowed herself to be so passionate in reply as Edmund was? She found herself writing a response to one of the letters as she sat at the table in the archive room, trying to imagine what it would have been like for Francesca to be waiting patiently at home for word of the man she loved. Would she have lived for the sound of the letters hitting the doormat, for news of him, and lived in dread of the news that he'd been lost to the horrors of the war?

This creative endeavour seemed to ease the block she'd been encountering the previous morning, and she found herself scribbling thoughts into the note-book she'd brought with her, putting herself in Francesca's shoes, and, she thought as she wrote, also tapping into some of that emotion that she'd felt when she'd been writing emails to Leo on the other side of the world. She couldn't conceive the devastation of discovering that the person she loved was dead: and the exercise helped her to put her thoughts into some perspective, and also gave her some more impetus to write the fictional, doomed love story.

Rory spent three hours poring over the archived material, and it was only when her rumbling stomach threatened to distract the archivist that she decided it was time to stop for a bite to eat. She carefully put the letters back in their box, but as she did so, she noticed that there was an unusual detail in the corner of one of Edmund's later letters. It appeared just to be a doodle: a sweet little squiggle that perhaps meant something to them both, a private joke or a reference to a shared experience. She wondered what it meant, and thought it would make a great addition to her novel – a sweet little Edwardian version of an emoji, perhaps?

'Everything all right?' Interrupting her thought processes, Simon Treloar, Tenth Lord of Roseford and current tenant of Roseford Hall, popped his head around the door. 'How's the research going? Is there anything else you need?'

Rory, eyes still blurred, thought for a heartbreaking moment that Edmund himself had risen from the grave. She'd noted the resemblance between Simon and his great-great-uncle from the moment she'd seen pictures of them both, but having spent so much time immersed in Edmund's letters, the lines between fiction and reality were beginning to blur.

'No, thanks,' she replied, her voice trembling slightly. 'This is all so interesting – it's certainly giving me a lot of inspiration.'

Simon smiled at her but seemed vaguely disconcerted by her emotional reaction. 'I'm glad. It's about time someone made use of the stuff here, instead of it just gathering dust for the next few generations.'

Rory smiled, more strongly this time. Simon seemed oblivious to the wealth of history and heritage around him, but in quite an adorable way. She'd been warned by Stella that Simon was 'one of life's eccentrics' when she'd told her friend that she'd arranged to look at the Treloar archives, and she was intrigued by his casual reaction to his own history.

'These are all fairly recent finds, too,' Simon said. 'They'd been chucked in a box in the attic for years, until the British Heritage Fund unearthed them and put them in proper archive boxes. I'm not sure any-one, apart from their preservation experts, has really looked at them properly.'

Rory's heart sped up. 'And have you had a look?'

Simon shook his head. 'I've had a quick glance, but some of dear old Edmund's communiqués were so densely written that I put them down again pretty quickly. After his death, the immediate family must have shoved everything away because of the grief.'

Including the unsent letters to 'F', Rory thought. She wondered again why the letters hadn't found their way into Francesca's hands. 'Well,' she said, 'it's certainly been a wonderful experience, getting the chance to handle them for myself. And to find out more about what Edmund was like.'

'I hope it's all helpful,' Simon replied. 'I'm just glad that the archives are proving to be of some use. There was so much stuff just lying around the place before the BHF took it on and started organising it that it's great to know someone's making the most of what's been collected.' He regarded her, a serious expression on his face. 'Are you planning on drawing on any of it directly for your own novel?'

Rory opened her mouth to answer, but before she could, a slightly strident voice echoed up the stairs to the archive room.

'Simon? Are you there?'

'Up here, my love,' Simon replied.

A few seconds later, an attractive brunette popped her head around the doorframe. 'Hi,' she said as she caught sight of Rory. 'I'm Lizzie Warner, Simon's better half.' She thrust out a hand for Rory to shake.

'Hi,' Rory replied, introducing herself to Lizzie. She'd had the lowdown from Stella about Lizzie and Simon's romance, which in itself could have graced the pages of a novel, but she hadn't yet had the pleasure of meeting Lizzie herself, although she'd passed Roseford Blooms, the flower shop that Lizzie owned, a few times on her mooches around the village.

'How's it all going?'

'Great, thanks,' Rory replied. 'It's lovely to spend some time with primary sources, especially when they're as fascinating as Edmund Treloar's letters and diaries.'

'It's about time someone unravelled the tale of

Roseford's most historical hottie!' Lizzie laughed. 'Present company excluded, of course, Simon.'

Simon shot Lizzie a wry look. 'Of course. I always knew you had a thing for Edmund. I could tell by the way you used to look at his portrait in the Long Gallery!'

Lizzie rolled her eyes. 'Jealousy is such an unattractive emotion,' she said, before breaking out into a grin. 'Anyway, I'm glad I found you. I've got a delivery of dahlias for the vases in the Great Hall, and I wondered if you could sign for them? And then we could grab some lunch?'

'Sounds good.' Simon smiled back at Lizzie, and Rory was tickled to see the obvious affection between this slightly odd, but obviously deeply in love couple. 'Just give the main office a ring when you're finished up here.' He turned back to Rory. 'They can sort out any photocopying that you need.'

'Thanks,' Rory replied. She felt slightly relieved that, due to Lizzie's arrival in the archive room, she hadn't had to answer Simon's question. In truth, she wasn't quite sure how much of Edmund's story she was going to use, but one thing was certain: it had given her plenty of food for thought.

That afternoon, bleary eyed in more ways than one from spending a few hours in the archives, Rory mooched back to the chalet to organise her ideas. She had a fair notion, now, of how the 'timeslip' angle of the novel was going to go, but it was tying the past and the present together that would prove difficult. Maybe she was being too ambitious for her first foray into novel writing? Perhaps it would have been better to have stuck to one time period, and given it her all, rather than trying to force links that were only there in her head?

She was surprised that, after thinking about this idea for so long, now she actually had time to write it, she was becoming more confused about it than ever. Perhaps it was the shock of seeing Leo again, after all these years, that had done it. She felt as though something in her brain had short-circuited, and she wasn't sure how to fix it. Instead of focusing on the historical part of the story, she found herself drawn to the more modern timeline, the one she'd loosely be basing on her own teenaged experiences of first love.

The problem was, one of the protagonists of that story was living a stone's throw away, and she felt the blurring of past and present every time she tried to think about the story she was trying to tell. It was one thing to draw upon personal experiences for inspiration: quite another to have a real, live character walking around in her life again.

Sighing, she opened up her laptop and tried to focus on getting her notes into some kind of order. She had to keep focused on why she was here in Roseford, and it wasn't to get sidetracked by Leo McKendrick.

14

Leo busied himself with the preparations for the next visitors to Roseford Villas, ensuring that the rooms that had been booked were spick and span, and the guests had access to everything they'd requested. The level of detail in the ring binder that Aunt Vi and Uncle Bryan had left him was certainly extensive, and he found himself wondering, if he himself had been in charge, whether he'd have bothered with a lot of it. However, he had to concede that Roseford Villas was a lovely place to stay, and perhaps that was because of his aunt and uncle's attention to every last detail. He was determined not to let them down.

If he was being honest, he needed the distraction. And not just because Rory Dean had turned up on the doorstep. The past couple of years had been hectic, to say the least, and he still found himself wondering, in the small hours when insomnia racked his brain, how it had all come to this. He had made a success of his life, and, for a while he'd truly believed, an equal success of his marriage. He and his ex-wife Corinne were both partners in love, and also in the law firm where they worked, and they'd been happy. Well, to a point. Then, on one fateful night, all of that had changed forever, and there was no going back.

Leo picked up the duster and the furniture polish and wiped briskly at the top of the chest of drawers in the bedroom he was preparing in an attempt to put a mental roadblock up to stop himself from wandering down another distinctly unpleasant lane of thoughts and memories. He'd been over it all a thousand times, both alone and with a counsellor: there was little use in going back over old ground. But every so often, when he felt the anxiety starting to creep up on him again, he was drawn to the bruising memories of his recent past.

He knew why he was heading that way, of course. Seeing Rory had awakened all kinds of memories that he'd shelved for many years. She was from a far different time in his life, a time when things were simpler. When all he'd had to think about was what his mum was cooking for dinner and when his next piece of GCSE coursework was due. They'd loved each other in that crazily passionate way that only teenagers really could, and they'd both suffered the agony of separation when it had come to an end. That they hadn't chosen to end things themselves had hurt beyond measure: it had been circumstance that had done for them in the end. You couldn't love someone from ten thousand miles away, no matter how much you wanted to. Especially back in the days before Zoom, smartphones and the multitude of other ways to keep in touch that people now used.

With those memories of Rory had come the seductive invitation from his brain to press on a few more bruises, just to see if they still caused him pain. But he knew he had to resist it. It wouldn't do him any good, and there was the present to consider. Balling up the duster, he went to throw it into the box of cleaning supplies he'd brought up to the first-floor rooms and missed. He shook his head: way off the mark, as always, he thought ruefully.

Fed up with cleaning what was already clean, Leo picked up the cloth and the box and headed back downstairs. He'd check the fridge, re-order whatever needed replacing for breakfast over the next few days, and then try to get his head around the finer details of the contract he'd been sent for his new job. *That* was the future, he thought, and it would be a decent compromise. While he was only going to be a mid-level solicitor in the London firm that were taking him on, and some way from the partner he'd been back in Melbourne, it was enough of a step down for him to be secure that he could handle it, both physically and mentally. To be fair, he hadn't thought he'd ever work again, so he was pleased and proud he was able to continue his career. There was plenty to sort out before he made the move, and he wanted to make sure that there weren't any nasty surprises in the contract before he made everything official and signed it.

A little while later, Leo sat at Aunt Vi's scrupulously tidy desk in the back office and pored over the details. The office window looked out over the garden, and his gaze kept flitting from the pages of the contract across to where the chalet – or Rory's chalet, as he was increasingly thinking of it – sat. He wondered what she was doing, and whether or not she was thinking about him...

Leo's mind kept drifting back to the early days of their teenaged relationship. He remembered the trip to the local cinema to see *Tomb Raider 2*, and how, despite how much he'd adored Angelina Jolie growing up, he'd barely watched any of the film. It had been their second date, and he'd spent half the movie plucking up the courage to hold Rory's hand across the armrest of the multiplex seats. When he'd finally taken the plunge, the warmth of that hand, squeezing his, had made his heart speed up faster than Lara Croft's death-defying stunts. Their first proper kiss had followed just before the end of the movie, and even now, if he happened to catch a clip of the film, he was taken back to that moment. That delicious, nerve-racking sense of anticipation seemed to be encroaching on him again, now, and he couldn't quite tear his mind away from the memories. He wondered if *Tomb Raider 2* still took Rory back to the same places.

He tried to stop that train of thought. It was clear from the awkwardness of their last encounter, even after they'd begun to laugh about the 'burglar' in the chalet, that Rory wasn't sure how to behave around him, just as he was uncertain about how to behave around her. There had been none of that easy banter and chemistry that they'd had as teenagers, and while he shouldn't have been surprised by this, he couldn't help but be a bit disappointed. Somehow, when he'd imagined bumping into her again, they'd had an instant connection. Even when he'd been married to Corinne, he'd allowed himself the odd fantasy about what might have happened if his path crossed again with Rory. The reality had been rather different, and far more awkward. But then, it had been twenty years.

Cursing himself for his inattention, he tried to focus on the contract again, but it wasn't the most riveting of reads. Fifteen years ago, he'd have killed for a job at this particular firm. Now, with a decade and a half of professional experience under his belt, it failed to excite him. It was a step down, but it was also a step back from all the stress that being a partner had entailed. He knew it was the right decision, so why was he suddenly having doubts?

Realising, after a couple of minutes, that he'd zoned out again, he felt his heart give a little lurch as he saw Rory making her way back across from the gate at the back of the garden to the chalet. She walked briskly, as if she didn't want to be waylaid by anyone, and he noticed the thoughtful expression on her face, and the way her ponytail swung as she headed for the chalet. The girl he'd known back then had turned into an extremely attractive woman, and for the first time in a long time he felt the stirrings of lust as he observed her. It had been ages since he'd touched or been touched by anyone, and he missed it.

Leo shook his head and grinned to himself. Rory would be mortified if she'd known he'd been watching her, and he had to admit, he felt a little uncomfortable about how easily he'd been distracted by the sight of her. But it wasn't like he had his binoculars out and was peering into the chalet windows, was it? They shared a space, and would be doing so for the next few weeks, so he'd better pull himself together and stop acting like a schoolboy with a crush. He'd been that schoolboy twenty years ago, and she *had* been his crush. He was surprised at how strongly that was coming back to him.

15

Rory, ravenous now, grabbed the remains of the loaf of bread and shoved a couple of slices in the toaster. She felt so excited by what she'd begun to unearth at Roseford Hall that she couldn't wait to get back there and chase up the leads that had been revealed to her. While she was munching on her toast, she fired off a WhatsApp to Stella.

When she was reading through the information in the archives, she'd discovered that Francesca and Frederick Middleton had lived in Halstead House and she wondered if Stella had come across any papers in Halstead's archives that would give extra context and colour to the story, especially if Halstead House still had copies of any more of Edmund's letters that actually had been sent to Francesca. She knew it was a long shot: the previous owners had probably cleared everything out when Chris Charlton had taken the place over, but she'd heard of similar situations when whole boxes of potential archive material had been found in cupboards and cellars after a property had been sold. It had happened to her parents when they'd moved into a house and found boxes of old birthday cards and letters to people who'd long ago moved on.

Chucking another round of toast in, Rory found herself waiting impatiently for Stella to reply. She smothered her toast in a thick layer of butter and Marmite, and rapidly gobbled it up. Then, realising that she couldn't just stare at her phone and wait for Stella's response, she cleared away and got her laptop out again, only to discover, with irritation, that it was very nearly out of battery. Since the setup of the chalet meant she couldn't sit at the table with the laptop while it was plugged in, she thought she'd head up to Roseford Villas and see if Leo could lend her an extension lead for the duration. It would make life a lot easier and would mean she wasn't limited by the battery life of her laptop.

The afternoon sunshine warmed her bare arms as she mooched up the path to the main house, and she was glad she was only wearing a T-shirt and capri-length jeans. The weather had been glorious since she'd arrived in Roseford, and although she was going to be working for a lot of her stay, it was still wonderful to be able to step outside the chalet and feel the sun. The grass, newly mown, wafted its sweet scent as she made her way to the French windows at the back of the main house, and, finding them un-locked, she wandered through the dining room and into the hall.

'Hello?' she called as she walked along the hall-way. Almost before she'd finished saying the word, a door opened, and Leo appeared.

'Hi,' he said, and his smile made her heart beat just that little bit faster. 'Everything OK?'

Rory smiled back. 'Fine, thanks. I was just won-dering if you had an extension lead I could borrow. My laptop cable doesn't quite reach the plug socket nearest the table, and I could really do with being able to work and charge it at the same time.'

'Of course,' Leo replied. 'I'm sure there'll be one in the cellar. Aunt Vi's got a whole basement full of spares for every conceivable emergency. I'll go and get you one.'

'Thanks,' Rory said. 'I'll, er, wait in the dining room, shall I?'

Leo hesitated. 'Or you could wait in the kitchen, and I could make you a coffee? That's if you're not too busy?'

Rory's face grew warmer at the invitation. 'Er... well, I was going to crack on as soon as I'd got the lead—'

'Oh, no worries,' Leo interjected. 'It was just a thought, and you must be busy. I'll run down and get it for you.'

Rory shook her head. 'No,' she said, and as she did so, she reached out a hand to stop Leo from brushing past her. 'What I was going to add was that yes, I'd like to have a coffee with you. Honestly, Leo, you haven't changed much, have you? You always used to try to pre-empt the end of my sentences when you were younger!'

Leo smiled ruefully. 'And you always used to bol- lock me for it back then, too. I'm sorry. I guess old habits die hard!'

Something about that exchange seemed to make them both relax, and as they smiled at each other, Rory found herself beginning to wonder what it would be like to spend a little more time with this new, grown-up Leo.

'I'll go and get some mugs out,' Rory said.

'Sounds good,' Leo replied. 'Won't be a sec.'

He moved past her to go to another door off the hall, pushed it open and switched on the light. Rory made her way to the kitchen, and before she could wonder exactly how the fancy coffee machine in the corner of the room worked, Leo had returned, brandishing a couple of extension leads.

'I wasn't sure which one would be long enough,' he said, 'so I thought I'd bring them both up with me and let you decide.'

Rory selected the one she thought would work best, and then, at Leo's invitation, sat down at the scrubbed oak kitchen table and watched Leo make her a latte. As he did so, they exchanged pleasantries, but Rory still felt as though they were two passengers who just happened to be sitting on the same table in a train carriage. There was something carefully measured about their words, as if neither of them wanted to broach the subject of their shared past. And the longer it went on, the more frustrated Rory felt that they were ignoring the large elephant in the room.

Leo eventually passed her a generous cup of latte, and as she took it, their fingertips brushed. She was too tense to feel anything from the gesture, but the sight of his hands did bring back memories, warm, tingling memories, of the way they'd once touched her. She fought to smother those thoughts: they weren't helping the awkwardness of the situation at all.

'So, have you had a productive morning?' Leo asked as he took a seat at the table, to one side of her.

'Very,' Rory replied. She hesitated, wondering if she should elaborate on what she'd found out about Edmund Treloar. Finally, she added, 'It's great to finally have time to get to grips with the ideas I've been thinking about for so long.' Briefly, she filled him in on her morning spent perusing the letters in the Roseford Hall archives.

'Oh, yes?' Leo raised an eyebrow. 'Have you discovered anything interesting? Or scandalous?' His eyes twinkled.

'I'm not completely sure yet,' Rory replied, 'but I'm hoping Stella might be able to help me decide.'

'Well, when you're ready to share, I'll be all ears!' Leo replied.

As they sipped their coffee and talked some more, Rory began to relax. Leo's genuine interest in her research felt flattering, and pleasing, and although she didn't divulge too many details, she liked talking to him about it.

Eventually, though, when they were nearly all the way down their coffee cups, the conversation began to flounder. There it was again, the thing that neither of them seemed able to discuss. And Rory knew, if she didn't broach it soon, it was going to become a huge distraction for her, and probably for him, too. She wasn't the kind of person who could just park things safely away in little mental boxes: she needed to face things head on, and the longer she and Leo did this crazy dance where they both pretended as though they hadn't ever been intimate, just for the sake of a quieter life, the more frustrating it was going to be.

'So,' she said, gathering up her courage as she gulped down the last of her latte, 'are we ever going to talk about when we were sixteen, or what?'

When she saw the look of shock on Leo's face, she wondered if it would have been better just to remain frustrated.

16

Leo gulped so hard at Rory's matter-of-fact question that he accidentally ended up inhaling his coffee instead of swallowing it. As his eyes filled with tears, and drops dripped from his nose, a flush of mortification spread over his cheeks.

'Christ!' Rory said, putting her own coffee cup down on the kitchen table and springing to Leo's side. 'I didn't mean to startle you!' Leo felt the slap on his back and he shook his head, coughing to dislodge the last of the fluid from his throat. Swallowing hard, he wiped his eyes with the back of his hand.

'It's all right,' he croaked. 'I'm fine, honestly.'

Leo looked up into Rory's distinctly amused face. Now she was seemingly sure he wasn't going to choke to death on her, a grin was plastered over her features.

'I'd never have been so direct if I knew you were that reluctant to talk about it,' she said, still smiling. 'I mean, was it really that triggering?'

Leo found himself smiling back through the spluttering-induced tears. 'Not triggered,' he reassured her, 'I just wasn't quite expecting you to be so, er, honest. The Rory Henderson I knew at sixteen wasn't into confrontation, or straight questions.'

Rory sat back down at the table. 'Well, fourteen years in a classroom has taught Rory Dean a lot about when to be diplomatic and when to just come straight out with it!'

'I can see that,' Leo replied. 'Whereas, in my line of business, we're used to couching things in rather more complex terms.'

'So, what's it to be?' Rory asked him. 'A straightforward discussion or something more, er, complicated?'

Leo let out a sigh. The coughing fit had, thankfully, subsided, and now he was just left to answer the questions Rory had posed. 'The honest answer is that I didn't know how to broach it with you, Rory. I mean, what can I say? I'm sorry I broke your heart? I'm sorry I never kept in touch? I'm sorry I didn't try harder to come back to you? Does that about cover it?'

Was that a head toss of exasperation he was observing from Rory? He waited for her response.

'Well, Leo,' she said eventually, 'it's like this. Yes, you did break my heart, but that wasn't your fault, was it? I mean, you can't tell me, with twenty years of hindsight, that it would have ended up any differently. We were a world apart, for heaven's sake!'

'I know that,' Leo said softly. 'But, for what it's worth... I missed you, and I'm sorry.'

'For what?' There was definitely a trace of annoyance in Rory's voice now, and Leo was struggling to understand why. 'I'm not sorry... for any of it. We've both had lives, good lives, away from each other.'

That's debatable, Leo thought, thinking of the mess of his own situation. But he could, at least, feel pleased that Rory seemed satisfied with the way her own life had turned out, and he did have some sort of hope for his future. 'OK,' he said, realising that Rory was waiting for some kind of a response from him. 'So, we grew up and did all right. What else is there to talk about?'

'Oh, how about the fact that we're living barely a hundred yards from each other at the moment, and you're my landlord for the summer? That's quite a power dynamic.' Rory sounded deadpan, but Leo noticed a familiar twinkle in her eye, downplaying her bald statement. He loved – he *had* loved – that about her.

'Well, I promise not to abuse that power in any way,' Leo replied. 'And, strictly speaking, I'm not your landlord. My Aunt Vi and Uncle Bryan are. They still own the place, even if I'm running it for the time being. So, I'm kind of *in loco avunculi et amitae*, if you will.'

'Oh, now you're just bamboozling me with dodgy Latin!' Rory gave a giggle, and it surprised Leo just how much he wanted to keep hearing that sound.

'So, it's not going to be weird for you, knowing that I'm at the bottom of your garden, then?' Rory asked. 'Because, Leo, if I'm being honest, it's kind of weird for me.'

'How so?' Leo asked. He knew how weird *he* felt about their situation, but he wanted to hear it from Rory's side, too. If they were on the same page, perhaps they could work on de-weirding it for them both.

It was Rory's turn to blush. Leo noticed how the colour creeping up her cheeks only enhanced how pretty he thought she was. He'd always loved making her blush, how that wild rose colouring deepened when she was on the back foot, and in the gentlest possible way, he used to try to fluster her, just so he could see the warmth in her cheeks and her green eyes widening in surprise that he should want to make her feel that way. He mostly used to do it by snatching a kiss, which never failed to make her flush, but as they'd become surer of each other, he'd utter a suggestive line from a favourite film, or tell her a naughty joke, just to watch her blush.

'Well,' she said, eventually. 'You know... you were the first person that I'd ever fallen in love with, and ever slept with. And coming face to face with you on the doorstep when I arrived kind of tilted my world on its axis. Not enough that I'd want to leave, but it's making concentration rather difficult, and as I'm here to *really* concentrate this summer, since I've only got a few weeks to break the back of this project, I'm finding that quite tricky to deal with.'

'So, you wanted to clear twenty years' worth of air, in the hope that we could be grown-ups and move on?' Leo asked.

'Something like that, yes.'

Leo let the pause develop between them for a few seconds while he chose his words carefully. There was so much he desperately wanted to say to her, now that he had her full attention, but his mind felt so sluggish sometimes. He was sure it was because of the accident, but also because he wasn't living at a hundred miles an hour any more. Eventually, he spoke.

'I'm not sure it'll be that easy to clear quite so much air,' he said, eventually. 'I mean, as you say, it's been twenty years. That's a lot of ground to cover in a few weeks!'

'So what do you think we should do?' Rory asked. There it was, that impatient toss of the head again. She couldn't help but seek solutions, he realised. Maybe it was her teaching experience that made her try to solve problems all the time. But this wasn't exactly a problem that needed solving: it was more of a pleasurable conundrum, if anything. He smiled inwardly. If that was the way she wanted to see it, then he didn't mind playing along.

'It seems to me that the only thing we can do is to *really* take our time and come to a solution that suits both our purposes,' he said, the seriousness of his tone completely belying the fact that inwardly he was smiling like the class clown.

'And how might we do that?' Rory asked.

Leo tried hard to maintain a straight face. 'Well, Rory Dean,' he said, in his most business-like tone. 'If you really want us to move on from this somewhat strange predicament in which we appear to have found ourselves, I strongly recommend you accept an invitation to dinner from me tonight, where we will be able to bash out the pros, cons and all things in between, of our current living arrangements. Would that be agreeable to you?'

Rory, to his shock, agreed.

17

How Rory walked out of Leo's kitchen, she didn't know. Her legs were shaking like jelly, and she realised that she'd fallen right into one of his traps. He always did have a way with words, and she could never resist it when he started verbally sparring with her. Often she used to tease him about his speech patterns: he spoke, and wrote, as though he'd been transplanted from an earlier century, but she adored him for it. It didn't surprise her in the slightest that he'd gone into law as a profession: the multi-clause contracts and impenetrable terminology would have suited him down to the ground. Some saw him as pompous, but she thought it was one of the things that had made him unique.

That being said, she'd never expected *that* discussion to have led to her accepting an invitation to dinner. She'd only wanted to clear the air so that she could devote her energy to writing her novel, and here she was, feeling as though she was living in the middle of her own bloody rom-com! They'd agreed that she'd come to the dining room of Roseford Villas at 8 p.m., and continue their discussion, and hopefully after that they could move on with things.

If nothing else, Rory thought, it would be nice to find out what Leo had been doing with his life for the past twenty years. And, of course, why he'd given up such a great career in Australia to help out with his family's B&B. It felt as though there was a story there, and from what Stella had already alluded to, she knew it wouldn't be an altogether happy one. But perhaps tonight would yield some answers.

What was she going to tell him about her life? She'd been content with where she'd got to, and although a flat share wasn't an ideal circumstance at her age, she was proud of what she'd achieved. This summer was meant to be something that would enhance that, a chance to finally follow a dream she'd been nurturing for a long time. But, apart from her job and her dream, what had she *really* achieved? She was a long way from who she'd been at sixteen, but was it enough? How would her accomplishments match up to Leo's?

Pushing away these thoughts, she plugged in the laptop to charge, and brought it over to the table. Thanks to the extension lead, she could work while the battery was charging, and she had plenty to think about, and note down, after her discoveries at Roseford Hall. She opened the document and began to type.

Perhaps it was the conversation she'd just had with Leo that had fired her up, but for the first time since she'd been in Roseford, inspiration seemed to pulse through her, until, an hour later, she leaned back on the bench seat to stretch out her arms, and realised she'd written nearly two thousand words. Even more surprisingly, some of them actually made sense. So this must be what *flow* felt like.

Deciding to quit while she was ahead, she closed the document and checked her messages. Stella had got back to her and suggested they meet at Halstead House tomorrow afternoon, and Rory, who hated leaving an opened message unanswered, sent back a quick reply saying she'd be there. If Halstead House held some of the missing pieces of the puzzle of Edmund Treloar and Francesca Middleton then that would make the novel a whole lot easier to write.

Buzzing with thoughts and ideas, Rory headed off to take a shower. She wasn't sure if she should dress up or not for dinner with Leo, but she wanted to freshen up and make herself look a touch more presentable. Fortunately, she'd brought a couple of smarter dresses with her, and as she slipped one on, a little later, she couldn't help remembering that crimson had always been Leo's favourite colour. That wasn't why she was wearing it, of course, she said firmly to herself. This was just dinner, and a chance to lay some old ghosts to rest, nothing more. All the same, as she applied a bit of light make-up and pulled a brush through her long, dark hair, if she was going to spend the evening talking about her life, she wanted to make damn sure she looked good while she did it.

At just before eight o'clock, she headed back towards Roseford Villas. As she drew closer to the dining room, she noticed a couple of tea lights in jars on a table just inside. She wondered why they were eating indoors, since it was still warm, but she walked up the steps and into the dining room. Should she call out to Leo to let him know she was there?

Just as she was about to say a brisk, 'Hello,' she saw a movement from the far end of the dining room, from the direction of the kitchen. She was flattered to see, when Leo came into view, that he, too, had got changed out of the polo shirt and shorts he'd been in earlier into something smarter. He was wearing a flattering pair of indigo-washed jeans, with a crisp white shirt, open at the neck and with the sleeves rolled up to just below his elbows. As he drew closer, she caught a tantalising waft of a spicy, jasmine-infused scent, the aroma of which was exotic and exciting. She wondered if it was a cologne he'd discovered during his time in Australia. He'd brushed his dark, curly hair away from his forehead, but it was already starting to break free from whatever product he'd used and was tumbling across his brow once again. He was still tanned from so many years living on the other side of the world, and she noticed the crows' feet crinkling around his eyes as he broke into a wide smile at the sight of her.

'Hey,' he said softly as he reached her. 'That's a knockout dress. Colour really suits you.' The trace of an Australian accent punctuated his words in a way she found decidedly attractive, and Rory wanted to hear more of it.

'Thanks,' she said, smiling back at him. 'You, er, don't scrub up so badly yourself.'

'Well, you know, thought I'd better make more of an effort than my Roseford Villas polo and scruffy shorts as this is the first time I've had dinner with someone since...' He trailed off. 'Well, since I came back from Aus, anyway.'

Rory thought about questioning him, but let it lie. She had all night to find out what Leo had been doing with his life since they'd last been in touch. And as he led her to the table, and asked her what she wanted to drink, she realised that she was really looking forward to finding out.

18

'So that was the first time one of the little buggers got into the house, and I don't think I've ever heard my mum screaming so loudly!' Leo leaned back in his chair as he finished recounting the story, and Rory couldn't stop howling with laughter.

'Wow,' she said, when she was finally capable of speech. 'I can't imagine being surrounded by so much potentially fatal wildlife. Your mum must have been terrified every time you and your brother and sister set foot outside.'

'She was, until one of her friends invited her round, fed her a bucket of margaritas and told her to stop being so bloody British about the whole thing. Eventually, she calmed down and realised that it was just a case of being a little more vigilant. But she never did quite learn to live with the redback spiders. Every time she saw one, she'd have to get Dad to come and remove it from the house.'

'But they're settled there, now?' Rory asked.

'Oh, yeah,' Leo replied. 'My sister's got two kids and they love being grandparents. I don't think they'll be coming back to live in the homeland any time soon.'

Rory paused. 'And what about you? Are you back to stay?'

Leo looked at her, and his serious stare sent her equilibrium a little off kilter.

'That depends,' he said. 'I'm only meant to be helping Aunt Vi and Uncle Bryan out for the next few weeks, and then I've got a job in London to go to, but I still don't know if I'll be here for the rest of my career.' He shrugged. 'Mum and Dad would rather I was back in Australia with them, where they can keep an eye on me, but then I suppose it's always the way when you're the youngest child.'

'Nice to have options,' Rory replied. 'I've been spending the past few years doing maternity covers at different schools in Yorkshire. I'm doing one at the moment, but I'm not sure what I'll do after that. To be honest, though, I don't want to keep doing temporary contracts. I've been teaching for fourteen years now, and I'm not sure if I've got any more left in me.'

'You sound tired,' Leo said.

'Not exactly.' Rory took a sip of her wine. 'More... bored, I suppose. There's only so many times you can teach the same poems and find something new in in them, and while Shakespeare will always be my first love, I think I need a break from him!'

Leo assumed a mock-affronted expression. 'I thought *I* was your first love. Now I find out I lost out to The Bard?'

Rory laughed. 'You know what I mean. We shared a lot in common with that couple from *Ten Things I Hate About You*, I always thought.'

Rory saw Leo preening slightly. 'Well, I always thought I looked a bit like Heath Ledger when I was sixteen!'

'Not *that* couple.' Rory kept on laughing. 'The Shakespeare-mad girl and the geek!'

'Gee, thanks,' Leo replied dryly. 'That's burst my bubble.'

Rory took a sip of her wine. 'I'm sure you'll recover,' she teased. 'And I do have to admit, dodgy fashion choices aside, we did have a rather spectacular leavers' ball, I remember. Maybe even one to rival Kat and Patrick's.'

A look of delighted recollection passed over Leo's face, and Rory knew he was thinking back to that night, so many years ago, when, slightly drunk from a surfeit of Hooch alcoholic lemonade, they'd danced the night away in the school hall, surrounded by their mates, and thought they were invincible. They were young, tipsy and having the time of their lives.

'I remember that night so well!' Leo laughed. 'I had that pastel-pink satin bowtie that we spent weeks trawling around the shops looking for, so that it was the perfect shade to match your dress.'

'That's right!' Rory shook her head. 'It felt like it was *so* important to get the right colour, as if no one would have known we were an item if we hadn't!'

'And then that bloke, God, who was it?' Leo wrinkled his brow, lost in the memory. 'Oh, that's right, it was Ed Truman who smuggled in a half bottle of vodka under his dinner jacket and poured double measures into our Cokes.'

'Then he puked up all over the curtains by the stage in the school hall!' Rory completed the anecdote. 'If we hadn't already finished our exams by then, I think he'd have been expelled!'

Leo leaned back in his chair. 'I suppose you get to see it all from the teachers' point of view now.'

'Yeah,' Rory replied. 'And there's no vodka involved when you're on that side of things, although still the odd bit of vomit!'

'All the consequences without any of the fun. Sounds like being a responsible adult.'

'Something like that.'

They fell silent, but it was a companionable one. Eventually, Leo broke it again.

'So, what do you *really* want to do, if you're fed up with teaching?' he asked.

Rory paused before she answered, feeling self-conscious again all of a sudden. 'Well, what I *really* want to do is write.'

'Why don't you do it, then?'

Shaking her head, Rory took another sip of the red wine that Leo had served with dinner. 'It's not that simple. I need something to live on while I do that, and it's difficult to walk away from a profession I've spent my working life in. But I'm not sure I can do both.'

Leo regarded her with his serious, brown-eyed gaze, and Rory felt her pulse quicken. 'The Rory I knew would have followed her heart,' he said.

'It's not so simple for me,' Rory replied, mildly irritated that Leo saw things in such binary terms. 'I can't live on fresh air, and I don't have the kind of funds, or options, that you do. I'm in a flat share that

I'm more than likely going to have to leave in the next few months, and I don't have a permanent job. I saved everything to come here for the summer, but once that's over, I've got to go back to York and earn some money, or I can't pay my rent.'

'I get that, I really do,' Leo said. 'But there has to be some way you can work it out.'

'You always were an idealist,' Rory smiled, despite her irritation. 'It's nice to know that part of you still exists.'

Leo laughed, but it sounded rather brittle. 'Sometimes it's difficult to be an idealist when your ideals have come crashing down around your ears, but I do my best.'

Intrigued, Rory probed further. 'So why aren't you still in Australia running some hotshot law firm and living the, er, Australian dream?'

Leo's face became serious, and Rory wondered if he was trying to avoid answering the question. But just as she was about to add a, 'Sorry, it's really none of my business,' he replied.

'If you'd suggested five years ago that would be my life, I'd have told you that you were probably right,' he said. 'But sometimes fate has a habit of smacking you on the side of the head just when you think you've got everything in nice, neat rows, and that's exactly what happened to me.' He winced, and suddenly got up from the table. 'Sorry,' he said. 'I've got some pretty hefty issues with my spine these days and I can't sit still for too long.' He went to grab her dinner plate to take back to the kitchen, and Rory stood too, to help him.

Having declined his offer of dessert, she nodded as he filled up both of their wine glasses. 'So that was a pretty cryptic answer you just gave me,' she said as they stood looking out over the darkening skies that surrounded the garden. 'What exactly did fate do to mess up your perfect life?'

'Oh, it wasn't perfect.' Leo gave that brittle laugh again. 'Far from it, but I didn't realise that at the time. I thought I'd achieved everything I needed to, but it turned out that wasn't true. And it wasn't until I lost it all that I realised none of it meant anything anyway.'

'So that's the second cryptic thing you've said to me in the space of five minutes,' Rory observed. 'The Rory Henderson who dated the Leo McKendrick of twenty years ago would never have stood for that!'

'Is that so?' Leo smiled at her. 'What about the Rory Dean of two decades later?'

Rory paused before replying gently. 'Rory Dean would like to know what you're alluding to, Leo, but she wouldn't want you to tell her anything that you didn't feel comfortable sharing with her.'

'Christ, and now we're speaking in the third person!' Leo laughed, and this time it was a heartier, more relaxed sound. 'Tell you what,' he said, 'so long as you don't mind possibly being dive-bombed by the local horseshoe bats, let's get some fresh air, and I'll tell you all about it.'

'Now there's an offer I can't refuse,' Rory replied. And when Leo's hand brushed hers on his way out of the patio doors and onto the terrace outside the dining room, it seemed the most natural thing in the world for her to take it.

19

Night was falling softly around them as they lingered on the terrace. The scent of honeysuckle, under-pinned by the heavier, herbier aromas of lavender and the late-flowering clematis wafted and weaved, doing battle with the freshly cut grass. It had been another warm day, and the night promised the same for tomorrow.

Rory sipped her wine and looked over at her little chalet, which lay in darkness at the bottom of the garden. It had only been a few days, and she was al-ready starting to regard it as hers. She hadn't even thought that much about Honeysuckle Cottage.

'You look miles away,' Leo observed as he stood

quietly by her side. She could feel the warmth of his hand in hers, and the slight heat of his body.

'So, are you going to tell me why you're really back here?' she asked. 'Or am I just going to get another round of verbal gymnastics?'

Leo let out a long sigh, and his breath brushed past her as he did.

'It's not a great story,' he said, 'and it doesn't really have a happy ending, or any ending at all, I'm afraid.'

'Life doesn't tend to,' Rory said. 'And as I said, if you don't want to tell me, that's fine, but if you do, I'd like to hear it.'

'You always were a good listener,' Leo replied. 'Weird as it is that you're here, now that you are, I'd like to tell you.'

'I'm all ears,' Rory said softly. She turned away from the garden view to look Leo in the eye. She remembered just how much she'd loved his eyes and now she knew she was at serious risk of losing herself in them once more. Trying to bring herself back to shore, she gave him a smile. 'You were saying...?'

Leo smiled back at her, but it was tinged with sadness. 'I thought I had it all,' he said as they turned back towards the garden. 'On paper, and to the outside world, I had a great life. Brilliant career, partner in a top Melbourne law firm, a wonderful wife, a great house... the only thing missing, as my folks kept reminding me, was kids. They were constantly hinting that grandchildren would make their lives complete, and, to be honest, I was hoping that it would happen, too.'

Rory tried not to struggle with the most unexpected pang of jealousy. Having children and the perfect life with Leo was something she'd dreamed about when she was a teenager, and it seemed odd to hear him talking about it now. Which was, of course, ridiculous.

'So I'm guessing it didn't?' Rory replied, trying to focus on Leo's story, rather than the emotions she was feeling as he was telling it.

Leo shook his head. 'Corinne, my wife, wasn't wild about the idea of kids. She'd always been so fixated on her career, and she wasn't too big on the whole family thing. She didn't have the greatest relationship with her own parents: they'd never really wanted kids, and they'd often told her and her sister exactly that, during family rows. And there were a lot of them, believe me!'

'Poor Corinne!' Rory replied. 'I can kind of see where she was coming from.'

Leo sighed. 'Me too,' he said. 'But it didn't make it any easier, trying to explain that to my folks, and as the years went by and we both got embedded in our careers, we just ended up trying to ignore that we both felt completely differently to each other. I married her because I loved her, and I convinced myself that not having kids wasn't a deal-breaker: maybe, eventually, she'd come around and we would try for a baby. It was unfair of me to assume that, and it put her under a lot of pressure at times. I began to realise that if you don't want kids as a guy, no one really seems to judge you, but if you're a woman and you don't want children, other people can be at best judgemental, at worst downright offensive. Why is that?'

'I don't know,' Rory replied dryly. 'Patriarchy, perhaps?'

'One nil to Rory Dean,' Leo said, equally dryly. Suddenly, he grabbed Rory's shoulders and pulled her back a step or two.

'What are you doing?' she squawked as she nearly lost her footing.

'Sorry,' Leo said. 'I should have warned you about the bats. They start flying in circles in the garden at this time of night, eating the insects. You were just about to have one land in your hair!'

Rory giggled nervously. 'I'm sure they won't hurt me.'

'Of course not, but I didn't want them to scare you.'

'So you grabbed me instead?' Rory shook her head. 'That's male logic, if ever I heard it.'

'Not exactly,' Leo murmured. He still had one arm around her. 'It gave me the excuse to get a bit closer to you.'

'Oh, you're such a charmer!' Rory began to laugh. 'I've kind of missed that.'

'I've missed you,' Leo said softly. 'I didn't know how much until I saw you on the doorstep.'

Rory shivered at the intensity in Leo's voice. On the one hand, she was electrified by his words, but on the other, it felt too much, too soon. She'd barely been in Roseford a few days and he'd only just begun to tell her about the past few years. She had the feeling that there was a lot more to unpack and she wasn't prepared to risk having her heart broken by Leo McKendrick again.

'Let's not get ahead of ourselves, Leo,' she said as gently as she could. 'We've had a bit of wine, and we're both probably still high on being able to spend time together after so long apart. I don't think either of us should be making any bold statements right now.'

Leo's eyebrows quirked in surprise. 'Again, I ask,

who are you, and what have you done with the Rory I used to know?'

'She's still in there,' Rory said, 'but she's a little more cautious than she used to be. And,' she added, with a twinkle in her eye, 'a little less bowled over by your blarney!'

Leo gave a laugh, and the tension that had settled between them dissipated. 'I'm hurt,' he said. 'I never told you anything that I didn't mean!'

'What, never?' Rory asked.

'Well,' Leo paused tantalisingly, 'almost never. I really didn't like those clumpy old brown suede moccasins you used to wear under your summer dresses. They didn't suit you at all!'

Rory giggled. 'But you insisted on walking everywhere! I'd have been covered in blisters if I hadn't worn something comfortable.'

'Yeah, but when you asked me if I liked them, I might not have been entirely truthful when I said that I thought they suited you!'

'Oh, how will I ever trust you again?' Rory put a hand over her heart. 'That's it, my faith has been destroyed.' She paused. 'Maybe if you walked me back across the lawn to the chalet, though, I'd find it in my heart to be able to forgive you.'

'It's a deal. And I swear to protect you from the bats, too.'

'Glad to hear it. I wouldn't want to be dive-bombed again.'

Rory watched as Leo hopped down off the patio and held out a hand to help her down the steps to the path that led back to the chalet. 'My lady.'

'Thank you, my lord.' Rory's hand settled in Leo's, and they meandered hand in hand across the expanse of lawn.

'Am I allowed to say that it's been really nice tonight?' Leo asked as they approached the chalet.

'I think that's all right,' Rory said softly. 'I think it's been really nice, too.'

They paused at the steps up to the decking that lay outside the front door.

'Well, this is me.' Rory smiled. 'Thank you for walking me home.'

'My pleasure.' Leo's eyes looked deeper brown in the evening light, and Rory couldn't resist putting a hand up to his shoulder and reaching up to kiss his cheek. 'Thank you so much for cooking dinner.'

'Any time,' Leo murmured and the sensation of his breath tickling her ear as she spoke sent a shiver right to the base of Rory's spine. She felt suddenly shocked at how much she didn't want it to end. But she'd just warned Leo not to expect too much, too soon, and she couldn't go back on that without raising his hopes.

'Goodnight, Leo,' she said gently. 'I'll see you soon.'

'I hope so,' Leo whispered into her ear. 'It's good to have you back, Rory.'

'Likewise,' Rory replied.

They paused, hesitating on the cusp of something, Rory's hand still on Leo's shoulder, and her lips close to his cheek, before both, rather regretfully, pulled away. Rory's knees gave a rather less than subtle wobble as Leo turned away from her and walked back down the path to Roseford Villas. She watched him grow less distinct in the gloom, and, heart hammering nineteen to the dozen, she let herself into the chalet.

20

The next afternoon, which was again drenched in sunshine, Rory headed out to Halstead House to meet Stella. She was fizzing with a different kind of excitement as she hurried down the hill. Whereas last night her tingles had been caused by spending the evening with Leo, now she was champing at the bit to get her hands on the papers from the Halstead House collection, in the hope that they might shed some light on Francesca's side of the relationship with Edmund Treloar. She was looking forward to discussing her Roseford Hall findings with Stella, who'd come back with the news, late last night, that Halstead did indeed have some documents in its own archive that might provide the other half of the story.

When she arrived at Halstead House, it was a hive of activity. The next group of artists had arrived, and were being shown to their rooms by Chris, Stella's partner, who waved a cheery but brief hello to her as she crossed the entrance hall.

'Stella's in the library,' Chris called as he passed. 'She said to tell you to go straight up.'

'Thanks,' Rory replied. 'And how do I get to the library?'

'Up the stairs and second on the right,' Chris called back.

Thanking him again, Rory followed Chris's directions and swiftly found Stella.

They greeted each other, and in no time Stella had opened a couple of archive boxes on the large mahogany desk off to one side of the library.

'These are all of the surviving documents that Chris inherited when he bought the house,' she said. 'They'd been languishing in the cellar for a while, since the house was left unoccupied, but over the past couple of years I've gradually been trying to sort through them and get them into some sort of coherent order. It's not easy – a lot of them have been damaged by mould. They weren't exactly Chris's priority when he took the place on, so it's fallen to me, now that the house is finally in better shape, to act as unofficial historian and archivist.'

'Looks as though you've got your work cut out,' Rory observed as she carefully took a sheaf of letters from the top of a pile in the nearest box. 'This could end up being a labour of love!'

'The whole place has been, really.' Stella smiled gently. 'But it's good to get a feel for Halstead House's past. Our local film director and movie star, Finn Sanderson, is trying to put together a pitch for a period drama about some of the earlier inhabitants of Halstead House, so it's given me an added incentive to try to find out as much as I can.'

Rory shook her head. 'I can't quite believe *the* Finn Sanderson lives in Roseford now! I remember watching him on the telly when I was a teenager. You could have knocked me down with a feather when I saw him in the pub the other night.'

'I know,' Stella laughed. 'It is a bit surreal, but you kind of forget it after you've spent some time talking to him – he's a lovely bloke and he and Lucy, who owns Roseford Café, are such a great couple. I think Lucy's hoping Finn's pitch gets green-lighted soon so he'll be able to spend more time at home. He's often away now his directing career has taken off. She misses him a lot when he's gone, what with their son Robin still only being a toddler.'

'Well, perhaps we'll be able to find some information that might help him to get his pitch accepted,' Rory replied. 'I mean, I've been inspired to write a pretty passionate story myself, just from reading Edmund's half of the letters from Roseford Hall.'

'Brilliant!' Stella exclaimed. 'Don't you just love it when you get that, that *fizz* when a story starts to take shape? It's one of the best feelings you can have, and it never gets old.'

Rory smiled. She felt grateful for the way that Stella treated her with equanimity, even though their writing careers were so wildly different. It felt like being admitted into a special club, where it was all right to talk in depth about things that were only imagined. Briefly, she filled Stella in on her research about Edmund Treloar and how she'd been reading through his last diaries, and the stash of unsent letters that had been sent home to the family after his death.

'Yes,' Stella said, as Rory paused. 'I know that Edmund was great friends with both Francesca and Frederick Middleton. They grew up together, and Edmund and Frederick went to the same small private school. I often wondered why they weren't in the same platoon when they were both sent off to war, but I believe, from what I could work out from the Halstead archives, that Frederick ended up in the Congo, whereas Edmund, holding a somewhat more senior rank, was posted out to the Western Front. It seemed odd, really. So many friends enlisted together and then shipped out to the same place. But those two were continents apart.'

'That must have made it even harder for Francesca, having been left at home,' Rory observed. 'At least, if Frederick and Edmund had been posted together, they'd have been able to keep a look out for each other, and it might have put her mind at rest, knowing that the man she hoped to marry and the brother she was so close to were in the same place.'

'I can't imagine what she'd have gone through,' Stella replied. 'She must have felt so helpless. Even if she ended up doing some kind of job to support the war effort, it must have been terrible, waving them both off. And then, to get the news eventually that Edmund had been killed...' She trailed off, and both women paused for a moment, lost in their own thoughts.

Soon, though, they were engrossed in the documents that Stella had salvaged from the boxes in the cellar. She'd begun the laborious process of sorting

them into a more coherent catalogue, but it was difficult due to the extent of the water and mould damage
on some of them.

'Oh, look!' Rory said suddenly, as she leafed
through a pile of papers, carefully trying to prise
them apart from where they'd got damp and then
dried. Between the pages of an old newspaper were a
couple of photographs. She carefully managed to
peel one of them from the other, and as she did so,
she immediately spotted the handsome face of Edmund Treloar staring out at her. This was a contrasting picture from the sombre portrait that hung in
the Long Gallery at Roseford Hall, and Rory was
amazed at the openness of his smile, the crinkling of
his eyes and the carefree way he was lounging on the
grass. Obviously taken in high summer, despite the
fact that the photograph was in black and white,
Rory could almost see the vibrant colours of the garden, and the looming presence of Halstead House in
the back of the shot. When her eyes had absorbed
the details of Edmund's smile, and his easy, relaxed
demeanour, she was then drawn to the other man in
the photograph, with darker hair, and the same con-
tented expression.

'That's Frederick Middleton,' Stella said, looking
over at the photograph. 'I assume the photo must

have been taken by Francesca, the way they're both smiling.'

Rory nodded. 'They seem really chilled out, and as if they don't mind having the picture taken – which is saying something, considering that it might have taken some time to set up.' In fact, the image felt very Bloomsbury, with the men in loose Oxford trousers and slightly scruffy-looking pale shirts. It conjured up a pre-war world of heady days, languid evenings, tea on the terrace and not a care in the world. How that world was going to change in the space of a few months, Rory mused.

'They look so happy there,' Rory observed. 'Awful to think how it all altered.'

Stella nodded. 'Frederick came back after active service in the Congo, but he never married. In fact, he lived with Francesca in this house until his death. Francesca married fairly quickly after the war ended, and went on to have several children, but Frederick was always with her. I suppose, being twins, they had a special bond. There was some evidence that he came back from the war suffering from shell shock. Perhaps Francesca wanted to keep him where she could take care of him. There were no counsellors in those days, of course.'

'Makes sense,' Rory said, still gazing at the photograph. Carefully, she put it down again and turned her attention to removing the other photo, which had stuck face down onto the newspaper it had been stored with. She didn't stop to think about the coronary she'd probably be giving the British Heritage Fund conservationists up at Roseford Hall by simply trying to peel it back off the paper, but she tried her best to keep it as intact as she could.

As the image finally came free of the paper, Rory drew in a sharp intake of breath. It was another picture of Edmund and Frederick, but this one felt different... more intimate. In a moment of affection, Edmund had put his arm around Frederick's shoulder, and his head was tilted downwards, eyes half closed, as he gazed down at Frederick, who was smiling, too, but looking directly at the camera. It felt, again, like a very personal shot, captured by someone who knew them both well. Once more, Rory suspected Francesca was behind the camera.

As she put the two photographs side by side, Rory wondered why she and Stella hadn't yet come across any pictures of Edmund and Francesca together. There were a few more shots of the three of them, but these looked far more staged, more formal. But as for photographic evidence of them as a romantic couple, there didn't seem to be anything that had survived.

'The boxes in the cellar were in a pretty bad state by the time I discovered them,' Stella answered when Rory asked her if she'd seen any more photographs of the Middletons and Edmund. 'And Chris, being the philistine that he is, had also dumped a load of stuff in a skip when he and his wife Olivia took the place on. He didn't see the point in keeping anything that the old owners had left behind. What you've got in front of you is what was left mouldering down there, shoved behind a load of old machinery. It's a miracle any of survived at all!'

'So it's possible that if there were any more photographs, they're long gone now,' Rory said. 'That's a shame. It would have been lovely to have been able to see some pictures of Edmund and Francesca together, but all we have is these ones of the two lads.' As she said that, Rory's heart did a little jump. Perhaps... but no, that would just be too heart-breaking for words. Especially when she knew that the young men had been separated and sent to different sides of the world.

'Any sign of Edmund's letters to Francesca yet?' Rory asked Stella, who was leafing through another box.

'Not yet,' Stella replied. 'I know I've seen some somewhere, though. I obviously wasn't quite as efficient as I'd thought at cataloguing things. I'll keep looking.'

The two of them carried on looking at their assigned piles of documents, and just as Rory was about to take a breather, and get five minutes of fresh air, she paused. Tucked between the pages of a waterlogged copy of Wilkie Collins's *The Moonstone* was a piece of paper, just poking out of the book. Carefully, she opened the book, and realised, to her surprise, that the letter, while water damaged at the edges, had mostly been protected from the damp by the book itself, and was largely legible.

As she peered at the closely written page, with a shock of recognition she realised that the handwriting was identical to the letters she'd been studying up at Roseford Hall. There was no doubt that this was one of Edmund's letters. It was just as passionately written as the ones that were in the Roseford Hall archives, and Rory's heart sped a little faster as she carefully deciphered the densely written prose.

'Wow,' she breathed as she came to the end. 'Francesca was a lucky, lucky girl. Edmund was obviously crazy about her. Listen to this, Stella... "I want to be lying in your arms, feeling the rightness of you pressed against me, making plans for our future.

You complete me, my darling, darling F, and I cannot wait until we are both back and at one once again."'

'Wow!' Stella laughed. 'He certainly had a way with words. To think that all of that passion was going on underneath that buttoned up Treloar exterior!' She took the letter from Rory and perused it for a moment. As she did so, she asked, 'Where did you find this? I haven't seen it before.'

'It was tucked inside this book,' Rory replied. 'Maybe we're the first to clap eyes on it since it was sent.'

'Maybe,' Stella, who was flipping carefully through the book, mused. 'Funny, though...'

'What?'

Stella paused. 'This book... it's got a plate in the front. I'm sure you must have had the same with some of your favourite novels if you were as much of a reading geek as I was.'

'Oh, yeah.' Rory smiled. 'I loved those "this book belongs to" stickers that you could stick onto the title page. It also stopped my mates from nicking my copies of the *Harry Potter* novels when I lent them out.'

'Well, this book plate looks like it's something similar.' Stella glanced back at Rory. 'But it's odd. It's not Francesca's name written inside it... it's Frederick's.'

'Maybe Francesca borrowed the book off her brother?' Rory replied. 'My sister and I were always pinching each other's stuff. Perhaps it ended up on her shelf instead of his.'

Stella frowned, then nodded. 'Maybe you're right. It just seems a rather intimate letter to keep inside a copy of a book that isn't yours, don't you think? I mean, I wouldn't stash something like this in a book that my brother might take back off me at any time. Imagine the embarrassment if he found it and read it!'

'Yes,' Rory agreed, 'when you put it like that...'

Her mind, still half-mulling over the contents of the letter, returned to the two photographs she'd peeled from the old newspaper. Suddenly, the idea that had occurred to her when she'd seen the old photos presented itself again to her so vividly that she nearly dropped the letter and the book that Stella had handed back to her. *What if...?*

But no. There wasn't any possibility of that, was there? She tried to push the idea away, but it remained, stubbornly, flitting through her brain so that she just couldn't leave it alone. Could it be possible? Should she tell Stella what she thought?

No. She couldn't be sure, just yet. She needed more time to think. She wasn't an investigative journalist, she was a first-time novelist. But she was intrigued, and she definitely wanted to spend more time looking into the details. She jotted a couple of things down in her notebook, and then went back to the contents of the box.

21

Leo kept himself busy, but he couldn't help the grin that kept stealing over his features every time he thought about the conversation with Rory the previous evening. Of course, they still had a way to go before the awkwardness of their two decades of separation had been fully breached, but he felt as though they'd made some decent headway. After Corinne, he didn't think he'd ever feel that fluttering excitement of desire again, but he was coming to realise that something was reawakening in him that had lain dormant for a very long time. And it wasn't just an emotional reawakening. Physically, he'd felt incredibly drawn back to Rory, and despite the challenges he'd felt recently in that area, he wondered if she was going to be the one who would help him to, so to speak, get back in the saddle. It had been a long time, nearly two years, since he'd been intimate with anyone, and while the thought of it definitely made him nervous, he was more than curious about what it would be like to be with Rory again. A lot had changed since they were each other's 'first': what would it be like to sleep together now they were fully grown adults? Less fumbly, he hoped.

But he couldn't just focus on the lust he was feeling for her. She'd put the brakes on his verbal outpourings last night, and he had the impression that she was even more likely to do the same if he tried to rush things physically between them. She'd always been cautious, but with maturity she'd developed a firmness to her manner that spoke volumes about what he could and couldn't expect from her. The last thing he wanted to do was to jump the gun. He had to be careful to curb his impulses and try to remember that they weren't kids any more.

But what could he do? He had to show her he was serious about spending time with her, but also that he understood the reason she'd come to Roseford was to work. She was writing a novel, he knew that. He also knew that RoseFest, the annual arts and literary festival, was coming up. He wondered if there were any events that Rory might be considering going to. Sitting down at the desk in the back office, he opened his laptop and searched for RoseFest. Soon, he was scanning the listings of speakers and events, and his eyes lit up when he spotted a familiar name. He was pretty certain that Rory had read a lot of that particular author's novels when she was a teenager, and it looked as though the author was going to do a talk and a workshop in one of the function rooms at Roseford Hall during the festival. Before he had the chance to second guess himself, he clicked on the Eventbrite link and purchased two tickets. If the worst came to the worst and Rory didn't fancy it, then at least the festival would get the income. It wasn't really his kind of thing, but he was pretty sure Rory would love it. Or, at least, like it enough to want to go with him.

The afternoon passed in a series of run-of-the-mill jobs: mindless stuff that was needed to keep Roseford Villas ticking over, and before he knew it, it was getting close to evening again. Rory hadn't yet returned from wherever she was, so Leo decided to send her a text, asking her to pop in when she got back. He felt a flutter of nerves in his stomach, followed by a jarring pain in the base of his spine that reminded him he'd been overdoing things. He had, for the most part, recovered from his injuries, but every so often when he did too much, his spine reminded him that he needed to take care of himself. On the way back to his room for a quick spray of deodorant and to run a brush through his unruly dark hair, he paused at the en suite and took a couple of painkillers. He didn't like to keep taking them, but sometimes it was necessary. There had been a while when his daily diet had included a hefty dose of opiate-based medication, just to allow him to function, and those days, thankfully, were long past. He had to remember how far he'd come since then.

Glancing in the mirror of the en suite, he briskly brushed his hair back from his face and considered chucking some product through it but paused at the last minute. He didn't want to look as though he was trying too hard.

God, why is this so difficult? he thought, frustrated. All he was going to do was see if Rory fancied coming to see a bloody author's talk, for goodness' sake! Why was he feeling so nervous? It was like he was sixteen again and quaking in his Dr Martens at the prospect of asking her out for the first time. He was an adult now, and he needed to start behaving like one. He couldn't stop his heart from leaping when his phone pinged, though. It was from Rory, asking if now was a good time to pop over? Texting back a quick yes, he found himself frantically taking a swig of mouthwash before he darted out of the en suite and hurried back downstairs to the dining room, where he could see Rory locking up the chalet and making her way down the path. Pausing in the doorway, paralysed by indecision, he sat down in the nearest chair, then sprang back up. He leaned against the wall, but then, worried he'd look too casual, stepped away again. Appearing relaxed was stressful!

In the end, he walked across the dining room and met Rory at the French windows. He pushed them open and smiled as she came through.

'Hi,' he said quickly. 'Thanks for coming over. How was your day?'

'Great!' Rory replied. As she proceeded to tell him what her research session with Stella had unearthed, Leo once again found himself drawn in by her enthusiasm. He was intrigued by her findings, and when she'd finished explaining, he wanted to know more.

'So you're feeling pretty inspired, then?' he said.

Rory grinned. 'You could say that and it's given me plenty to think about in terms of how I might use a relationship like that in fiction. It's the perfect counterpoint to the modern story that I wanted to tell. The two ideas will complement each other beautifully.'

'And what's the modern story?' Leo asked. 'I don't think you've actually told me anything about that aspect of it. I thought you were writing a historical novel?'

Leo noticed the pause that Rory took before she spoke. 'Well,' she said carefully. 'I've been meaning to talk to you about that...'

22

'You want to write *what*?' Leo's tone of incredulity was about what Rory had expected as she delivered the news that she was planning on drawing on their past relationship for inspiration. Of course, if he'd stayed on the other side of the bloody world, she'd never have had to tell him. At least, not face to face.

'Well,' Rory said, beginning to feel very self-conscious. 'I, er, have this idea about linking the two tragic love stories together. I wanted to use what happened to you and me as the base for the modern love story, and then the original idea was to make it a kind of parallel with the historical relationship, when I'd done the research into Edmund and Francesca, of course.'

'And how much of it is really going to be fictional?' Leo asked. He suddenly looked a whole lot more serious than he had when Rory had walked in. 'I mean, am I going to cringe every time I think about it? How much of our teenage angst are you going to be sharing with your readers?'

Rory laughed. 'What, the millions of people who will pick up a romance by a new author off the shelves? You do know this book might not even get published, Leo? Chances are, my readers, as you call them, will be my mum, and my flatmate, Alex!'

'You don't know that, Rory,' Leo said. She watched his face carefully. 'Look... I'm not going to tell you not to write it. But do you think you could, oh, I don't know, think carefully before you write about anything that might be difficult for me to read? I know that makes me sound like the biggest, most conceited twat, but I just don't want to be hung out to dry in public for things we both did twenty years ago.'

Rory laughed, strangely tickled by the earnestness in Leo's expression. 'Seriously? I'm not out to do a hatchet job on you, Leo. And I'm not going to go into the gory details about what we got up to when we were teenagers. If anything, my main characters will be a little older and wiser than we were. But I can't ignore the emotions I felt when I fell in love for the first time, and I need to draw on some of those to make this book feel authentic.' She paused. 'If you hadn't opened the door to me when I arrived here, chances are you'd never have known about this project. After all, you didn't even know I'd changed my name. So just because you know about it now, why should it worry you?'

She watched as Leo mulled over what she'd said. He'd leaned back in his chair, and a lock of dark hair had fallen over his forehead, which he brushed impatiently away. 'I get it,' he said eventually. 'And I trust you. But can I ask you a favour?'

'Sure,' Rory replied.

'If you're unsure about anything... don't write it. You always were good with your gut feeling. If anything feels off, then think about it.'

'So not exactly a "publish and be damned" then?' Rory said, smiling slightly. Seeing he was still concerned, she added, 'I promise to think very carefully.' All the same, she thought, he need never have known...

Leo pushed himself up from his chair and straightened his back. Rory was sure she didn't imagine a slight grimace of pain crossing his features.

'Are you OK?' she asked. She rose from her chair

and they were suddenly standing in front of each other, both a little wary.

'Yup. Just had a hectic couple of days,' Leo replied.

'So, er, why did you want me to come over?' Rory said.

'Oh, yeah, right. I'd nearly forgotten.' Leo fumbled in his pocket and pulled out a piece of paper, which he handed to Rory. 'I thought you might like to come to this. With me. If you want to, that is.'

Rory felt a surge of excitement as she unfolded the paper and saw the name of her favourite author, Shona Simmonds, written on the page. 'Oh, wow!' she said. 'I had no idea she was coming to RoseFest. She wasn't mentioned on the website anywhere.'

'She was a last-minute booking,' Leo replied. 'The event didn't go live on the website until this morning. I was, er, looking for something that you might like, and this seemed perfect.'

Rory felt her face begin to warm at the tone of Leo's words. It was clear he'd really put some thought into it, and she couldn't help feeling flattered. 'Thank you,' she said, and before she could stop herself, she'd leaned forward and kissed him on the cheek. She caught a waft of his scent, and her senses felt as though they were suddenly on high alert. Pausing, so that her face lingered next to his for a long, delicious few seconds, she breathed in, and the memory of what it felt like to be so close to him tugged at the back of her mind. She felt more definitely those stirrings of attraction that she'd been trying to keep a hold on threatening to cloud her caution and judgement, and when Leo put a warm, gentle hand on her waist, she felt the distinctive rightness of that gesture. She let out a breath and turned her face closer to his.

'And don't worry,' she said softly. 'I promise I'm not going to write anything that you'd be embarrassed to read!'

Leo laughed. 'Or, more importantly, that my mum would be embarrassed to read. I'm pretty sure she guessed most of it, but there're a couple of things I *really* wouldn't want to see in print!'

'Such as?' Rory raised a teasing eyebrow.

'Oh, you remember,' Leo replied. 'I'm sure, even after all this time, there are some things we did that must be seared into your memory as much as they are in mine! I mean, surely you won't need to mention the time I escaped out of your bedroom window at 2 a.m., when your folks had thought I'd left at ten! Or those more, er, "experimental" things we thought we should try, just because *More!* magazine had them on their back page?'

Rory's face grew even warmer. She knew all too well what Leo was alluding to, and, despite having her diaries as an aide-memoire, she didn't need reminding of the times when enthusiasm had overwhelmed expertise. The fact that she was still teasingly close to him made her even more nostalgic. But this wasn't just nostalgia. If she wasn't careful, she could end up making some pretty heated new memories with this man. She pulled away a little regretfully. 'Well,' she said, as Leo's hand dropped from her waist. 'On that note, I'd better get back to the chalet and try to make sense of the scribbles I made during my time with Stella today. I'll see you soon.'

'Definitely,' Leo replied. He looked a little disappointed that she wasn't going to stay longer, but Rory still had facts and ideas buzzing in her head from her day's research, and she was desperate to get them into some kind of order. As she wandered back through the French windows, she glanced back over her shoulder to see Leo still standing there, watching her, an unreadable expression on his face. She got the feeling that he still wasn't sure about being used for 'inspiration', and that maybe this wouldn't be the last conversation they were going to have about that strand of her novel.

23

Did I just agree to a first proper date – a second *first date – with Leo McKendrick?* Rory turned the question over and over in her mind as she let herself into the chalet. She'd left Roseford Villas determined to get straight into making sense of the notes and discussions she'd had with Stella, but as she switched on her laptop again, she found her thoughts occupied with what had just happened between herself and Leo. She couldn't ignore the chemistry between them: she'd used kissing his cheek as an excuse just to get closer to him, to touch him, to get a sense of his familiar geography again. Her thoughts were overtaken by an odd feeling of excitement and nostalgia, and as she began to type, words tumbled from her brain to the page, not about Edmund Treloar, but about her own emotions, past and present. She knew she'd have to fictionalise it, but for the moment she just revelled in the unedited ideas as they came to her. As much as she'd assured Leo that she wouldn't write anything that could identify him or embarrass him, she found herself recalling those early, ecstatic days, when they thought they'd be together forever, and the discoveries they'd made about one another in subsequent months, as they grew closer.

An hour later, she saved the document to her desktop and leaned back in her seat. What she'd written would never be published: at least, not in its current form, but it had been cathartic to get it out of her head and onto the page. Before she closed the laptop, she looked again at the last paragraph she'd written and smiled.

Leo seemed to have that instinctive and assured touch, and I responded to it every single time he reached for me. We fitted together perfectly, as if no other two people could ever be such a fit. He used to luxuriate in my hands, and I in his, until we lost ourselves in each other, for those precious moments we were alone. He was my first, and at that point, I re-

ally believed he'd be the last. How wrong
I was.

Rory shook her head. It was pure, saccharine
nonsense, and it would never make any kind of final
draft (as were the frankly rather pornographic de-
scriptions of their more assured lovemaking sessions
in the later stages of their relationship), but it was
what she needed to write. She had a funny feeling
that writing about it wasn't all she needed, though.
She tried to slow herself down. She'd agreed to go to
Shona Simmonds's talk with Leo, and she'd see how
that went. It would be nice to spend time with him
doing something different, away from that obsessive
introspection that seemed to dog them in all their
interactions so far. What they needed was time: time
to get to know each other again, and a little lightness.

With that in mind, she spent the evening determined to make some progress on the section of the
book she was working on. If she was going to play
hooky with Leo and go to see and hear Shona Simmonds, she wanted to have plenty of her own words
under her belt before she did so. That way, perhaps,
she could really make use of Shona's knowledge and
experience.

* * *

When the morning of Shona's talk dawned, Rory was keen to get out of the chalet. She'd binged on her own writing for a productive twenty-four hours, only stopping to eat and sleep, and she definitely needed to get some sunshine and talk to people. As she got ready, putting on a pair of denim shorts and a pretty striped top, she felt excited both for the talk and that she was going to be spending some time with Leo.

A knock at the chalet door brought her back to the present. She shoved a notebook in her backpack and hurried to answer it. Seeing Leo on the other side, dressed in a plain white T-shirt and dark blue cargo shorts, she drew in a quick breath. He looked absolutely gorgeous. His dark olive skin, that always looked great whatever the season, had tanned to a darker colour as a result of all of the outdoor work in the garden, and it was offset by the bright white T-shirt to very attractive effect.

Oh, God... she thought as she realised that whatever happened today, she was more than willing to let it.

'Hey.' Leo smiled as she pushed open the door. 'Are you ready to meet your literary idol?'

Rory nodded, and then decided she probably

should respond in words. 'Can't wait,' she stammered. 'I hope you won't get too bored.'

'I'm sure I'll learn a lot.' Leo grinned. 'Although if the discussion gets too saucy, I might have to get some fresh air. I wouldn't want to discover too many trade secrets!'

Rory laughed nervously. 'I'm sure she'll be very interesting, even for a listener who's never read any of her novels.'

'I read one once,' Leo admitted, rather sheepishly. 'Mum had one on the shelf back when we still lived in the UK. I was twelve and *very* bored in the summer holidays. Let's just say that Shona Simmonds's work opened my eyes, in more ways than one.'

'You never told me that!' Rory, nerves suddenly abating with Leo's revelation, shook her head. 'When I spent all that time banging on about how amazing she was, and how much I loved her books, why didn't you admit you'd read one?'

'I was shit scared you'd think I was some kind of weirdo for reading my mum's books,' Leo replied. 'I mean, what sixteen-year-old is going to admit to that?'

'I'd have loved to have talked about it with you,' Rory said. 'I think it would have been great.' She paused, then smiled broadly. 'But I suppose I can understand why sixteen-year-old you might have been worried about 'fessing up!'

'I hope my confession hasn't put you off the grown-up me,' Leo laughed. 'I mean, I'd hate to think, as we were getting on so well, that I might have blown it.'

'Not at all,' Rory replied. 'In fact, I think it's very brave of you to admit to it. And I can only imagine what twelve-year-old Leo might have made of Shona's more, er, "grown-up" work. Which one was it, by the way?'

'*Boundaries of Desire*,' Leo replied immediately. 'Kara and Kayden Chance's story *really* gave me a lot to think about.'

Rory's eyes grew wider. 'I bet it did. I mean, I've read every single word Shona Simmonds has ever published and even I was, er, "moved" by that one.'

'Certainly gave me some ideas about what was and wasn't physically possible on top of a snooker table!' Leo laughed. 'Can't say I've ever wanted to try *that* out.'

'I might have attempted it once, at university,' Rory admitted, flushing slightly. 'But it definitely wasn't as, er, exciting as Shona's version.'

'I'm going to refrain from cracking jokes about potting balls and long, hard cues.' Leo was openly laughing now. Rory found herself thinking what a lovely sound it was, to hear him so happy. 'And as for polishing the end...'

'Oh, stop!' Rory was giggling, too.

'Puts me in mind of that night we all stayed over at Matt Thurston's place,' Leo continued. 'Do you remember? He had that massive house, with a games room. His folks were away, and he threw a huge party, and got in a massive keg of cider. We all ended up passing out in the games room, and you and I fell asleep on the pool table. It was the most uncomfortable night's sleep I'd ever had!' He shook his head. 'Closest I ever got to shagging someone on top of one, I can tell you that.'

'If I remember rightly, you were so pissed, you just crashed out anyway,' Rory observed. 'Just as well really, since there were about twenty of us in there, all trying to sleep.'

'If I hadn't been so drunk, there's no way I'd have got any shut-eye,' Leo replied. 'I can barely remember any of the night, apart from waking up the next morning with the most stonking hangover, and being freezing cold.'

Rory laughed. 'I don't think I was much better. I couldn't do it now.'

'I wonder what's he's up to, these days,' Leo

mused. 'If there's ever a school reunion, I'd be tempted to go.'

'Not sure I would.' Rory shuddered. 'Or maybe I've just seen too much of schools, over the years.'

They'd walked most of the way down to the centre of Roseford while they were teasing each other, and Rory marvelled at how easy conversation now was between them. It felt lovely to be able to relax in each other's company.

'Did you want to grab a coffee before it starts?' Leo asked. 'I think we've got half an hour or so.'

'That sounds great,' Rory replied. They were walking down Roseford's picturesque main street, which was a pleasing array of independent shops and houses. Roseford Reloved, the vintage clothing shop that Rory had noticed when she'd first arrived in the village, had an eye-catching display in its front window of pretty summer dresses in contrasting colours. The small art gallery a couple of doors down looked to be doing good business and the florist, Roseford Blooms, which was positively overflowing with buckets and stands of fresh, fragrant flowers, looked inviting on this warm summer's day.

'This place is so lovely.' Rory breathed in the scents of the flowers as they passed Roseford Blooms.

'I can't imagine anyone wanting to leave, once they lived here.'

Leo gave her a brief smile. 'I have to admit, it's been growing on me since I came back to help out Uncle Bryan and Auntie Vi. I used to spend summers here when I was a kid, and I got bored silly, but as an adult, it feels like the kind of village that I could live in. If things were different, of course,' he added quickly. 'But job offers wait for no man, and London definitely won't wait longer than September.'

Rory felt an unidentifiable pang of something as Leo said that. It felt so plain, so clear that he only saw this summer as a stop-gap. She was fooling herself if she thought he wanted anything longer term. All the same, it was lovely to be spending time with him while she could. And if things were different...

'So, what would you like?' Leo's voice interrupted her thoughts as they stepped over the threshold of Roseford Café.

'Oh, a latte to go would be great,' Rory replied.

'Two lattes it is,' Leo replied. He spoke briefly to the attractive blonde woman behind the counter, and in very little time they were sipping their drinks and mooching towards Roseford Hall, where Shona Simmonds's talk was scheduled to take place in the Great Hall.

'I feel so nervous!' Rory admitted as they walked through the wrought-iron gates towards the grand, imposing building that was Roseford Hall. 'I've loved Shona Simmonds's work for my whole life. What on earth am I going to ask her?'

'I would have thought you'd have written down a million questions in your notebook,' Leo replied. 'I mean, there must be so much you want to know.'

'Yeah, but so many of them just seem so daft. And I don't want to come across as just another aspiring novelist who doesn't know anything about anything.'

'Rory.' Leo stopped her in her tracks. 'You don't have to worry. Shona Simmonds will have seen and heard it all a thousand times. Just be yourself. She'll love you.'

Rory blushed. 'You're sweet. And I almost believe you.' She looked up into Leo's open, sincere face, and if it hadn't been for the coffee cups they were holding, she'd have given him a hug. He met her gaze, and something seemed to pass between them. Once again, as they both stood there for a fraction longer than they needed to, Rory found herself thinking, *Careful.*

24

Dropping their coffee cups into one of the many recycling stations that were placed at strategic points around the Roseford Hall site, Rory and Leo made their way to the already crowded Great Hall. Shona may have been a late addition to the programme, but she'd proved to be a popular one, and the chairs that had been arranged in the generous space of the Great Hall were already mostly occupied. Wondering where on earth they were going to sit, Rory was pleased to spot Stella near the front, with two empty seats beside her.

'I heard through the grapevine that you might be showing up for this one,' Stella said as they approached. 'Thought I'd save you a couple of seats.'

'Thanks,' Rory said, sliding gratefully into one of them. 'Have you, er, met Leo? He's staying at Roseford Villas, helping out his aunt and uncle for the summer.' She knew Stella had heard about Leo, but she wasn't sure if they'd actually met.

'Yes,' Stella replied, smiling at Leo. 'We've bumped into each other a couple of times.' As she made polite small talk about running similar businesses for a few minutes, Rory was content just to listen. If Stella was surprised that she and Leo had turned up together, she wasn't showing it.

'Well, looks as though Simon gets to introduce this very special guest,' Stella observed as the man himself took to the front of the Great Hall. 'Bet he loved being told by the BHF he had to do that.' She caught Rory's eye and smirked good-naturedly. 'He might not show it, but he hates speaking in public, even though he's actually quite good at it.'

'I should think he's probably used to it, isn't he, having been head of the family for quite a while.' Rory again observed how much Simon resembled Edmund. It really was like looking at a living version of history, when she saw him.

'Bless him,' Stella said fondly as Simon cleared his throat. 'He's such a dork.'

Rory turned to her friend in surprise. 'You know

him well, then?'

'Oh, yes – he's a good mate. We spent some time together when I was Writer in Residence here, and he's known Chris forever. He's a sweetheart, but sometimes he forgets what century he's living in.'

Stella paused as Simon began his introductory speech. He was a good speaker, with just the right amount of humour and interest, and Rory found herself enjoying listening to him. Then, she felt a frisson of excitement as Shona Simmonds herself appeared in the archway of the Great Hall, to thunderous applause.

It was if a rock star had entered the building as the audience rose to its feet. The diminutive woman, dressed in a simple but chic dark plum trouser suit, with a pastel-pink embroidered scarf wound elegantly around her shoulders, paused and smiled to acknowledge the welcome. Still spry and agile at eighty years old, she walked with a slow but confident step to the armchair that had been provided for her at the front of the hall and waited for the applause to die down.

'I can't believe she's here!' Rory whispered to Leo as they took their seats once again. 'All these years I've so desperately wanted to hear her speak, and she's right in front of me.'

Leo smiled down at her, and Rory's heart did a little flip in her chest. He looked, in his white T-shirt and dark shorts, like the perfect hero of a summer romance, and she felt the attraction growing stronger, the more time she spent with him. Wrenching her gaze from Leo's eyes back to Shona, who was about to begin her talk, Rory glanced at Stella, who was as excited as she was to be in the presence of such greatness. She was sure she didn't miss the crooked eyebrow and the glance in Leo's direction that Stella made, as well. Perhaps Rory's attraction to Leo wasn't quite as well disguised as she'd hoped.

'It's so wonderful to be here,' Shona Simmonds began, in that precise, clipped King's English voice that Rory had heard so many times in interviews. 'I can't tell you how delighted I am that so many of you have made the journey to see me today.'

A flutter of spontaneous applause greeted this opener, and Shona looked around and gave an all-encompassing smile to her audience. Then, she consulted the iPad she'd brought with her. 'As you know, I don't often give interviews, or do events any more, but when my old friend Margaret Treloar asked me to be here to celebrate the second year of the Roseford Literary and Arts Festival, I couldn't refuse. Margaret and I go back years, you see, and while she ended up bagging the lord of the manor, I was fortunate enough to marry his best friend, my dear, much missed Laurence.'

'I never knew Simon's mum was friendly with Shona Simmonds!' Stella whispered. 'He kept that one under his hat.'

'Oh, you know Simon,' Lizzie Warner whispered back from Stella's other side. Rory hadn't noticed her arrive, but she'd taken a seat just after Simon had started his introduction. 'He's got zero idea about popular culture, or at least, he hadn't until he set up RoseFest. He mentioned "Aunt Shona" to me a while back and then the penny dropped.'

Rory had one ear on Shona's talk and one ear on the conversation happening by her side.

'Rory, Lizzie, Lizzie, Rory,' Stella said quickly. 'Proper intros later, after Shona.'

'It's OK, we met in the archives!' Lizzie grinned. 'Nice to see you again, Rory.'

Rory smiled at Lizzie, and they both turned back to the armchair where Shona was sitting.

'After fifty novels and numerous short stories, you'd think I'd be more than happy to offer you the benefit of my so-called expertise,' Shona was saying, 'but, to be honest, when I started out it was as a way of paying the bills. I was rather broke, you see, and when someone, the editor for the local newspaper, in fact, told me I could write, then I just decided I would.'

Oh, how times had changed, Rory thought. But she appreciated Shona's lack of pretension. In fact, as the interviewer probed a little deeper, it became clear that Shona was a mine of information, and, sometimes, barely concealed frustration about how women writers were often seen as lesser to their male counterparts. In a wide-ranging discussion over the next hour that covered her 'bonkbuster' years in the 1980s to the rather more sedate output of the turn of the twenty-first century and beyond, Rory found herself hanging on every last word.

An hour flew by, and then it was time to open questions to the floor. Did she dare ask her question, Rory thought, or should she just stay quiet? Suddenly, all the imposter syndrome she'd been feeling since she'd arrived in Roseford came rushing back to her, pouring over her like molten lava. Weirdly, as Leo sat quietly beside her, she realised she didn't just feel like an imposter because she was calling herself a writer: she was beginning to feel like a stranger to her own life, too. Everything she thought she'd known two weeks ago had changed, and she felt swept up by it all. A new 'identity' as an author, a fledgling relationship with Leo and a whole new set of emotions about both of those things seemed to have taken her a long way away from the person she'd been before the holiday started.

'Yes? The woman in the third row in the striped top?'

Rory flushed as she realised she still had her hand up. The interviewer looked quizzically at her. 'Did you have a question for Shona?'

Rory opened her mouth and then shut it again. 'Sorry,' she said swiftly. 'I've completely forgotten what I was going to ask.' Mortified, she sank down in her seat. She felt the comforting presence of Leo's hand squeezing her own as her heart thudded uncomfortably in her chest, but it didn't quite assuage the embarrassment.

As she listened carefully to the questions that followed, and tried her best to take in the answers Shona was giving, she realised that Leo's hand was still holding hers. She relished its warmth for a while longer, until, finally, and with a trace of regret, she moved it to give Shona a last round of applause.

'Well,' Stella said as the audience stopped clapping and some of them began to move out of their seats, 'I never thought I'd learn so much in an hour. Shona Simmonds is truly one of the greats, isn't she?'

Rory nodded. 'I just wish I hadn't looked like such an idiot when I forgot my question.'

Stella gave her a sympathetic smile. 'It happens to the best of us. You should have heard my first words to Finn Sanderson when Lucy introduced me to him!' She stood up, and, obviously noticing that Rory was still downcast, added, 'Look, Simon's invited me to have some tea and cake with Shona now she's done her talk. Why don't you join us? I'm sure she'd be delighted to speak to you.' She glanced over at Leo. 'And I'm sure she'd be more than happy if your, er, friend came along, too.'

Rory felt a surge of excitement. A personal audience with Shona – that was beyond her wildest dreams! Rapidly, she agreed, before turning to Leo. 'Are you OK coming with me?' She felt as though she needed the moral support.

'Sure.' Leo smiled, and Rory felt a tingle of a different kind as he did. 'I'd be intrigued to hear a little more from her, too. Maybe I'll get to ask her about *Boundaries of Desire!*'

They got up from their seats and followed Lizzie through the archway that led to Simon's private rooms in Roseford Hall. Rory couldn't wait to see what else Shona might reveal over a cup of tea.

25

Shona Simmonds did not disappoint. As Rory sipped tea from an exquisite bone china cup and tucked into a delectable slice of carrot cake, baked by Simon's mother Margaret, who also now graced the gathering with her presence, Shona continued to talk as though she had an audience, albeit a far smaller one. She'd had a long and fascinating career as a novelist and regaled them with off-the-record tales of the rich and libidinous, some of which had made it, heavily disguised of course, into her novels. A writer of the romantic old school, she'd made her living and then some selling romantic ideals to readers, and now lived comfortably off the proceeds of her labours. As Rory listened, enraptured, she finally plucked up the courage to ask Shona what her best piece of advice would be for a novelist starting out.

'Darling,' Shona replied in the genteel tones that were almost as much of a trademark as the novels themselves, 'you must set out to give the reader what they want. But remember, if you don't want it, the reader won't either. So, make it matter.'

Rory nodded. The good, but vague advice made sense. 'Thank you,' she stammered. 'I'll try.'

'Make the reader a part of your world,' Shona continued. 'Don't try to speak in anyone else's voice. If you love your characters, readers will love them, too.' She paused mischievously. 'Except for the ones who don't, and never will, of course, but there's always five or six of them!' Laughing quietly, she sipped her tea.

'To be honest, I'm not sure this idea will even get off the drawing board,' Rory admitted, 'but I'm having fun finding out.'

'That's half the battle,' Shona replied. 'My first novel was an act of pure self-indulgence and was rejected by sixteen publishers before it found its rightful home.' She raised an eyebrow speculatively at Rory. 'And the other half of the battle is learning to live with rejection!'

'Amen to that,' Stella said dryly. 'But it only takes one editor to say yes.'

'Quite right, my dear,' Shona said. Rory listened to Stella and Shona talking about the business of writing for a few minutes in slightly awed silence. This was the world she was aching to be a part of, and listening to those who moved within it was an education. She leaned back in her chair and took another sip of her tea. There was something almost alchemical about listening to writers discussing their trade, and she hoped, one day, she'd be able to do the same. A writer she might be, she thought as she tried to brush away the encroaching imposter syndrome again, but she wasn't even on the same page, let alone the same shelf as Stella and Shona.

Rory's thoughts were interrupted as Leo ambled back into the room. She looked at him carrying a freshly brewed pot of tea on a tray, and thought how attractive he was, even in this rather odd setting.

'And who might you be?' Shona's gaze had also come to rest on Leo, who'd largely made himself useful ferrying tea from Simon's kitchen and making sure everyone's plates and cups were filled up. Rory knew that romantic fiction wasn't really his thing, but his quiet, reassuring presence in the room stopped her from getting too nervous in front of Shona.

'Just a friend of Rory's,' Leo replied.

Shona laughed. 'Well, if Rory here just keeps you as a friend, you're not working hard enough!'

Leo, flustered, gave a laugh. 'I don't know what to say to that.' He beat a hasty retreat back to the kitchen, and Shona's eyes, with that mischievous sparkle, came to rest on Rory again.

'Tall, dark and handsome. And good with a teapot. He's pure Mills and Boon material, that one,' Shona said, giving Rory a wide smile. 'Of course, that's where I started out, back in the very early days...'

Shona was off again, regaling the small group with more tales of the workings of the publishing world. Rory listened, but this time she was somewhat off balance from Shona's clear statement of the very obvious. Leo *was* gorgeous, and she *was* really attracted to him. Maybe she should stop dithering, throw caution to the winds and see where her bravery led her?

Eventually, thanking Shona for an entertaining morning, Leo and Rory made an exit into the sunny grounds of Roseford Hall.

'So that's what you aspire to, is it?' Leo teased. 'Can't say I blame you. She's had a hell of a life and she's not afraid of speaking her mind, is she?'

Rory, feeling her face growing warm, wondered if Leo had heard what Shona had said about him. 'She certainly isn't,' she replied. 'Maybe, when you get to your eighties, that's not a bad thing.'

'Honesty is the best policy, eh?' Leo's eyes bore a teasing expression. 'What is it that you honestly want, Aurora Henderson?'

'At the moment, I'd be happy just to get my first novel written,' Rory replied lightly, still not willing to be completely honest with Leo about how he was making her feel. Joking seemed so much easier, for now. 'I think the champagne and caviar comes much later, if ever!'

Rory and Leo were approaching the ha-ha, which was a stone wall built into the bank that separated the manicured gardens of Roseford Hall from the broader sweep of lawn that sloped slightly upwards to the horizon. There were a couple of stone steps down to the grassy area, but Leo took a jump down the two-foot wall, and then, grinning, turned back to Rory.

'May I assist you down, my lady?' He bowed, then held out a hand for her to grab.

'But of course, my lord,' Rory replied, smiling. She took Leo's proffered hand in her own, and made a small jump down, feeling herself drawn into Leo's arms as she landed.

'Well, hello,' he said softly. 'Fancy meeting you down here.'

Rory could feel the warmth from his body emanating towards her as she stood, happily encircled in his arms. There wasn't much room between them, and as she drew a breath, she found herself moving even closer, so that their bodies were just about, and rather deliciously, touching. A fizz began in Rory's abdomen, and she was shocked at just how powerful it felt.

'Fancy,' she murmured, looking upwards into Leo's deep brown eyes, and, in pleasure, watching them widen. 'And what brings you to this wonderful place on such a beautiful day?'

'Oh, this and that,' Leo teased. 'What about you?'

Feeling happily reckless and heeding her own previous advice to throw caution to the wind, Rory lifted her chin, and placed a gentle, warm kiss on Leo's lips. It felt like a first, but also achingly familiar as she felt the pressure of her own mouth returned, their lips discovering each other, and becoming reacquainted. She shivered as she felt one of Leo's hands moving carefully upwards to tangle in her hair, and allowed herself, for a few moments, to become lost in those thrillingly familiar sensations. His mouth was warm, and tasted faintly of carrot cake, and she found herself wanting to deepen that kiss, and thinking of more passionate things she wanted to do with this incredibly gorgeous man.

'Well,' she said as they eventually broke apart. 'That's got the awkward first kiss over with. Where do you suggest we go from here?'

26

The answer to that question took them on a walk around Roseford Hall's extensive and beautifully maintained grounds. The grounds were packed with people milling between the different events that RoseFest boasted, and the atmospheric vocals of a famous local folk singer drifted through the air as they meandered.

'Simon's done a great job, organising all this,' Rory said as, hand clasped firmly in Leo's, she tried to anchor herself, despite a persistent train of thought that was intent on carrying her away to more intimate places. 'I can't believe the festival's only a couple of years old.'

'Well, I think he's had a lot of help with the logistics from Lizzie,' Leo said. 'It's not so much "behind every great man" as "in front of him, reminding him there's more to organising a festival than just making speeches", from what I've heard!'

Rory cocked an intrigued eyebrow. 'You say that with the knowledge of a true local!'

'Aunt Vi has an ear for the social dynamics of the village—' Leo grinned '—and she gave me a crash course on who was who before she and Uncle Bryan left.' He paused, looking down at Rory before brushing a loose strand of hair back from her face. 'Of course, you don't become *truly* local in Somerset until you've lived here for at least twenty years.'

'That leaves Simon and his family in the clear, then!' Rory giggled. 'I mean, I've heard the Treloars go back at least ten generations.'

'Fancy the lord of the manor, do you?' Leo teased. 'I'm pretty sure he's taken.'

'Oh, my interest in the Treloar family is purely academic,' Rory replied. 'You've nothing to fear on that subject.'

'I'm glad to hear it.' A husky note, quite in contrast to the innocent, almost pastoral scenes around them, had crept into Leo's voice, and Rory suddenly had visions of what it would be like to be wrapped in his arms, somewhere far less crowded.

Leo seemed to sense the effect his tone was having on her, and he slid an arm around her waist. 'Have you seen enough, or do you want to keep wandering?'

Rory tilted her head up and met Leo's lips with her own. 'Well,' she said softly, 'I can think of other things I'd rather see...'

If Leo was shocked by her directness, he didn't show it, but a slight stiffening of his back suggested surprise. The kiss lingered, and for a warm, sensual few moments, they lost track of the rest of the world.

Breaking apart, Rory noticed the flush to Leo's cheeks, and smiled. 'Shall we get back?' she asked softly.

Leo nodded. 'I think that's a great idea.'

They walked, arms around each other, through the field that led to a footpath back to the village and back to the front door of Roseford Villas.

'Well, here we are,' Rory said nervously, trying to keep hold of the adventurous mood that had led to many more kisses on their walk. She looked up at Leo from under her lashes where he was pausing on the doorstep. It was as if she was seeing him in duplicate: the adult Leo of the present day was overlaid with the younger Leo of their adolescence, and for a few precious moments while he pulled his front door key from his pocket, the duality was confusing. Realising she was probably overthinking it and trying to heed her own advice to just live in the moment, she shook her head.

This gesture did not go unnoticed by Leo. 'Are you sure you want to do this?' His gentle voice wrapped around her like the arms she was aching to feel. Rory looked at him as she shifted on the doorstep and was nodding even before he'd got the words out.

'I want this, Leo,' she said softly. 'I want you.' They stood there for a moment, the weight of their shared history hanging in the air between them. Then Leo's hand reached out, gently cupping Rory's cheek in a touch that held both familiarity and longing.

'I never thought I'd see you again,' Leo murmured, his thumb tracing the curve of her cheekbone.

'Life has a way of surprising us,' Rory said, the touch of Leo's hand making her heart pound against her ribs.

Leo's gaze dropped to her lips, a mixture of hesitation and desire dancing in his eyes. 'Rory, ever since you showed up on the doorstep, I haven't been able to stop thinking about you. Knowing you were at the bottom of the garden, but not being able to touch you. It's been almost as bad as being so far away from you when we were teenagers.'

'You always had the gift of hyperbole.' Rory gave a nervous laugh. She had the feeling they were both playing a kind of verbal gymnastics, as they had when they were younger, just to get them through the potentially mortifying moments.

'It's true,' Leo insisted. 'I've wanted to level with you so much, Rory, but I didn't know if that's what you wanted. I was scared of being rejected and looking like an idiot in front of you.'

A rush of emotions swirled within Rory, and before she could overthink it, she replied, 'I think we're both on the same page, Leo, don't you? Let's make the most of it.' Leo's arms encircled her, pulling her closer as the kiss deepened, until Leo was leaning against the blue front door, and Rory was enthusiastically pressing against him. When they finally pulled away, their breaths mingling, Leo rested his forehead against hers, his eyes closed. 'We'd better get inside before we get arrested on the doorstep.'

Rory smiled. 'Yes,' she said. 'I mean, we wouldn't want to bring scandal upon Roseford Villas, would we? Imagine the reviews on Tripadvisor!'

'Don't mention that website!' Leo replied. 'Aunt

Vi's banned all talk of it under her roof.' He went for his keys again, and Rory followed him through the front door, until it was closed securely behind them.

'Have you got any guests in who are likely to want anything?' Rory asked, mindful that this wasn't just Leo's current home, but that he was also in charge of the business for the duration.

'I'll leave a note on reception to call me,' Leo replied. 'But there's only one occupied room for tonight. More coming in tomorrow for the next couple of days of RoseFest.'

Rory waited with increasing anticipation while Leo scribbled out a note and left it at the desk, then, as he turned back towards her, she smiled. 'Ready?'

Leo, eyes wide, nodded.

Hand in hand, they wandered up the stairs to Leo's bedroom and Rory felt the strangest sensation of complete familiarity and apprehension. It was confusing, but oddly right.

'Do you remember the first time we did this?' Leo asked as they headed towards the bed. 'I was so shit scared of messing things up, I don't think I stopped shaking the whole way through.'

'I was scared, too,' Rory replied. 'Not because it was you I was with, but because everything was so new. We really did learn with each other, didn't we?'

She gave him a warm smile. 'But if it's any consolation, I'm feeling pretty nervous now, too.'

'Me too.' Leo gave a gentle laugh. 'Stupid, isn't it? We're both adults. What have we got to be afraid of?' He sat down on the edge of the bed. 'Except...' He trailed off.

Immediately, Rory was on the alert. 'What is it, Leo? Have you changed your mind? Are we going too fast?'

Leo shook his head. 'It's not that.' He shifted uncomfortably on the bed and looked down at the floor. 'I'm actually quite out of practice at doing... this. And, if I'm being completely honest, I haven't been, er, "close" to someone since before I had the car accident. So I'm feeling ever so slightly petrified...'

Rory's heart swelled with compassion, and she sat down on the bed next to Leo, taking one of his hands in hers. 'It's all right,' she said softly. 'We can take it really, really slowly and just see what happens.' She gave a little, nervous laugh. 'In a way, it's similar to what we were like when we were younger – both of us wondering what all of the fuss was about, but desperate to do it anyway!'

Leo looked up and his eyes met Rory's, full of affection. 'I might not be able to, er, fully get my act together,' he said, and his face flushed again. 'I've been having a few issues in that area since the accident. The doctors said it might happen, because of a combination of anxiety and the back injury, so this is all going to be kind of new to me.'

'If it doesn't all happen the way you want, it's fine,' Rory said softly. 'We can just cuddle. We've got time.' She sat down next to him on the bed. 'Shall we start with that, and see how things go?'

'I remember you saying something similar to me, the first time we slept together,' Leo replied. 'And we ended up getting rather carried away!'

'Didn't we just! Thank God my parents were away for the weekend. I'd never have gone through with it if I'd thought they were going to burst in on us.'

'But you don't regret it?' Leo asked. 'Me being your first, I mean? Even though we both knew I was going to have to leave.'

Rory shook her head so hard her ponytail slapped her on the neck. 'No,' she said. 'I never regretted a second of it. Did you?'

'Absolutely not,' Leo murmured. He reached a hand up to her face and cupped her cheek, bringing her mouth towards his. 'Now, about that cuddling...'

27

A little time later, the cuddling was getting rather heated. Leo had discarded his T-shirt and Rory slipped off hers, too. The kisses had warmed them both, and Rory knew, without a doubt, that she was more than ready to take another step.

'So,' she said softly, 'when you told me that there might be a problem, is that something that you can control? Is it, er, physical, or mental?'

Leo smiled. 'A bit of both,' he said. 'Being in certain positions makes things easier for me, and I'm afraid my days of *any time, anywhere* are over, but I know what my limits are, and the further away I get from the accident, the easier things seem to be. My therapist and my physio both suggested a "suck it and see" approach, but to be honest, I've not had any opportunities since my marriage ended.' He shook his head, but they both started to laugh at his physio's expression, which defused the tension somewhat. 'I must sound like a really sad, lonely twat,' Leo admitted, with a rueful smile.

Rory propped herself up on one elbow. 'No, you don't,' she said. 'You sound like someone who went through a terrible experience and is quite rightly being cautious about things, especially when it comes to getting close to someone else.'

Seeing Leo swallowing hard, Rory reached out a hand and ran it through his hair. Encouraged as he leaned into her touch, she moved forward and kissed him gently. 'I meant it when I said we didn't have to do anything you don't want to.'

'I know,' Leo murmured. 'And the longer I'm lying here with you, the more I want to experiment, see what my limits actually are.'

'Well, we'd better make sure we embrace an experimental approach, then!' Rory smiled into the kiss.

'You always did have a way with words,' Leo said dryly.

'Suck it and see, you said?' Rory glanced down

the length of Leo's body. 'Is that something you'd be happy for me to, er, explore?'

Leo's eyes widened. 'More than happy,' he said, a husky note in his voice.

'Well, let me know if that changes,' Rory said. Carefully, she began to kiss Leo's neck, and as he arched his back in pleasure she ran a hand down his chest, following that movement with featherlight touches of her lips. 'Is this all right?' she murmured between kisses.

'That is definitely all right,' Leo breathed as she progressed downwards. 'Definitely, definitely all right.'

Rory smiled into the kisses. She remembered, back in the day, just how wild Leo had been driven by this, and as she moved down the bed, she ran a hand through his hair, and down, over his chest and to the top of his shorts.

'I really want to test things a little further,' she said gently. 'Are you OK with that?'

In response, Leo raised his hips, and Rory could see his arousal outlined through his dark blue shorts. 'I am OK with that.' She ran a hand over his abdomen, and further down, squeezing and touching until he was rocking against her hand and moaning into her kisses.

'Christ, I feel like I'm sixteen,' Leo groaned as he pressed up against her hand. 'I can't decide if this is too much of a tease, or not enough...'

Rory smiled. She remembered the thrill she had felt, as a teenager, holding Leo in the palm of her hand, and was ecstatic that she still seemed to be able to have the same effect on him.

'Do you remember the first time we saw each other naked?' she whispered into his ear. 'We did everything but go the whole way that night, and God, it felt incredible.'

'I don't suppose you fancy recreating it?' Leo breathed. 'I think I'm more than up to that.'

Rory nodded. 'I am definitely up for that.' She momentarily took her hand away from Leo's fly and unhooked her rose-pink bra and was wildly encouraged to see Leo's expression change to one of barely disguised lust as he caught sight of her half un-clothed. He pulled her on top of him, and as their torsos touched, she felt a rush of warmth through her body that left her wanting and needing to feel more.

'You look amazing,' Leo murmured, 'and even better than I remembered.'

'Flattery will get you into my underwear!' Rory laughed. She rolled back off him and wriggled out of her shorts and knickers. Leo, in a slightly less elegant way, did the same until they were both completely naked.

'So, where did we start?' Rory asked. 'My memory's a little hazy, after all these years...'

'Somewhere about here,' Leo said, running a warm hand over her breast and down her waist. Rory arched her back towards Leo's touch, and it was soon very clear that they remembered a lot more than they thought about each other. The years had matured their responses, but there was a familiarity that both were thrilled to discover was still there. It certainly made things a lot easier.

For a few moments, Rory had felt self-conscious about her body: after all, twenty years did a lot to alter things physically, but Leo's enthusiastic response to her closeness soon dispelled any worries she might have had. It helped, too, that he was cautious about what he could and couldn't do. She didn't want to push him, and she didn't feel as though she was under pressure. Getting older definitely had its advantages, she thought as his hands began to explore her. She knew what she liked, she remembered how much they'd learned about each other, and this time, she was more than happy to tell him when something was working, and when it wasn't.

'How am I doing?' Leo asked as he caressed her.

'Just a little to the left,' Rory breathed, feeling the tingles starting to build. 'Yes... that's perfect...' She let herself float for a moment on the sensations, before she turned her attentions back to Leo.

'What was that phrase your therapist used? Suck it and see? I don't think I got around to that just now.' She raised herself up on one elbow. 'Shall we give it a try?'

Leo drew in a sharp breath. 'I'm willing if you are...'

Needing no further encouragement, Rory moved back down the bed and soon had Leo gasping beneath her. Unlike twenty years ago, he had a modicum more control, and, though his hands gripped the sheets in pleasure, he kept himself the right side of the precipice.

'It's all right,' Rory replied. 'You don't have to hold back if you don't want to...'

It gave her the greatest thrill when Leo took her at her word. After all, they had all summer to rediscover each other: this was just the beginning. As the afternoon wove into a delicately falling evening, they talked, and touched, and soon drifted off to sleep.

28

The next morning, Rory awoke before Leo. Lying there, in his bed, she felt the strangest sensations of familiarity and excitement. It was a twinning she was gradually getting used to, but it didn't stop it feeling odd. Leo was turned on his side, away from her, and she couldn't help but notice the scars on his back. After a glimpse of them in the garden, she was literally eye to eye with them, and she realised just what a mountain it had been for him to climb to fight his way back to health and mobility. No wonder he'd been so cautious. She couldn't imagine how terrible it must have been for him. But, on the basis of last night, she got the sense that he was more than ready to test his limits, at least as far as making love was concerned.

She couldn't help thinking about what might have been. What if she'd taken the leap and gone to university in Melbourne? Or if he'd decided to come back to the UK? How might both of their lives have been different? Would they still have been together, or would first love have petered out once they'd reached adulthood? Teenage infatuation was one thing, but adult love quite another.

But what ifs were pointless. They were where they were, and she couldn't complain. Last night had been gentle, and sexy, and promised a new beginning and she couldn't wait to see where things were going to go next.

As she was contemplating all this, Leo stirred and rolled back towards her.

'Hey,' he murmured. 'How did you sleep?'

'Beautifully,' she replied, smiling. 'You?'

'Like an absolute log. Haven't slept like that since I got here.'

Rory grinned. 'I'm glad to hear it.' She glanced over at the alarm clock by the bed. 'God, it's eight thirty. We *did* sleep well.'

'Eight thirty? Shit!' Leo jumped out of bed. 'I was

supposed to have breakfast on the table for 7 a.m. Mr and Mrs Cross are going to be livid!' He hastily pulled on his boxers and shorts and reached for his T-shirt.

Rory reached for her own clothes and threw them on. 'What can I do to help?'

'Can you go and switch the coffee machine on in the dining room? I'll check if they're still about and go and apologise, see what they want to eat.'

'Sure thing.' Rory hurried out of Leo's room and downstairs to the large dining room. She filled up the reservoir on the coffee percolator and hastily spooned the ground coffee into the filter. Just as she was heading to the kitchen to see if she could find some milk, Leo appeared in the doorway, looking sheepish.

'They've gone out for the day,' he said, ambling over to where Rory had paused. 'They, er, left me a rather snotty note on their bedroom door, requesting a refund for breakfast.'

'Shit!' Rory began to laugh. 'That's your perfect, five-star rating on Tripadvisor toppled, then.'

'Oh, well.' Leo smiled, and Rory felt that fizzing tingle low down in her belly again. He drew closer to her, and wrapped an arm around her, bringing their bodies together. 'I guess it's one thing to own up to

Aunt Vi about when she FaceTimes me next!' He leaned down and kissed her lingeringly. 'In the meantime, though, I've got a load of croissants and jam in the kitchen, and the coffee'll be ready in a few minutes. How about we head back upstairs and have a picnic in bed?'

The morning, and most of the afternoon, with a brief stop for more snacks, consisted of much of the same activity that they'd spent the night indulging in. Rory was still very aware that Leo might have limits, and worries, and although she was beginning to *really* want to take the final step and feel all of him, she silenced that thought and tried to focus on their voyage of rediscovery. And what a journey it was. With no anxious parents to interrupt them, and very little else to occupy them once the guest house was empty, they took their time, until, sweaty and sated, they lay next to one another in Leo's bed, chatting and giggling like the teenagers they used to be.

'So, what are your plans for the next few days?' Leo asked as they both stared at the patterns of sunlight rippling across the ceiling.

'Well, I should be cracking on with looking at the material I photocopied from the Roseford Hall archives,' Rory replied. 'It was fascinating stuff, and it's really given me a lot to think about. Simon Treloar's been great about wangling me access to whatever I need, and Edmund's diaries have been really enlightening. I can see the parallels with the contemporary story I want to tell already. It's just a question of working out how best to link the two, so it makes sense to someone else outside my own head!'

Leo propped himself up on one elbow, and his expression showed how fascinated he was by what Rory was saying. 'So, you're still dead set on using the contemporary story that's kind of about us, then?'

Rory paused. 'Oh, I haven't got my head around it all yet. You know how it is when you're trying to pin down an idea.' She didn't quite feel comfortable discussing that part of the story further with Leo. Something told her that she needed to have it straight in her own mind before she presented it to him.

'Well, I'd love to hear about it when you're ready to talk it over.' Leo smiled. 'I always told you that you should be a writer, back when we were in school. It's wonderful to see that finally starting to happen.'

Rory shook her head. 'I'm a long way off *being a writer*,' she said, making quotation marks in the air with her hands. 'I mean, what I end up with might not be any good.'

'I don't think you really believe that, or you wouldn't have given yourself so much time this summer to work it all out,' Leo replied. If he could express things with so much clarity and certainty, Rory thought, she could see why he'd been so good at the law. He was certainly persuasive.

'Well, I guess it's now or never, really,' Rory said. 'I mean, the time just felt right, you know.' She grinned and made jazz hands in the air this time. 'Perhaps it was written in the stars! I mean, who knew I'd come to Roseford and find you again?'

Leo pulled her close once more. 'Well, something was in play,' he said huskily. 'I don't really believe in fate, and stuff being written in the stars, but whatever it was that brought me back to you, I'm so glad it did.'

Rory luxuriated in his closeness again. She remembered how desperately she'd clung to every last second with him, the first time around. How every kiss, every touch, every sentence they spoke mattered. It was partly the intensity of first love, she knew that, and now they were together again, it had more of the feeling of a holiday romance, but she was increasingly reluctant to get out of bed and get back to the real reason she was here.

'I'm glad too,' she said softly. She kissed him again, long and lingeringly. 'And I hope, no pressure, that at some point, if you're ready, we might... you know.'

Leo smiled. 'I'd like that, too. At the moment, if I was fifteen, I'd be high fiving myself for having a beautiful, naked woman in my bed, but as an adult, I'd like more.'

'Well, we're on the same page, then,' Rory said, and kissed him again. 'But, speaking of pages, I've got some to write. And you've got some ground to make up with Mr and Mrs Cross when they come back for the evening. Not to mention some other guests, I'd imagine, now RoseFest has started. So, we should probably get up and get on with what we're supposed to be doing.'

Leo groaned. 'If you say so. But can I see you later?'

'I'd like that. Dinner at mine?'

Leo looked wary. 'I don't know how great the oven is in the chalet, to be honest. How about I bring something round?'

'It's a deal.' Rory reluctantly prised herself out of Leo's arms and grabbed her clothes. 'I'll see you later.'

The sight of Leo, still reclined in the rumpled bed, tousled dark curls falling over his forehead and eyes regarding her with a lustful stare, almost made

Rory change her mind. But she knew she needed a few hours to come back to earth and have a good think. Things were moving very fast, and she needed to take a breath and remember what had brought her here to Roseford in the first place.

29

Rory, returning to the chalet, showered and settled down for a few hours on the manuscript. She'd loved being with Leo, but she needed to focus on the real reason she'd come here. She grabbed her notes from the Roseford Hall archives and started work, fleshing out the story of the growing relationship between her two fictional historical protagonists, and giving them the voices that had been singing in her head ever since she'd decided to write the story. It was a relief to have the distraction from what was going on in her romantic life.

But now wasn't the time to be thinking about Leo. She had a book to write, and plenty of things to write about. Grabbing a cup of coffee, she settled back down to the table, and before she knew it, she'd written two chapters of the historical story, words flying from her fingertips. She felt the ebb and flow of the ideas as she worked, teasing out the subtleties of her characters, and drawing upon her research where she could. After another hour she was satisfied, and saved her work.

As she shut her laptop, her stomach growled. She realised she'd basically been surviving on cake and pastries and decided it was definitely time to do some shopping. The chalet had a decent-sized fridge and an ice box, so she locked up and set out for the nearest supermarket.

Having taken a lightning trip to the supermarket in the early evening and restocked the chalet, she buckled down to work again. She felt her fingers falling into the now accustomed routine of typing, and the words flying from her brain and onto the screen. This time, she focused on telling the contemporary love story, and spent an hour or so alternately smiling and wincing over the collection of photographs that she'd tucked into one of her diaries. The vibrant yellow Von Dutch T-shirt and low-slung cargos she rocked in one snapshot made her wince, although she had to confess that Leo had looked great in a David Beckham-esque pairing of dark blue scruffy Diesel T-shirt and baggy jeans. *May Y2K fashion never rear its head again*, she thought, noting the pink velour leisurewear her best mate from school wore in another picture. Some looks deserved to be consigned to history.

Before she knew it, dusk was falling. Her phone pinged with a message, and she smiled to see it was Leo, asking if it was all right to come over. She was pleased that he asked permission and didn't just land on her doorstep. The fact that she was living at the bottom of the garden and was his tenant for the summer could potentially prove awkward, but it was a good sign that he respected her space. Texting a quick 'Yes,' she just about had time to brush her hair and squirt on a bit of deodorant before there was a knock at the door.

'Hi,' he said softly. He was brandishing a bottle of fizz, and he set it down on the table as she opened the door. In his other hand he was carrying a thermal bag, which he also put on the table. 'It's alcohol free, but the best one the West Country can claim.'

'Sounds perfect,' Rory replied. 'I really do need to keep my wits about me if I'm not going to lose my momentum while I'm writing.'

'How's it going?' Leo asked.

Rory took down a couple of glasses from the cupboard and watched as Leo popped the cork and filled them.

'Not bad,' Rory said. 'I feel like I'm getting into the story, now, which helps. How were Mr and Mrs Cross? Did you see them to apologise?'

Leo looked sheepish. 'I did,' he said. 'And I've knocked this morning's breakfast off the bill and given them a complimentary bottle of wine by way of compensation. I think it's what Aunt Vi would have done, not that she'd have missed breakfast in the first place!'

'I feel kind of responsible for that,' Rory replied. 'I mean, I'm sure if I hadn't distracted you...'

Leo paused in the act of filling the glasses and straightened up, sliding an arm around her waist. 'I was more than happy to be distracted by you,' he murmured, beginning to kiss her neck. 'And I rather hope you might distract me some more, if I earn that right tonight with what I've brought us for dinner.'

'OK, but I'm sending you home before you have to get breakfast on for your guests!' Rory grinned.

They broke apart, and Leo began to unpack the thermal bag. Inside was a still warm lasagne and foil-wrapped garlic bread, which both tucked into with gusto. As they chatted over dinner, Rory found herself wanting to know more about what had brought

Leo back to the UK but didn't know how to broach it. Eventually, she decided the direct approach, much as it had been the last time, was best.

'So,' she began, having taken a sip of her wine. 'Here we are, and I still don't know why you're really back in this country. If you want to tell me, I'm all ears.'

Leo leaned back on the bench seat and paused for an almost unbearably long time. 'Well,' he said, 'it's like this...'

30

'Look, this is hard for me to talk about,' Leo said. 'Can you bear with me if it all seems a little disjointed?'

'Of course,' Rory replied. 'Take your time. I'm here for you.' She waited while he gathered his thoughts, and then, taking a deep breath, Leo began talking.

'You already know that physically I'm a bit of a wreck these days.' He gave a nervous laugh. 'I think I made that clear when we spent the night together. There was a pretty nasty car accident about two years ago which left me with a column of metal in my spine, and I had to have several discs removed as a result of the impact. It also left me with a lot to work through, psychologically. That had some, er, interesting physical effects, too, as you know.' He coloured slightly. 'Nothing I can't handle, but it's something I always have to be aware of.'

'So, what happened?' Rory asked.

'My wife Corinne and I had been out to a fundraiser for a local charitable foundation just on the outskirts of town,' Leo said. 'It was late, and we were both tired. We'd had a long few months, but the law firm was starting to take off, and the contacts were spectacular. It finally felt, after years of graft, that we were getting somewhere. It was just as well. We were a great business partnership, but our marriage was into injury time. We'd patched things up as best we could, but after five years, we were both beginning to realise that we were better lawyers than we were husband and wife. I don't think, even if things hadn't worked out in the way they had, that we'd have been far off a divorce.'

Leo took a gulp of his drink. They'd switched to red wine as they ate, but neither had drunk much from the bottle, both mindful that they had a lot to do the next day. 'Sorry,' he said as he began to cough. 'I don't actually drink much any more. Too many meds since the crash.' He looked at her and resumed the story. 'Corinne and I were arguing, as usual. It was all we seemed to do. Corinne... she was over the limit but she insisted on driving us home because I had a fucking awful migraine. I should never have let her behind the wheel, but I was kind of past caring. We were five miles from home when she lost control and smashed into a tree. The passenger's side of the car took most of the impact.'

'Christ,' Rory breathed. 'That sounds horrific. Was Corinne injured?'

'Only superficially,' Leo replied. 'And thankfully, we were fully covered in terms of insurance, so I was well taken care of. But when I finally got out of hospital... well, you can imagine. We were past injury time and into penalties, as far as the marriage was concerned. I didn't move back home, as I needed a more adaptable place to live, and although we were working together, we haven't lived together since. The divorce has been going through, slowly, but with the business in the equation it's been difficult to wind everything up. It got to the point when I just had to get out of there, so I applied for a job in London.'

'Doing a similar thing to what you were doing in Melbourne?'

Leo smiled. 'The job starts in September. It's a step down from being a partner, but it's with a decent firm in Canary Wharf, and it'll give me a way in to practising business law in the UK. I'm their contact for their Australian arm, which is right up my alley. In the meantime, when Aunt Vi and Uncle Bryan contacted me, it made sense to come over here a few weeks early and have a change of scene. They're planning on selling up and wanted someone to look after the place while they look for somewhere in a warmer climate. They're in Spain as we speak.'

Rory tried to silence the voice that was reminding her just how far away London was from York. After all, just because they'd started something, it didn't mean that either of them was ready to jump into anything more serious. She would be back up north in September, and it sounded as though Leo still had a lot to work through, fresh start or no fresh start.

'So, when will everything be finalised?' Rory asked.

'Well, the job's all sorted, and my divorce is done in all but name,' Leo replied. 'These things take a while, but Corinne's not contesting much. Potentially, it could have been so much nastier, but, weirdly, now the relationship's over, we're getting on better again. The space has been good for us, and ultimately, it's made sorting out the business side easier. The piece of paper that says I'm a free agent should be through by Christmas: Hallowe'en, if I'm lucky.'

'And how do you feel about that?' Rory asked.

Leo shook his head. 'Relieved, for the most part. Corinne's guilt about the car accident was difficult to come to terms with, even though she knew I felt responsible, too. I should never have let her get behind the wheel that night. Luckily, she wasn't too far over the limit, and she kept her licence, but it was too much to move on from, in the end. Compounded with the fact that we were already in trouble, there really was no going back.' He looked downcast for a moment, but Rory got the feeling it wasn't regret, merely the acceptance that things, however difficult, had to change.

There was a pause, and suddenly, she was sixteen years old again and madly in love with him. 'Oh, Leo,' she murmured. She reached out and pulled him close. 'I keep forgetting that all the time we were apart, we had our own lives. And I keep having to remember that I'm not the kid I was, and neither are you. But this is all such weird territory.'

'Tell me about it!' Leo laughed nervously. 'This is not what I expected to be doing this summer.' He paused. 'Don't get me wrong but meeting you again does rather complicate things.'

'The London job?'

Leo nodded. 'When I came to Roseford, I was dead sure that I'd be packing up my stuff again and starting at the law firm in Canary Wharf in September. Now... I'm not so sure.'

Rory's heart began to beat faster. 'It's early days, Leo. You can't base decisions on what might or might not happen between us.'

'I know,' Leo replied. 'But I also know that, after everything I've been through over the past couple of years, there's no point sticking with something that you know is wrong. The accident taught me that.'

'But you can't rush into things, either,' Rory observed.

'Rory.' Leo's voice was suddenly calmer, more gentle. 'We've had twenty years apart... do you honestly think we're rushing now?'

As he enfolded her in his arms, Rory wanted to believe that he was right, but her own inner voice was telling her that it would never be as simple as all that.

31

Rory, fearing for Leo's back in the chalet's bed, had insisted that he return to Roseford Villas before he fell asleep and regretted it. The bed, while comfy for one, wasn't really a great solution if you had any kind of injury, so, it was with a pang of regret she saw him back to the main house. She'd dropped off for a few hours, but then woken while it was still dark, mulling over what he'd told her. There was no doubt that his life was tangled. She'd expected some complications, but *nearly* divorced wasn't the same as actually divorced, whatever the extenuating circumstances. Did she really want to get involved with someone who was starting something new, in a totally new place, and who carried so much baggage with him? Did she have the emotional capacity for that?

She cursed herself for overthinking it. If she'd learned one thing during this endeavour of hers to write her novel, it was that the course of true love didn't so much never run smooth as become a raging, uncontrollable torrent on occasion. But that didn't mean it wasn't worth trying to navigate. The trouble was, she'd never been one for holiday romances. All of her previous relationships had been long term, and whilst she'd never found *The One* to settle down with, she was optimistic that one day it would happen. Much as her heart was starting to tell her otherwise, in practical terms, she couldn't see that Leo was going to be The One. She was hard-wired for commitment, and holiday flings just weren't part of her emotional vocabulary.

In frustration, she rolled over in bed. She knew she wasn't going to get any more sleep tonight. It was 4 a.m. and she'd been lying awake since at least two. Hoping a cuppa and a read might settle her back down, she went to put the kettle on.

As she did so, she checked her phone, and was surprised to see she'd received an email from the trust that ran her school in York. As she read it, she nearly dropped the phone. Suddenly, the decision to blow the money she'd been saving on this indulgent few weeks in the West Country was coming back to bite her right on the arse. The trust, much to its regret, was giving her notice that after October half-term, she would be ceasing her employment with them. It was through no fault of her own, merely that the person she'd been covering had expressed their intention to return from their maternity leave somewhat earlier than expected. The Trust would like to express its thanks for all of her work over the past seven months and wished her well in her future endeavours.

Well, shit. Rory took an unguarded sip of her tea, forgetting how hot it still was. As it burned the roof of her mouth, tears stung her eyes and she dived for the cold tap. Gulping back several mouthfuls of cold water, she then slumped down on the bench seat. That was that, then. She might as well tell Alex that she'd be moving out a little earlier than she'd thought. At least Alex would have a new housemate in no time, since Luca was going to move in soon, anyway.

The email had pulled the rug out from under her feet. Without a steady income, and somewhere to live, she was going to be scuppered. While she knew that Alex wouldn't chuck her out on the street, the thought of sharing the flat with a loved-up couple, and being unemployed, was about as far from ideal as it could get. She knew she'd be able to pick up supply teaching work, but the thought of that filled her with dread, since she'd probably end up going to different schools every day if she was unlucky.

At least, she thought, she had the money she'd saved from her change of accommodation this summer. That ought to tide her over for a month or so and would certainly help to pay her last couple of months' share of the rent. Rory wasn't a great believer in fate and the universe, but as she sipped her tea and the sky started to lighten towards another day, she couldn't help wondering if someone up there was having a laugh at her expense. Not only was she in a quandary about Leo, but being served notice on her job, and with her flat share in the balance, she wondered what the next bomb was going to be that went off in her life. Sighing, she finished her tea and, feeling exhausted again, sloped back to bed for a couple of hours.

It was after eleven o'clock before she woke up again, and, groggy from the depth of her sleep, it took her a minute to get her bearings. Then, slowly, it all came back to her. She couldn't help groaning aloud. But there was little time for introspection: she was due to meet Stella at twelve o'clock to spend some more time on what was now their joint research project into the relationships that linked the past residents of Roseford Hall and Halstead House. Shaking off her tiredness as best she could, she made a coffee, chucked herself under a shower, dressed and then hurried out.

Stella greeted her at the door of the Victorian mansion with a smile and an air of excitement, which turned rapidly to concern when she saw the expression on Rory's face.

'What's wrong, hon?' she asked as Rory crossed the threshold. 'The last time I saw you, you were floating on a cloud of literary enthusiasm and lust!'

Rory allowed herself a quick smile at her friend's turn of phrase. 'That was then,' she said, 'and this, I'm afraid, is now.'

As they settled down with a mug of coffee and several substantial box files, Rory recounted all the layers of mess that had occurred since she'd seen her friend a couple of days ago.

'So not only are Leo's circumstances rather more complex than I could have guessed, but I'm going to be out of a job come the end of October, and without a steady income I can't pay my half of the rent, which in itself won't be a problem for Alex, but is a huge problem for me, unless I take the supply teaching route.'

'You can't be doing that,' Stella replied, sipping her coffee. 'I mean, it's not a guaranteed income for one thing, and I can't imagine what it would be like to have to rock up at a different school every day.'

'It might not come to that,' Rory conceded. 'My current school will probably put me on the books, but that could just be a day or two a week, and nowhere near enough for me to live on.' She dropped her gaze to the tabletop. 'I just don't know what I'm going to do, Stella.' Rory had always been afraid of financial insecurity, ever since her dad had walked out on her mum and they'd struggled, when interest rates were high, to put food on the table. That had happened shortly after Leo had left for Australia, and had driven Rory to change her last name to 'Dean', her mother's maiden name, later in life. She was terrified of being in a similarly financially unstable situation again as an adult. Her mother, who had remarried and now lived in a small village in the Cotswolds with her husband, couldn't offer her a place to live as the cottage was so small, and the cost of living was even more prohibitive in that area than in York. Rory knew she'd have to try to sort this out

herself, but she didn't have the first clue how she was
going to even start.

During their conversation, Rory had been mind-
lessly leafing through the sheaf of papers from the
box Stella had handed her. In an attempt to take her
mind off her current predicament, she tried to lose
herself in the events of the past, if just for a little
while. As she carefully read through the letters, she
noticed a strange little symbol in the corner of a
couple of them.

'Are these Edmund's letters to Francesca?' Rory
asked. 'Only I've seen this odd little squiggle before
in the margins of the ones that were returned to the
Treloar family after his death.' Idly, delicately, she
traced her index finger over the small, repeated doodle. It was so simple that, had she not seen it before
on a couple of the other letters, she might not have
noticed it, but it was starting to ring a distant bell in
her mind.

Stella reached over and checked the index
number on the archive box. 'I thought they were,' she
said, brow wrinkling in confusion. 'Hang on, let me
check my spreadsheet. I've been trying to get the papers into some kind of order, mainly because Simon
and the British Heritage Fund were keen to tease out

the links between Halstead and Roseford Hall, but it's very much a work in progress.'

Stella flashed up her laptop and within moments she'd located her spreadsheet. 'Bear with me,' she murmured as she did a search for the number on the box file.

Rory waited. As she did, she saw Stella's expression change from one of curiosity to confusion, and then all-out surprise.

'Rory,' she said softly, 'can I just take a look at the letter?'

'Sure.' Rory handed over the letter, and started to look at the next one from the box. 'What is it you've found?'

'You're not going to believe this,' Stella said slowly, 'but I think you might have unearthed the real reason why Edmund's letters remained with the Treloar family and were not sent on to Francesca Middleton after he died. I mean, why wouldn't the family have wanted her to have them, if they'd been intended for her?'

'Maybe they just wanted to keep them as last mementoes of their lost son,' Rory volunteered. 'After all, they were written only days before he died.'

'But we already know he wrote to his mother and

father at the same time,' Stella said. She shook her head. 'I think there's more to it than that.'

'How so?'

Stella raised her eyes triumphantly. 'What if I told you that the letter you're holding was never intended for Francesca Middleton at all?'

'But how could that be?' Rory asked. 'I mean, it's written to "F". Who else could it be?'

'Take a look at this.' Stella rummaged in one of the boxes she'd pulled out. She pointed to the bottom corner of the letter. 'See that?'

Rory's eyes widened. 'That's the same little squiggle.' She looked more closely at the letter. 'But this isn't Francesca's handwriting. It's totally different to the script on the diaries in the other box.'

'Exactly!' Stella met Rory's eyes triumphantly. 'There's no way Francesca wrote this letter, and yet here's the doodle in the corner.'

'So, who's the recipient, then?' Rory asked, but even as she did, the penny dropped and she felt a fierce, emotional excitement that, for a moment at least, made her forget everything that was worrying her. 'Oh...' she said softly. 'It all makes sense now.' The theory that had been percolating in the back of her mind since she'd seen the two photographs taken out the front of Halstead House, and read the letters that had been returned with Edmund's possessions after his death, suddenly gained traction.

'Stella,' she said, eventually, realising her friend was waiting for her to elaborate. 'I think the letters in the Roseford Hall collection weren't intended for Francesca Middleton, but were actually written to her brother Frederick.'

Stella raised an eyebrow. 'Then I wonder why the archivist hadn't made that connection already. Or if they had, why this hadn't become public knowledge. I mean, times have changed since the Great War.'

'I know it seems a little unlikely that I'm the first to be picking up on this,' Rory said, 'and for my purposes, fictionalising the story is perfectly fine, but I'm pretty sure that I'm right. I don't think Edmund ever had any intention of marrying Francesca. I'm pretty sure his heart lay elsewhere. Thousands of miles away, in fact, in the Congo.'

Stella's eyes gleamed. 'Well, if you're right, that means Roseford Hall has another intriguing legacy, and one that Simon would be really interested to find out about, I'm sure.' She carefully reached into the archive box in front of her and pulled out another sheaf of letters. 'I've got a few hours free while the guests settle in. This week it's mainly artists in the retreat, and we've got a couple of external tutors coming in, so that frees me up a bit. How do you fancy a research buddy?'

'You're on!' Rory grinned. She and Stella had often collaborated on projects when they were at university, and they made an excellent team. She felt sure that, with both of them sifting through the Halstead House letters, they'd soon get to the bottom of the mystery.

32

Rory reeled back to the chalet, giddy with excitement. She and Stella had spent another couple of hours looking through the correspondence, and by the end of it they were in no doubt: Francesca and Edmund hadn't ever been more than friends. The letters that Edmund had written, the last, passionate letters he'd written in his life, were to his lover, but that lover wasn't Francesca. In fact, the 'F' that Edmund had expressed such love and adoration for was none other than Francesca's brother, the male heir to Halstead House, Frederick.

The more they'd looked into it, the surer they'd become. Even more tellingly, through the lens of that particular reading, it had become clear that

Francesca had been the keeper of their secret, and she'd kept it to the grave. She'd obviously adored her brother, and felt equally strongly about Edmund, and the news of Edmund's death had affected her greatly. Francesca's diaries had revealed her great affection for Edmund, and she'd written passionately about him, but, alongside the letters between Edmund and Frederick, all of the puzzle pieces had revealed the true nature of the relationship the three of them had shared.

Rory's excitement at finding all of this out had been tempered with a depth of sadness. In the early years of the twentieth century, Edmund and Frederick would have been forced to hide their love, and most likely would both have lived clandestine lives. If they had maintained their relationship as lovers, it would have been at enormous risk to themselves. Who knew what would have happened if they'd been discovered? Edmund's loss at the Somme was heartbreaking, and the knowledge that Frederick would have returned to Roseford and would have had to have lived with that grief was even more so.

Musing on this lost love, and the risks that the two men must have taken before their deployment, Rory let herself into the chalet. Theirs was a lesson in taking chances, in following your heart despite what the rest of the world might think. She wondered, given the fact that the two men had been sent to completely different parts of the world, whether someone had had suspicions about the true nature of their relationship, and aimed to put a stop to it by separating them for the duration of the Great War. Edmund, as the heir to Roseford Hall, would have been expected to marry and continue the line. While his death could never have been said to be a release, it did make her wonder if, had he lived, Edmund would have ended up returning to the cells of some other kind of prison. Where was the freedom and liberation for someone who couldn't be free to love who they wanted to? What would have awaited Edmund Treloar back in Roseford other than the need to hide his true self, and conceal the love he so passionately felt for Frederick? At least for a short time before the war, and while they wrote their impassioned letters to one another, they'd found some sort of solace. What would have awaited them back home other than separation, frustration and the pain of a broken heart?

Mulling all this over, she couldn't help thinking about her own situation, and while the risks she might take with her own heart paled in comparison to those taken by Edmund and Frederick, she felt the parallel with herself and Leo. She wondered what he was doing tonight, and whether she'd see him. She still wasn't sure how she felt about the way things were moving between them. Years ago, they'd had the recklessness of youth and inexperience on their side, and nothing to lose. Now, she didn't feel so confident. This might just turn out to be a nostalgic holiday fling, but her heart was already beginning to tell her that she felt more than that. But what was the point when they were going to be separated again at the end of the summer? She wished she didn't feel so confused, and spending the afternoon musing on another doomed relationship hadn't helped.

She was overthinking things, she knew it. What did it matter if it was all just for the summer? After all, they'd been having fun so far, and who said that it needed to stop?

Smiling at her train of thought, she decided to head up the garden to Roseford Villas and see what he was up to. Maybe they could have dinner together, or, if he'd already eaten, she could nip back and grab a sandwich and they could meet again later. Spontaneity wasn't really in her nature, but she could learn, she was sure of it, and after their nights together recently she was aching to feel his arms around her again. They'd still just played around, but she really wanted to take things to the next level...

These thoughts took her to the French windows, and as she breathed in the sweet evening air, she pushed them open and walked into the dining room. She was just about to call out to him when she heard the laughter. Rory froze in her tracks. Peering through the interior door of the dining room down the hall towards the kitchen at the back of the house, she caught sight of Leo, glass of water in his hand, smiling across at someone who was seated just out of Rory's field of vision.

It was the smile that really did her in. She never could resist him when he'd looked at her that way, and it hit her like a bolt between the eyes: whoever he was talking to, and giving that smile to, meant a lot to him.

'You really didn't need to get on a plane, you know,' he was saying. 'I mean, FedEx would have done the job just as effectively, and you'd have had them back in a couple of days, too.'

'I couldn't trust something as important as this to the postal service,' the voice, a woman's, emanated from the kitchen. 'I mean, knowing you, you'd have sent them to the wrong address anyway.'

Leo gave another laugh. 'I'm sure they'd have got to you eventually.'

'This is too important, Leo.' The voice, mellow, Australian and very obviously female, continued. 'This is the future. *Our* future. I had to make sure you took it seriously. Why do you think I came here otherwise?'

In rising confusion and horror, Rory watched as Leo crossed the kitchen and disappeared from sight. As his voice came to her again, her heart gave a painful thud in her chest.

'I wouldn't do anything to put the future at risk, Corinne, you know that. We've both been through too much.'

Turning away again, tears threatening, Rory stumbled back to the dining room and hurried out of the French windows. Corinne was here. Corinne, Leo's ex-wife. But from what Rory had just overheard, 'ex' was the last thing Corinne was. No one spoke with that amount of affection about the future to someone who was meant to be a part of the past. It was clear, from what she'd heard, that Leo had been less than honest with her than she'd believed. Who travelled all the way across the world to see someone when the relationship was over?

As she let herself into the chalet, the thought of

everything that Leo had told her made her even more confused. Perhaps he'd decided to forgive Corinne after all for her part in the accident. He'd said they were getting on better than they had in years. But if that was the case, why had he been so willing to start something with her? Had she just been a stop-gap? Someone to break the sexual drought he'd faced since the car accident? Switching off her phone, pulling a bottle of Cava out of the fridge and firmly closing the curtains of the chalet, Rory tried her best to make it all disappear.

33

Rory didn't know, in the end, if Leo made the walk across the garden to the chalet that evening. She'd taken the bottle of Cava and a glass to the bedroom, propped her laptop up on a pillow and fallen asleep with her headphones on watching the new series of *Bridgerton*. It was approximately halfway through the fourth episode when she'd drifted off, and she awoke several hours later with an empty bottle, a dry mouth and a thumping headache.

Swearing under her breath at her own stupidity, she staggered off the bed, necked a couple of painkillers, drank a pint of water, brushed her teeth and crashed out again. Her last thought was irritation and disappointment that she'd reacted so badly to what she'd overheard. Gaining a hangover was hardly going to help.

When Rory next awoke, the sun was streaming through her bedroom window and she felt somewhat more human. Sleep, while induced by the alcohol in her bloodstream, had calmed her racing thoughts, and she felt as though she was able to put things into perspective a little more. Perhaps what she'd heard last night wasn't Corinne and Leo getting back together? Perhaps 'our future' was just a figure of speech? She washed the night out of her hair, threw on some clothes and forced down a bowl of cornflakes. There was only one way to find out.

She was due back at Roseford Hall at midday, but she wanted to make time to talk to Leo first. She knew if she didn't, she wouldn't be able to concentrate on her manuscript. So, taking a deep breath, she headed out across the garden and made her way towards the dining room, a now familiar route.

As she got to the French windows, she could see an attractive blonde sitting at one of the tables that looked out onto the garden. She was sipping a cup of coffee and reading something on an iPad that was propped up in front of her. Rory paused at the door, wondering if this was Corinne. She certainly looked the part – she could have walked straight off the set of *Neighbours*. In fact, she was a dead ringer for Margot Robbie. Rory felt a distinct prickle of jealousy as she dithered at the door.

The woman, obviously sensing she was being watched, glanced up from the iPad and set clear blue eyes on Rory. She gave a brief, polite smile before turning her head back towards the interior door of the dining room, and Rory heard her call out, 'Leo, there's someone on the patio. Should I let them in?'

Leo came bustling through from the direction of the kitchen and his face registered a mixture of emotions as he came into view. Rory struggled to read them.

'Rory, hi!' His voice was unnaturally hearty as he crossed the dining room and pushed open the French windows, which had, for the first time since Rory had been staying at Roseford Villas, been locked. 'What can I do for you?'

Something about the formality of the question threw Rory off even further, as did the way that he took a step back from her as he opened the doors, as if he needed to put some space between them.

'Er, well,' Rory stammered, trying to get some

sense of equilibrium back. 'I, er, just wondered what you were doing today. Did you want to, er, meet for a coffee or something?' Her face burned as the feelings of gaucheness crept over her. Something about the coolly curious eyes that Corinne was regarding her with was throwing her off balance.

Leo, looking like a cornered hare, glanced from Rory to Corinne and then back again. 'Sure, sure,' he said quickly. 'Look, I've got a couple of things to sort out here, but why don't I pop over to the chalet sometime this afternoon? I'll, er, text you.'

Rory wondered if the 'couple of things to sort out' included explaining to his wife just what he'd been up to over the past few weeks, and how Rory herself fitted into the picture. She felt her anger and jealousy starting to rise, taking over from the early confusion.

'Of course,' she said stiffly. She glanced back at Corinne, who was still staring, transfixed, at their exchange. 'I'll look forward to hearing all about those things later.' Pausing for a moment longer, she added, in an undertone so that only Leo could hear, 'And hopefully, you and your wife will have sorted out "the future". Wasn't that what you said? Do let me know as soon as it's convenient to talk about ours as well.'

Rory turned on her heel and strode back across

the garden, steeling herself not to give Leo a second glance.

'Rory, wait!' Leo's voice, and the sound of his hasty footsteps, caught up with her when she was halfway down the path. 'Let me explain...'

Rory stopped, took a deep breath and plastered the most confident smile she could on her face. She was damned if she'd let Leo see how upset she really was. 'What would you like to explain?'

Leo shook his head. 'I don't know what you think you know, but believe me, it's not what you think.'

'Really?' Rory's voice, in contrast to her smile, was flat. 'And what is it you think I'm thinking?'

The ridiculousness of her words wasn't lost on Rory, but at this point she couldn't focus on being more creative. She watched as Leo shook his head. 'Look, I really need to get a few things sorted out, but please, please don't get the wrong end of the stick. I need to talk to you, badly, about what's going on. Can you promise me you'll give me a chance to do that?'

Rory felt the twin sensations of wanting to walk away with the moral high ground and desperately wanting to hear what Leo had to say. In the end, her heart won.

'All right,' she said softly. 'I'll see you later.'

She went to move, but Leo's gentle hand on her

arm stopped her. 'I promise you, there's nothing for you to worry about.'

Rory gave a brief smile. 'I hope not,' she said. But as Leo let go of her arm, she felt as though a connection between them had been severed.

34

'So that was the infamous Rory Henderson?' Corinne's voice broke into Leo's troubled thoughts as he walked back to the dining room door. 'I have to say, she's not what I imagined.' Leo watched her calmly filling up her cup from the cafetière on the table and taking another sip. 'She certainly seemed to put you in your place just now, though, I'll give her that.'

Leo felt the familiar irritation rising. Corinne knew just how to push his buttons, after a decade of working out just how much pressure to apply, and the time apart from her had done nothing to temper that skill, it seemed. 'Oh, just leave it, Corinne,' he said wearily. 'I don't want to talk about Rory.'

'Well, I do!' Corinne knocked back the rest of the coffee and stood up abruptly from the table. 'How long has this little affair been going on? Have you been in touch with her all this time? Rather coincidental, isn't it, that the summer you come back to the UK, there she is, living in a shed at the bottom of the garden. How very quaint.'

Feeling frustration adding to irritation, Leo tried to force it back down again. Getting angry wouldn't help. He'd been used to Corinne's nitpicking jealousy all the time they'd been married: now they were on the last leg of divorce, he wasn't going to allow himself to get drawn into it again. There had been too many spirals in the past for that, drenched in booze and recrimination.

'You know that's not the case,' he said carefully. 'Rory being here was just a huge coincidence. They do happen, you know.'

Corinne's raised eyebrow suggested that she rather thought they didn't. Leo, not wanting to be drawn, began to clear away her breakfast dishes.

'So, this is what you're going to do with the rest of your life, is it?' Corinne mocked as he did so. 'Playing host in the family's B&B and wondering where it all went wrong?'

Leo, who hadn't yet mentioned the London job,

stayed silent. He didn't want to get into it with Corinne and didn't see why he should.

'Maybe,' he said carefully. 'Maybe not.' He placed the cafetière back down again on the table. 'But whatever I do, it's my decision now, Corinne. I don't have to consult you, or anyone else. And after all these years, and everything I've been through, I think I deserve that, don't you?'

He wasn't too late to see the flash of guilt in her eyes. It was a low blow, to make a reference to the car accident, but he just wanted this to be over, and for Corinne to be back on a plane, as soon as possible.

'So, what are your other plans while you're here?' he asked, resuming the clearing away.

'I've got a couple of friends to see in Manchester, and then I'm flying back out of there in a few days' time,' Corinne replied. 'Then it's back to work. The firm want me on a merger when I'm home again.'

'Anyone I know?' Despite himself, Leo couldn't help the enquiry. He and Corinne had been a great professional team, even if their personal life hadn't worked out.

'No,' Corinne replied. 'This is new business. A fresh case and a fresh start.'

'Well, I'm glad you've got plenty coming your way,' Leo replied carefully. He paused again. 'I know how hard you've been working for this. It's good to see it all paying off.'

Corinne looked at him intently. 'You know there's a place for you back in the company if you want it,' she said softly. 'Mike always said he shouldn't have let you go, even though he understood why you felt you had to leave. The door's always open, Leo.'

Leo smiled. 'I appreciate that. But it's time to move on. You can't ever go back; you know that as well as I do.'

'Funny,' observed Corinne, 'from what I've just seen, going back seems to be exactly what you're do-ing, to the sweet little girl you fell in love with back in the dark ages. Maybe you should take your own advice.'

Leo shook his head. 'It's not the same. There's too much water under the bridge now for me to go back to the firm, and I wouldn't want to cramp your style. You don't need me as a reminder of everything.'

He went to pick up the breakfast dishes for the third time, but Corinne's hand on his arm stopped him. 'I miss you, Leo,' she said gently. 'Even after everything that's happened, I wish you and I...'

Leo shook his head. 'We were over long before the accident, Cor, you know that. We were going nowhere. If we'd stayed together, we'd only have made each other miserable in the end. No matter how successful we were professionally, that's not enough for a marriage. It's time to move on.'

'You always did have the knack of putting things into perspective, no matter how much I tried to ignore it,' Corinne replied. 'But you can't blame a girl for trying!' She blinked, and Leo noticed the tears that threatened. 'I'll let you know when I'm off.'

As Corinne walked out of the dining room and back to her bedroom to pack, Leo shook his head. He knew they'd done the right thing by calling time on their marriage, but he still felt that sense of disappointment in himself that they hadn't been able to find a solution. But there was relief in knowing that, with the final papers signed, that part of his life would soon be over. And with a new chapter beginning, he only hoped that Rory might agree to be a part of it. Just as soon as Corinne was out of here, he'd go and see her, and explain everything.

35

Rory was damned if she was going to mope around in the chalet waiting for Leo to amble down the garden path and speak to her. She had enough to do that day to keep her occupied, and although she wasn't due at Roseford Hall until later, she thought she'd text Stella and see if the offer of a hot desk at Halstead House was still open. The more time she spent at Halstead House, the more she liked it, and she was really glad that she and Stella had renewed their friendship. Rory vowed to keep in touch with her when she left Roseford at the end of the summer.

As she wandered through to Halstead's library again, she forced a smile onto her face, but it was a fraction too late, and Stella asked her what was wrong.

'Oh, where shall I start?' Rory sighed. She filled Stella in on the strange meeting with Corinne, and Leo's odd behaviour, and as she finished explaining, Stella gave her a sympathetic look. 'So,' Rory concluded, 'on top of being out of a job and potentially out of a home, it looks as though I've just been a shag buddy for Leo since we reconnected. I kind of figured it was going to be a holiday romance, but I didn't expect him to be so blatant about it.'

'I'm sorry, Rory,' Stella commiserated. 'Leo didn't seem to be the type to pull something like this. What a twat!'

Rory shook her head. 'He really had me fooled. He seemed so sincere, all the time we were together, and now his gorgeous soon-to-be-ex has rocked up and I just don't know what to think any more. It's not as if I can just head back to York, either. Alex is playing house with Luca while I'm away, and they definitely won't welcome the intrusion.'

'Surely Alex wouldn't chuck you out on the street?' Stella replied. 'I mean, you've been sharing for ages, haven't you?'

Rory nodded. 'She definitely wouldn't, but sooner

or later I'll have to move out for good. It would be unfair of me to expect Alex to pick up the shortfall while I'm out of work when the other option is a ready-made flatmate. They've been wanting to take things to the next level for a while, so it would make sense for them.'

'But leave you jobless and homeless.' Stella shook her head. 'I wonder...'

The ensuing pause made Rory put down the letter she was perusing and look at her friend, whose brow was furrowed.

'What are you thinking?'

'Well,' Stella said, 'and it's only a possibility – I'd need to check with Chris to see when the tenancy is up, but I seem to recall the gatehouse at Halstead is going to be vacant again at the end of October. The current tenant is relocating and we were going to put it back up for rent as soon as we've had the chance to redecorate, probably after Christmas. It's a bit shabby, as we've had holiday lets in there before this current guy, who's been renting it while he works on a contract in Taunton, but if you don't mind a few marks on the walls, I wonder if you'd fancy being our tenant for a while? The gatehouse needs someone living in it, so you'd be doing us a favour, really.'

'I'm broke, Stella!' Rory laughed. 'I can barely afford a flat share up north. What makes you think I could afford to rent your gatehouse?'

'Well, I need a part-time tutor for the winter retreats we're planning on running,' Stella continued. 'And Gabe, Chris's son, is sitting his GCSE exams next June. Chris keeps saying he thinks Gabe could do with a bit of tutoring in his core subjects, especially English.' She paused mischievously. 'Shakespeare doesn't exactly set his world on fire, and my knowledge of *Macbeth* is shaky at best! Maybe you could do that? Let me know what your hourly rate is, and we can do some maths and see where that leaves us in terms of the rent?'

Rory's heart leapt. Stella could well have come up with a solution to her woes but did she really want to relocate to Roseford, especially after what had just happened with Leo? But then Leo wasn't going to be here after September anyway – he'd be off in London, living his best corporate life, and she'd be here, with a roof over her head and the possibility of a steady job for the next few months, at least. Leo wouldn't be in the equation, and the way she was feeling about him now, that was a bonus.

'It's a lovely offer,' Rory said carefully, 'and it's not that I'm not grateful but I'd need to run some numbers. After all these years of a steady salary, I'm not sure how I feel about being self-employed, and doing tutoring on the retreat is a different ball game to being in the classroom.'

'Yeah, your students will have paid good money and want to be there, for a start!' Stella grinned. 'You can't tell me that the prospect of willing participants doesn't sound lovely?'

Rory laughed too. Admittedly, teaching Shakespeare to a bunch of bored Year Tens on a rainy afternoon in November seemed, in theory, to be far less inviting than delivering a course to enthusiastic adults who desperately wanted to learn, but she was still unnerved.

'What do I know about teaching creative writing to writers?' she persisted. 'I mean, I've got a few thousand words of my own novel that I've slaved over for a short time, and no idea about how to finish it. What's to stop your paying customers from calling me out as a total fraud?'

'You've been in the classroom for over a decade, Rory,' Stella replied. 'And yes, I know that's not quite the same, but have you ever heard of the phrase "transferrable skills"? Not to mention the fact that I've got a ton of resources you can use for your first course. And speaking of phrases, here's another one: "fake it till you make it". How about that?'

'I don't know, Stella,' Rory murmured. 'It's a lot to think about.'

'You've got time to think about it,' Stella replied. 'After all, you've got a term back in York to get through first. And if the worst comes to the worst, I can teach the course. It's just that Chris wants me to scale back a bit and focus on my own writing for a little while, too. I've been banging on for years about writing a screenplay, and with Finn Sanderson's interest in creating something based in Roseford, this is the perfect opportunity. If you took over some of the teaching at the retreat for a few months, it would give me the breathing space to work on that, too, so you'd be doing me a favour.'

Rory felt reassured by Stella's reasoning, and she was relieved that Stella was making the effort to try to convince her to stay. It didn't seem quite so much like a sympathy offer now that her friend had explained it. It would also be good to know she had some security when her contract at her current school ended.

'It sounds great,' Rory said, enthusiasm for the idea beginning to ignite inside her. 'I promise I'll let you know as soon as I know if it can work.' She reached out and gave her friend a quick, slightly awkward hug. 'I'm so glad I came to Roseford this summer. It's been lovely to be back in touch with you.'

And even though she was still in at least two minds about Leo, Rory realised that she was telling the truth.

36

Later that day, Rory's enthusiasm was re-ignited by Simon Treloar's surprised, bemused but definitely positive reaction to the information that she and Stella had been able to unearth about Edmund and Frederick. As she passed him the copies of the letters from the Halstead House archive that Stella had entrusted to her, he looked intently at them, and then, with Rory's guidance, compared them to the unsent letters in the Roseford Hall archive boxes.

'This is quite something,' Simon murmured as he mulled over the fruits of Rory and Stella's labours. 'I can't believe it was a secret that's been so effectively buried until now. But, given the state of Roseford Hall when the British Heritage Fund took it over, I'm not terribly surprised. There's so much material here, and it would seem that it was something that Edmund's generation hoped would stay buried.' He looked keenly at one of the photographs that Rory had found between the pages of the old newspaper. 'I mean, when you look at them, it's so obvious, really, isn't it?'

Rory's heart sped up a little. 'And are you happy that we've found all this?' she had to ask. It was, after all, quite a revision to Simon's family history.

'Of course.' Simon looked up, and seemed surprised by the question. 'It might seem contradictory, given the sheer amount of material in this house, but it's taken so long to get things into a kind of order. The middle years of the twentieth century weren't a good time for this family: that was when the money started to run out, if my father was to be believed. We lived in a state of fading disorganisation for two generations at least, when the last thing anyone was interested in was keeping tabs on the thousands of documents that made up the family history. Most families have a few photo albums and birthday cards in shoeboxes: the Treloars had whole cellars full of paperwork!' He paused and grinned briefly. 'Even Stella, as Writer in Residence some years ago, couldn't have been expected to chase it all down. Although it's fitting that you and she unravelled this mystery together: she became very fond of this place when she worked here. And the BHF archivists have enough to keep them busy well into the next century, I'd say.'

'She was,' Rory agreed. She could tell from Stella's excited reaction once they'd found the real links between Halstead House and Roseford Hall just how much both places meant to her, and again she felt that the stars had aligned in allowing them to make the discovery together.

'Well,' Simon continued, passing the letters carefully back to Rory. 'I hope that what you've found out has inspired you. Will you be including much of Edmund and Frederick's story in your novel?'

Rory nodded. 'If you're happy for me to fictionalise their account, then I'd very much like to draw on their experiences.'

'I'm more than happy,' Simon replied. 'And I'm sure the BHF will be, too. They're always on the lookout for engaging ideas for exhibitions. This will provide them with a great deal to work with. And who knows, perhaps, when your novel is published, they could sell it in the shop.'

'It's still in the drafting stage,' Rory laughed, 'but it's a lovely thought!' She carefully put the letters back into the cardboard document wallet she'd brought with her. 'Thank you so much, Simon, for giving me access to the archive. It's been more inspiring than I would have ever thought possible.'

'You should be thanking the BHF, really,' Simon said. 'But on behalf of the family, I can at least say you're welcome.' He sighed, as if, suddenly, the story of Edmund and Frederick's doomed love was hitting home. 'I wish we'd known about all this sooner,' he said softly. 'Poor Edmund, and poor Frederick, returning from war carrying so much trauma, and losing the man he adored.'

'At least they both knew they were loved,' Rory said gently. 'Even if they weren't together after the Great War, there was a time when they were, with Francesca's blessing. Those moments, however brief, would have given Frederick some solace, I'm sure.'

'I'm sure you're right.' Simon smiled. 'And now Edmund and Frederick's truth can be brought into the light where it should have been, instead of buried in boxes in the dark. I'm sure, if either of them is keeping an eye on the comings and goings here, from the great beyond, that they'd be pleased to see it.'

'I think they would,' Rory replied. She felt her own emotions bubbling to the surface as she said goodbye to Simon and headed back to Roseford Villas. Simon's reaction to the information she and Stella had discovered had been so positive and so welcoming, she felt as though she'd really accomplished something. She wasn't given to thoughts of what happened after people shuffled off this mortal coil, but she hoped that somewhere Edmund and Frederick would be together, and happy with how things had turned out.

37

Rory headed back to the chalet feeling a whole lot more optimistic about her future than she had that morning. Despite the nagging doubts about what was happening with Leo, the fact that she had another option to consider in terms of her career and her living situation was a definite bonus. The lovely meeting with Simon had been the icing on the cake. Suddenly, the prospect of leaving her job at October half-term didn't seem quite so scary. It now felt exciting. Galvanised by the prospect of a fresh start, she spent the afternoon on the main teaching recruitment websites, submitting her CV to a few, just in case she needed some supply teaching hours to top up her work at Halstead House. Schools were always looking for reliable supply teachers, and she had enough experience for them to put their trust in her. And with the prospect of some extra income from tutoring Gabe, too, it seemed as though there really could be a solution. Not to mention the possibility of getting more work done on her own novel if she had more time to spare.

That done, she cracked open the notes she'd been making about the modern-day section of her novel. She'd been so caught up in the historical narrative that she'd not written much about the twenty-first century romance lately, and she felt as though she wanted to get to grips with it again.

She glanced at the notes she'd made the other night and tried not to cringe. She'd been high on the endorphins that being with Leo had released and re-alised that a lot of it would have to be cut, or at least rewritten. Stella always used to laugh at her for her 'Mills and Boon tendencies' when they'd had creative writing assignments at university, and the stuff she'd written so far was purple prose of the highest order. Grinning to herself, she decided not to just delete it, but added to the page, trying to refine, explore and get a handle on her two modern lovers and their predicament. She'd spent so much time with her fic-tional versions of Edmund, Frederick and Francesca lately that it took her a while to get back into a modern mindset. But eventually the words started to flow and the ideas came back to her as she began to explore the love story that had been so heavily influenced by her own early experiences of a broken heart.

She worked for so long, sitting at the table in the chalet, that she hadn't realised how late it was getting until her stomach started to rumble. As she stood up from the desk to put the kettle on and grab a quick slice of toast, she was startled to see Leo walking across the garden towards the chalet. Grabbing two mugs out of the cupboard, she flipped the switch on the kettle and waited for him to approach the door.

'Hey,' he said as she crossed the small floorspace to let him in. 'I'm sorry I took so long. I had a few things to sort out, and time got away from me.'

Rory nodded. 'I've been pretty busy myself. Tea?'

'Please.'

The next few moments were taken up with making two mugs of tea, and by the time Rory had brought them over to the table, Leo had settled into one of the chairs on the decking outside the chalet. Feeling a little awkward, she sat down next to him. After their previous intimacy, it felt odd not to know quite where to put herself, but the encounter with Corinne had changed something between them.

'So...' Leo began.

'So...' Rory echoed.

Leo let out a nervous laugh. 'It feels as though we're right back at the beginning again.' He turned towards her. 'I wish it didn't.'

'Me too.' Rory, who was used, in her career, to waiting for students to respond, didn't add anything further. Whatever it was that Leo wanted to say, she needed to hear it.

'Look, Rory,' Leo finally began, 'I don't know what you're thinking about what you saw this morning, but I swear to you it's nothing you need to worry about.'

'Well, what I saw was Corinne sitting at the table, and smiling at you as if you were still her husband, right?'

Leo's look of surprise at Rory's directness showed her that it was the last thing he'd been expecting.

'Yes,' he admitted. 'She'd come over to see me. To talk to me. But now we've talked, I can assure you that there's absolutely nothing left for us to say. Corinne knew that, really, but she felt she needed to see me in person.'

'Because she wants you back, and she thought

she could convince you to go back with her?' Rory asked. 'I mean, that's what I'd do, if I was your wife.'

'Ex-wife,' Leo reminded her. 'As of the moment I signed the papers, very much an ex-wife.'

'So why would your ex-wife come here all the way from Australia then? She must have thought she'd be able to talk you round.' Irritated now, Rory took a sip of her tea, and wished she'd put more milk in it when it scalded her mouth.

'Rory, it's not like that, I swear!' Leo's voice was shot through with frustration, and Rory wanted so desperately to believe him. She watched as he jumped up from his chair and began to pace up and down the decking, unable to keep still. 'Corinne's part of my past. It's not what you think!'

'No one who's part of somebody's past flies halfway around the world to see them,' Rory replied. 'From the way she was looking at you, it was clear that she still loves you, Leo.'

Leo put his fists up to his temples in frustration. 'No, Rory, you've got this all wrong. Corinne wasn't here to get me back. Well, not in the way you think.'

'And what does that mean?' Exasperated, Rory leaned back in her chair. 'Maybe you can explain it to me?'

Leo paused. 'Look, Corinne wasn't just my wife.

As you know, she was my business partner in the law firm back in Melbourne. When I came to the UK, I was on the verge of signing my share of the company over to her. I wanted to get out, and I'd had a job offer in London that would, finally, get me away from all the crap that's happened over the past few years. And to be honest, Rory, I needed that. I *really, really* needed it. The problem was that Aunt Violet and Uncle Bryan contacted me about this place just when we were on the verge of winding up the company. Corinne wasn't prepared to wait for me to come back, and so she came over to make sure everything was signed so we could dissolve our business partnership.'

'But surely she could have just emailed you the papers?' Rory said. 'What aren't you telling me, Leo?'

Leo paused. 'You're right,' he said quietly. 'There is more to it than that, but... it's complicated.'

'Try me,' Rory replied. 'If I'm going to trust you, I need to know.'

Leo let out a long sigh. 'Corinne's been going to Alcoholics Anonymous,' he said. 'She realised, after the accident, that her drinking had got out of control. We were both well used to the corporate life, and with that comes a lot of opportunities to overindulge. Corinne's drinking was out of hand, and the night of the car accident, she should never have been behind the wheel. The law firm agreed to keep her on if she started receiving treatment for alcohol abuse, and while I was recovering in hospital, she decided that enough was enough, and, to keep her job, she agreed. She's been working through the twelve-step programme ever since. She's been sober for two years now, and intends to stay that way.'

'So why did she come here?' Rory asked.

'Part of the programme is atonement,' Leo replied. 'That means she needs to make amends to those she's wronged. I wasn't just the catalyst for her to stop drinking, I was her biggest mistake. She's had a lot of trouble coming to terms with that. I've told you that our marriage was over long before the accident, which is true, but it would be wrong to blame alcohol for that. We'd just come to the end of the line. The trouble is, Corinne can't quite accept that. She had to see me one last time, to see my name on the papers for the business and the divorce, before she could truly accept that it was over. So that was why she was here. Now she's seen what she wanted to see, and that I'm well, and better than I ever was when we were married, she can move on.'

'But she could have just Zoom called you for

that!' Rory exclaimed. 'Did she really have to come all the way across the world just to apologise?'

Leo gave her a grin. 'She was always one for the grand gesture, and even after everything, she wanted to make an impression.' He held up a hand, as if anticipating what Rory was going to say. 'I know it's bizarre, but it was what she felt she needed to do. Now she's done it, I hope that'll be the end of it. I've signed the papers for the company, and for the divorce, and now we can both move on with our lives.'

'Has she left already?' Rory asked.

Leo nodded. 'She left this morning. She's going to stay in Manchester with some university friends who emigrated here a few years back. She thought it would be a good chance to catch up with them. I think, probably, that's the real reason she came here, but making amends with me while she was this side of the world seemed a sensible detour.' He paused. 'She's not a bad person, Rory, in spite of everything that's happened. She's trying to move on with her life just as I'm trying with mine. We both have a lot to work through, but it's one step at a time. I was her next step, and now she's taken it.'

Rory let the silence extend between them for a few moments. She couldn't really dispute anything that Leo had said, but it didn't make seeing the woman who had held his heart for so long any easier. She'd be lying if she'd said she wouldn't have preferred Corinne to remain on the other side of the world. However, it seemed counterproductive to keep going around in circles about it. She was only here for a few more weeks, and Leo was heading off to London at the start of September anyway. Was it really worth spending any more time obsessing about a person who was clearly part of Leo's past?

'Well,' Rory said finally, knowing that Leo was waiting for a response from her. 'If Corinne's made peace with herself, and with you, then I need to make peace with her having been here. I'm too old to be worrying about what happened in the past. Let's just try to enjoy the present, shall we?'

'Amen to that,' Leo murmured as he drew Rory to him. As their lips met, Rory felt a lightening of the burdensome thoughts she'd been carrying around with her all day. This might just be for the summer, but she was determined, from now on, to enjoy every single minute of it.

38

'So, what do you want to do?' Leo asked as they broke apart from their kiss. 'The night is young, and so are we. Sort of!' He paused. 'Sorry, that was really cheesy, wasn't it?'

Rory smiled. 'I've heard worse. Mostly from you, in fact.' She remembered the ways he'd tried to impress her in the old days, when he sent her song lyrics and sonnets, and tried to learn snatches of poetry to quote during their soppier moments.

Leo tried to look offended, but was clearly so relieved that Rory had accepted his explanations about Corinne that he didn't quite manage it. 'Well, I was thinking, if you didn't have any other plans, we could get out of Roseford for a bit, go and do something different.'

'Such as?' Rory hadn't really looked into what else there was to do in this part of the West Country, she'd been so caught up with her writing, but she did feel like exploring a bit.

Leo paused. 'Well, there's a ten-pin bowling alley just outside Taunton, or we could see a film if you wanted?'

Rory couldn't help the laugh that escaped her. 'That was *not* what I thought you were going to say.' She held up a hand as he started to backtrack. 'But actually, I've been sitting at my desk for so long, bowling might be just the ticket. I don't think I've done it since I went on a school trip with a bunch of Year Nine students a few years ago.'

'Well, I haven't done it since I was in school back in Aus,' Leo replied, 'so you've had a bit more recent practice than me, anyway.'

'Do we need to book a lane or anything?' Rory asked. She reached for her laptop. 'I'll take a look, shall I?'

As Rory found the place, an All Star Bowling franchise about twenty minutes away, she noticed, with a grin, that there was a burger joint on the premises, too. It might not quite be the 'grown-up' date that she and Leo should be going on, but it would be fun to pretend to be teenagers again for the night. The grown-up stuff could wait...

Lane booked for an hour's time, they were soon pulling up to an out-of-town retail and leisure park on the outskirts of Taunton. It couldn't have been more of a contrast to the quaint historical buildings of Roseford, but Rory felt a childlike sense of excitement to be doing something a bit silly, and being on a 'proper' date with Leo again.

'All set?' she asked as they found their lane.

'Hit me with your best shot, Rory Dean!' Leo replied.

The bowling alley was noisy, neon and full of families and teenagers making the most of a night out during the summer holidays. As Rory typed in their names to the computer, she couldn't resist a daft selfie to go alongside her score on the screen, and, after a little persuasion, Leo did the same. Rory realised that getting away from Roseford Villas was exactly what they'd both needed, especially after the weight of their discussions about Corinne, and she found herself getting really into the game, even though her enthusiasm definitely overwhelmed her expertise, as ball after ball rolled into the gutter without hitting any pins.

Some time later, having both collapsed in helpless laughter over the crapness of their scores compared to those of the group of teenagers in the lane next to them, they conceded that they were both a little out of practice. As the pins stubbornly stayed put for Leo's last ball, Rory drew a deep breath, took her ball off the loader and prepared to make her last shot her best one. The bowling gods were obviously smiling as the ball made firm contact and took all of the pins out.

'Result!' she crowed, waggling a finger at Leo. 'It's all coming back to me now.'

Leo, not to be outdone, picked Rory up and gave her a squeeze. 'Pride comes before a fall, Aurora.'

'Is that so?' As she was locked in his arms, her stomach gave an almighty rumble. 'But I think it's about time for dinner, don't you? I'd rather eat a burger than my words.'

'Fair enough.' Leo let her go. 'And I never could resist a really greasy burger.'

'Sounds perfect,' Rory replied. 'Shall we get a table?'

In a short time, they were ensconced in a booth in the corner of the restaurant, tucking in with great gusto to the 'Everything But The Kitchen Sink' burger with a generous side order of fries each.

'This has been fun,' Rory said, between bites. 'I didn't realise how chained to my desk I'd been lately. Thank you for suggesting it.'

Leo sat back in his seat. 'It has been fun,' he agreed. 'I didn't think my back would be up to it, but so far so good.'

'You don't feel too bad, then?' Rory asked. It was all very well acting like a teenager for the evening, she thought, but she couldn't quite get away from the fact that they were still adults, after all.

'Nope.' Leo gave her a seductive smile. 'And if you're not too blown out from your fast food, I'd love to show you how absolutely fine I am...'

Finishing their food quickly, they headed back out to the car. Rory had driven, and as the car covered the short journey back to Roseford, she felt a tingle of anticipation. She hoped, as they drew up in the driveway of Roseford Villas once again, that this might be the night that Leo wanted to take things to the next level.

39

A sweaty, sensual night commenced, and Rory found herself, once again, hoping that Leo would feel confident enough to take that final physical step. She'd been worried about the sturdiness of the double bed in the chalet, but as they slipped off their clothes and sank down onto it, they found that it was more than adequate.

This time, maybe because of the discussions they'd had, or perhaps because Rory was feeling much more at ease about what this relationship was, both relaxed into the rhythm, and when it came to the moment of decision, Leo looked up into Rory's face with a confidence and a certainty that she couldn't help falling for.

'Are you sure?' she asked softly, shifting position so that she was sitting back on her knees, astride his thighs.

Leo nodded. 'Absolutely. Got to try it sometime, and I can't think of anyone I'd rather try it with.' He shifted upwards, so that his lower back was supported by two firm pillows. Then, after a brief stop for a condom, Rory moved downwards, never breaking eye contact with him as they became enticingly and excitingly connected. She let out a long sigh of pleasure and began to move, both of them feeling the sensations as they touched and caressed one another to the summit. As Leo gave a deep thrust inside her, Rory felt the oddest combination of happiness and heartbreak: the thought crossed her mind, not for the first time since they'd rediscovered each other, that she really didn't want to let him out of her life again.

The next morning, as they lay entwined, Rory breathed in Leo's scent, and realised that she'd never felt so content. She knew it was probably the endorphins, but she couldn't help wondering whether or not they could make a plan to keep seeing one another when the summer break was over. Surely there had to be a way? Especially if she was going to be moving to the West Country for a while. She knew

Stella's solution wasn't a permanent one, but the more she thought about it, the more she found herself wanting to accept. Of course, Leo would still be in London, but they could see each other at weekends.

'What are you thinking?' Leo asked her, sounding sleepy.

'Oh, you know,' Rory replied, trying to sound as if she hadn't just been contemplating their whole future, and looking up train timetables in her head. 'Just stuff...'

'Stuff? Sounds riveting!' Leo propped himself up on one elbow and looked down at her, his dark brown eyes alight with amusement. 'And you, a writer. I'm sure you could do better than that.'

Rory grinned up at him. 'Well,' she said teasingly, 'if you must know, I was deciding just how many marks I'd award you for that little performance. I was thinking, perhaps, a seven!' She put on her best impression of the late *Strictly Come Dancing* head judge, Len Goodman.

'Oh, really?' Leo cocked an eyebrow at her. 'From where I was sitting, it most definitely felt like at least a nine, *dah-ling*.' His Craig Revel-Horwood was impeccable in response.

Rory giggled. 'Well, we can always give it another

go if you'd like. But I must just use the loo first and I'm desperate for a glass of water. Did you want one?'

'That'd be great,' Leo replied. 'I'll, er, use the loo after you, too. Try not to be long.'

Grabbing Leo's T-shirt from the crumpled pile of clothing by the bed, Rory headed out to the bathroom. As she was sipping her water, she flashed up her laptop to see if she had any new emails, and to check that what she'd written the previous evening had saved to the cloud. She plugged in the laptop to recharge the battery and saw, with a glance, that the document had updated. Despite the dodgy prose, she was getting a much clearer idea of who the modern characters were now, and how the story was going to progress. Remembering that she owed Leo a glass of water, she brought it back to the bedroom and then headed off to the shower, with a teasing 'You're welcome to join me,' as she walked back out of the bedroom. The shower room was in a separate little space to the loo, so as Rory stepped in and started running the water, she heard a muffled flush from the other end of the chalet and waited in anticipation for Leo come into the shower.

After about five minutes, she'd finished washing her hair and was wondering if Leo had just gone back to bed. It didn't matter; she was probably just going to join him back there, anyway. Switching off the shower, she wrapped herself in a large, fluffy white towel and ran a brush through her wet hair, slicking it back from her forehead. She worried that she looked a bit pink and dishevelled, but then reasoned that Leo had seen her in a much more dishevelled state so tried to put it out of her mind. Taking a deep breath, she opened the shower room door and froze.

There, sitting in front of her laptop, was Leo, an expression of hurt and confusion written all over his face.

40

'Hey,' Rory said softly. 'What are you doing?'

'I could ask you the same thing,' Leo replied bleakly.

Rory's back stiffened. 'Were you reading my novel?'

Leo's eyes swivelled from her, back to the screen. 'If that's what you can call the thing on the screen, then yeah, I suppose I was.' He shook his head. 'And to be honest... it's all a bit of a shock.'

Rory hurried across the chalet towards the table. 'You shouldn't be looking at this, Leo. The screen-saver should have kicked in. I can't think why it hasn't. And it's a first draft, too.' She gave a nervous laugh. 'No one's supposed to see it yet.'

It was as if the last few hours hadn't happened. Leo's expression had gone from confusion to anger, and he didn't seem to register what she'd just said. 'Christ, Rory, I had no idea you were going to make this so personal,' Leo said. 'What you've written about us, about me... it's too much.'

Rory's hands started to shake, but she tried to keep calm. 'As I said, it's a first draft. Most of it's probably going to get cut anyway. I was just emptying out my head onto the page. Trying to get my ideas, and my research, into some kind of order.'

'Is that what all this has been, then?' Leo shot back. 'Am I just part of your "research"?'

'No!' Rory exclaimed. 'Of course not! But you already knew I was going to be using some of what we used to have as inspiration. What you read was just the raw stuff coming out of my head and onto the screen.' She felt irritated that Leo had taken it upon himself without permission to read what she'd written, but also seriously worried that he'd clearly got the wrong end of the stick. She reached out a hand to touch his upper arm, but he shrugged her off and stood up. He'd put on his boxer shorts, but little else.

'I never really felt particularly happy you were going to be delving back into our history for this book, Rory, and now, reading this, it seems my gut feeling was the right one. You just can't go writing this kind of stuff and expecting me to be OK with it.' He paced away from her, and, looking around for his T-shirt, which Rory had discarded in the shower room, he slipped it back over his head.

'But no one who reads it will know it's based on what happened between us. And it was all so long ago, Leo. Surely you can see that?' Rory clenched her fists in frustration. She felt exposed by what Leo had read, as if he'd reached somewhere personal and was now putting everything he'd found up for questioning, but she also felt angry. The laptop might have been on, but he'd had no right to delve into what she'd written. It was a Pandora's box of ill-formed thoughts, half-narratives and stray ideas that she hadn't yet had the chance to refine. In short, the worst possible thing for him to have read.

'I don't know, Rory,' Leo replied. 'It's one thing to be nostalgic, but it's another to spill your guts all over the page about a time in our lives when we're just stupid kids. Anyone who knew us back then is going to make the connection.'

'It's fiction, Leo!' Rory retorted. 'And by the time it's finished it'll be a literary parallel with the tragedy that Edmund Treloar faced in his own life. He never got the second chance that we've got. Can't you see how those two stories make sense together?'

'So that's all this has been, then? Fact finding? Christ, Rory, I gave myself to you and you know how hard that was for me to do. And now... it feels like a betrayal, both of what we had when we were kids and what we've had since you came here. Then you expect me just to smile and say it's all fine?'

Rory tried to reach out a hand to him, but Leo took a step back, as if making contact with her would burn. 'Leo, it's not like that. Yes, I drew on some of what happened between us, but the rest is complete imagination. There's nothing in there that you need to be afraid of or embarrassed about. If you could just let me explain how it works as a whole piece...'

'Don't bother,' Leo snapped. 'I'm glad I've provided some "inspiration" for you while you've been staying here but that's as much as I'm prepared to give you. If you need anything else while you're staying, I'd appreciate it if you could leave me a note. You're *so* good at writing, after all.' And without a backward glance, he stormed out of the chalet, slamming the door as he left.

Shit, shit, shit! Rory sank down onto the bench and put her head in her hands. This was absolutely the last thing she'd wanted to happen. Leo, clearly reading out of context, had happened upon part of the book that was raw, and intimate, and nowhere near as polished as it should be. Now he was convinced that this novel was going to be an embarrassing confessional about their relationship! Whoever had said you should write what you knew had clearly never had a doomed teenage romance, and a conversation about said romance two decades later.

She knew she'd shattered his trust in her, after everything they'd done to build it over the past few weeks. After their glorious night together, when things had certainly gone with a bang, she felt as though she'd damaged what had seemed to be the beginnings of a more serious relationship.

The question was, how on earth was she going to fix it? In the midst of her upset about the way Leo had reacted, she also heard a little voice in her mind questioning why she felt she now needed to run things past him in order to tell the story. After all, if he hadn't been in Roseford, wouldn't she have written it anyway? What difference did it make that he'd seen an early draft? Perhaps she'd been influenced by their new relationship, and written with a little more immediacy than she would have done otherwise, but what was narrative, if not some kind of representation of a greater truth?

Shaking her head, realising that this was getting her nowhere, she decided to take herself off for a couple of hours, and lose herself once more in the Roseford Hall archives. If one line of plot was causing her grief, perhaps the other strand, the one that concerned Edmund Treloar and Frederick Middleton, would provide her with a little distraction.

41

It was amazing, Leo thought, as the next couple of
weeks passed, just how easy it was to avoid someone,
even when they were living at the bottom of the garden. He'd been keeping on top of things at Roseford
Villas before, but now he really threw himself into it,
cleaning and scouring everything, making sure he
was up long before his guests, even hoovering the
communal areas three times a day, just to keep himself busy. He'd always kept the darkness at bay
through work, and now it was his salvation. Every
time he stopped to think about Rory, and what had
happened between them, he thought of another job
to do, and by the time he collapsed into bed each
night, he was beyond insomnia. The house and gar-

dens had never looked so good, even if he did tend to the back gardens when he was sure Rory wasn't around. The mental energy he was expending by keeping out of her way was tiring enough but, combined with the endless jobs he manufactured for himself, he had no time to brood.

Which was just as well, as Aunt Vi and Uncle Bryan were due home in the next week, and he wanted to make sure that Roseford Villas looked even better than when they'd left. Leo had even managed to set up a database for customer feedback which they could manage on their return. He hoped they'd find it useful. Keeping his mind on administrative tasks, the careful, predictable inflow of data, also kept his mind busy and away from more emotional things.

He'd also had confirmation that, having signed the papers when Corinne had visited, his marriage was officially over, and his old life in the law firm was, too. Now, he had a future in London to anticipate, a new job and the chance of a brand-new start.

So why did he feel so unmotivated by it all? Why did he feel as though he was walking away from the most important thing in his life? And this time, rather than being forced to do so by his parents' change of circumstances, he was choosing to do it himself.

The problem was, he wasn't prepared to go to Rory and apologise. Reading what he'd read, no matter how rough the draft on the computer was, had frightened him. The intimacy in those pages, laid bare, for anyone, eventually, to pick up and read wasn't just a reminder of what they'd experienced the first time they'd been together, but also a manifestation, in black and white, of the emotions he'd been experiencing ever since they'd met again. He knew, now, that he'd fallen in love with her, hard. And while she'd been affectionate, and passionate, and he'd seen a hopeful light in her eyes about what *might* have been going on in her heart, something told him that she wasn't in the same place as him yet. Leo was so afraid of rejection, after everything he'd been through, that he couldn't bear to put himself in that position. So he'd jumped first, using the manuscript as a good reason to call the relationship to a halt.

What was the worst that could happen? he'd reasoned. Rory was going back to York, anyway, and he was off to London. They couldn't sustain a relationship over that distance, even as adults. He wasn't in the market for a long commute every weekend, he just wasn't physically up to it, and the thought of spending hours on a train for a couple of days at a time filled him with exhaustion. It would have been nice to have continued the illusion of a pleasant holiday fling for a few more weeks, but ultimately, it would have had to have come to an end. Leo knew, if he hadn't read the manuscript, he'd probably have found some other excuse to end it. He wasn't proud of himself for that, but he was certainly self-aware enough to draw that conclusion.

All of this knowledge didn't solve the problem of his aching heart, though, and that was why he'd thrown himself, hook, line and sinker, into managing the hell out of the B&B until it was time to hand it back to Bryan and Vi. The funny thing was, he was really enjoying the work. The business suited him, and once he'd begun to formulate his own rules and routines, adapting those that his aunt and uncle had so fastidiously left him, he found himself feeling as though he had a real stake in the place. It was liberating to take control, and as guests came and went during the closing weeks of the summer season, he was feeling a great reluctance to step away and start again in London, to go back to the corporate grind. When he'd started looking after Roseford Villas a few months ago, he'd been doing it out of a sense of duty to the family, and purely as a time filler before his new job started. But over the time he'd been in Roseford, he'd found himself warming to the place and its people, and his fledgling relationship with Rory had been the icing on the cake. The fresh summer air of Roseford at its most attractive was winning him over, and more than once he found himself wondering: what if he could stay?

Not that it would solve the problem with Rory, of course. Rory would still be in York, and, if he stayed in Somerset, he'd face even more of a commute to see her. But what if staying in Roseford allowed him to continue to heal, to make his own life better? He'd spent two years working on his physical rehabilitation: it might now be time to really focus on his mental health, and what he needed to improve things in his own head.

All this, however, was a pipe dream, as much as making a future with Rory was. He'd signed the contract with Palmer, Dennis and Wright and he was committed to them for the near future, at least. And really, that was all there was to it. Wondering what might have been, with both Roseford Villas and Rory, simply wasn't in the equation.

When Bryan and Vi returned, he welcomed them back with a smile and accepted a huge hug from his aunt. She'd always been someone he could talk to, and despite the fact that her standards when it came to Roseford Villas had been, in the beginning, very hard to live up to, he loved and respected her. Uncle Bryan, always the quieter of the two, had greeted him with a warm smile and a promise to show him their holiday photos that evening. Leo was looking forward to the distraction. Anything that stopped his thoughts from wandering in the direction of the chalet was definitely welcome.

42

'So it looks as though we'll be looking to get this place sold over the next few months, if we're to move to Spain in the new year.' Uncle Bryan sat back on the sofa, having talked Leo extensively through the many photographs of their prospective retirement property that had been screen casting on the television in the family's private lounge area. 'The vendor wants rid of it as soon as possible, so the family can divide the spoils, and so we'd be looking to do the same with Roseford Villas.'

'It looks fabulous,' Leo commented, not for the first time since the slide show had commenced. 'I can see why you'd want to take your next steps over there.' He gave his uncle a brief smile. 'And is that an outbuilding in the garden? Potential to run a small holiday let, if you wanted to?'

Uncle Bryan's eyes twinkled. 'We're going to walk before we run, but I would never rule something like that out.'

'Well, I'm glad the trip was successful,' Leo replied. 'And I'm sure you'll find a buyer for Roseford Villas very quickly. Anyone who's interested in hospitality will snap it up, I'm sure.'

There was a long pause between the two men, during which Leo took a sip of the glass of red wine that Bryan had poured him.

'Yes,' Bryan said, eventually. 'You've done a good job keeping an eye on the place while we've been away. It seems as though you've really enjoyed being here, too.'

Leo nodded. 'I have. It was just the change I needed. Thank you for trusting me with it.'

'I'll be sad to see it going out of family hands,' Bryan observed. 'But I suppose all good things must come to an end eventually.' He looked around the room, and then topped up his and Leo's glasses. 'We changed a lot when we came here. Roseford Villas was in a time warp when we took it on, and ran more like a smaller version of Fawlty Towers than a proper B&B. We focused on what was important to us, and we moved with the times. But now it needs to move again, and I'd like to think it was going to someone with the vision to do that. Even in the time you've been here, the small changes you made when you were in charge show that you might be the one who has that vision.'

Leo's heart sped up a little. He saw the look in Bryan's eyes and knew that his uncle was suggesting a move that would make the process of selling up easier for him and Vi. After all, if they sold to Leo, things could progress quickly. But that didn't alter the fact that Leo had committed to a job in London or negate the arguments he'd had with himself about what staying in Roseford would mean.

'I've had such a lovely time working here for the past few months,' Leo said carefully. 'And I would be lying if I said the thought hadn't crossed my mind that I should like to be here for longer.'

Bryan arched an eyebrow at him over his wine-glass. 'I sense a "but" coming.'

Leo smiled slightly. 'Well... as you know, my situation is rather complex. Having accepted the job in London, I'm not quite the free agent I was six months ago when I was looking for something to do. I just don't know if I'm the right fit for you. But I am grateful that you'd consider me a decent proposition.'

'I'm glad of your honesty, lad,' Bryan replied. 'But there's no need to make your mind up just yet. You're the lawyer... couldn't you get yourself out of that contract if you wanted to?'

Leo laughed. 'If only it were that simple, Uncle Bryan!' He took another gulp of his wine. 'Now, why don't you tell me a little bit more about your plans for La Vista Marítima?'

'Well, lad,' Uncle Bryan warmed to his subject once more. 'Given the proximity to the beach, we were thinking about adding an oceanside bar...'

* * *

A little while later, Leo mooched off to bed. He'd had a couple of glasses of wine, which he was sure was making him sentimental, but he couldn't help wondering what it would be like to really be in charge of Roseford Villas. The house felt different to him when he'd been the one making the decisions. At first, he'd been terrified of making mistakes, of getting things wrong and putting his aunt and uncle's business in jeopardy through his own inexperience. When he'd forgotten Mr and Mrs Cross's breakfast, he'd panicked that an error like that would mean the end of their good reputation. Now, with a few months' work under his belt, he felt much more in control of it all. But his aunt and uncle were back now, and they'd be assuming the mantle again from tomorrow. He'd just be a helper again, and in a few more days he'd be off to London. He felt the loss of that independence, illusory as it might be, keenly. If he took on Roseford Villas, he'd be his own boss, responsible to no one. He had some money in the bank from the sale of the house in Melbourne, and his payout from the law firm when he'd had to leave his post through ill health. It was meant to be something to put towards a more substantial base in London, once he'd settled into his position in the firm, but what if he used it as a deposit for Roseford Villas instead?

Leo sighed. He was in no position to start making decisions like this. Roseford Villas had felt like home in the time he'd been here, but it wasn't. He was committed to London, and while his heart was beginning to feel as though he'd like to stay, his head was telling him it was a daft idea. Better to just get to London and get on with things. That was the sensible thing to do, and sensible was what he needed. He tried to quiet the other, rather insistent voice, that was telling him to face his feelings and follow his heart. That had got him into nothing but trouble recently. Heaving a hefty sigh, he decided that, rather than hang around any longer and brooding, he'd be better off heading up to London sooner rather than later. His accommodation was available whenever he wanted it, so there seemed very little point in hanging around Roseford any longer.

43

For the last couple of weeks of her holiday, Rory continued to keep her distance from Roseford Villas. It was easier than she'd thought it would be: she was spending a lot of time up at Roseford Hall, and when she wasn't there, she was hot-desking at Halstead House. She hadn't told Stella what had happened between herself and Leo, but she noticed that Stella was checking in with her regularly, and she was pretty sure it wasn't just to see how the novel was going.

Added to that, she'd finally decided to take Stella up on her offer and move down to Roseford in the autumn. If Leo wasn't going to be around at that time, having already started his new job, she wouldn't have to run the risk of any awkward meetings. She could concentrate fully on finishing her novel, teach on Stella's course, tutor Gabe and, hopefully, pick up some supply teaching at the local secondary schools if she needed extra funds. There were three within ten miles of Roseford, so she was in no doubt that some work would be forthcoming if she wanted it.

It was probably just as well things had cooled off between them, Rory thought. Leo was already at an intense point in his life, and with her own circumstances changing significantly, perhaps now wasn't the best time to be starting something new. Better to consign it to the 'holiday fling' category, than wait in hope that it could be resolved.

All the same, her heart ached, when she had time to allow it. Knowing Leo was so close, but that he didn't want to see her, felt as bad as when he was thousands of miles away and she couldn't see him. Many times, she'd considered just knocking on the door, forcing him to sit down and speak to her, hashing it all out and coming to some kind of conclusion, but she just didn't know what to say. She hadn't lied to him when she'd told him what the book was going to be about, and she wasn't going to change things just because he'd read part of the first draft. Out of context, the section he'd read was pretty embarrassing and intimate, but by the time it was finished, it would be unrecognisable. She thought he was being unreasonable, and he thought she'd abused his trust, and tainted their past, not to mention their possible future. She couldn't see a way forward for them that didn't involve some kind of conflict.

If I was writing their ending, what would I write? She asked herself that question a lot, in the ensuing days. But in truth, she was no closer to finding an answer. Better just to press on with the historic element for now and worry about the modern one later. So, pushing all thoughts of Leo to one side, she did just that.

Looking back over the past few weeks, Rory was pleased that she'd made so much progress. After the initially difficult times when she'd first come to Roseford, she had settled into a kind of routine, and even though she didn't have the excitement of a developing relationship with Leo any more, she still felt content enough that she'd done what she'd intended, and made some headway on the project. So it was that, by the time she was due to go back to York in the last week of August, she had almost two-thirds of the first draft written. It felt time to go back: to get some distance between herself and Roseford. She didn't feel sad about leaving at the end of the summer holiday; she'd be back at the end of October, after all. She'd spoken to Alex about it the week before she was due to go back up north. Alex was surprised but pleased that what could have been a tense situation had been sorted out, and they were both now very much looking forward to their fresh start.

On the day she was due to check out, Rory packed up her things and gave the chalet a last clean. She'd taken care of it while she'd been living there, and it had, in the end, been a good space for her to occupy. It might not have had the period charm and quirkiness of Hyacinth Cottage, but the Roseford Villas chalet had felt like a decent alternative.

Casting her eye around the chalet one last time, Rory picked up her bag and locked the door. She'd drop the key off in reception, and then do the 'check out' option online for Airbnb. She wondered if Leo would be about, and wasn't sure if she wanted to see him or not. It might be easier if she just didn't. He'd made no effort to approach her since their row about the novel, which felt hurtful, but if that was the way he wanted it, then she wasn't going to argue.

Rory walked up the garden path towards Roseford Villas and, instead of heading through the dining room as she had so often during her stay, she mooched around to the front of the building. The main door was open, so she walked into the hall and put the chalet's keys down on the reception desk. Just as she was about to turn and leave, a trim-looking woman in her early sixties popped her head out from the back office behind reception.

'Oh, you're off now, are you?' she asked as she saw the keys. 'I hope you enjoyed your stay.'

Rory smiled. 'I did. The chalet is lovely, and I've really enjoyed being here.'

'I'm glad.' The woman smiled. 'I hope my nephew took good care of you. He's new to the business, but he assured me we were leaving the place in safe hands.'

Rory twigged: this must be Leo's Aunt Vi.

'He did, thank you.' Well, Rory thought, for most of the time here that had been true, at least. 'Did you have a good holiday?'

'Oh, heavenly, thanks.' Vi smiled. 'I think we might just have decided where we're going to spend the rest of our days! Of course, Roseford Villas is a joy to run, but it's never too late to dream, is it?'

'Quite,' Rory replied, smiling back. 'Is, is Leo around? I'd, er, like to say thanks and goodbye before I head home.'

'Oh, I'm sorry, love,' Vi replied. 'He left for

London earlier this morning. His new job starts soon, you see, and he wanted to get himself settled properly in his new digs before it did. Being here was only ever a stop-gap, you know.'

Rory fought disappointment. In spite of the way she and Leo had left things, she'd thought, and hoped, that he might have said goodbye. Clearly even that had been beyond him.

'Oh, well.' She forced another smile at Vi. 'Never mind. If you speak to him, could you say that I said goodbye, and thanks?'

'Of course,' Vi said. 'And if you'd like to leave us some positive feedback on the website, that would be fabulous. Every little helps, you know!'

'I will,' Rory replied. She suddenly felt the need to escape Roseford Villas, put a lot of distance between herself and everything that had happened over the summer. 'And thanks again.'

With Aunt Vi's cheery farewell echoing in her ears, Rory hurried to her car. She wondered what kind of review she could write that wouldn't sum up her stay at Roseford Villas. 'You will love the place, and lose your heart to it,' seemed rather apt.

44

For Rory, the start of the autumn term usually felt like a new beginning, even more so than the start of an actual calendar year. She looked forward to the scent of immaculate exercise books, and the sight of students beginning to write in them in their neatest handwriting. She redecorated her classroom with fresh posters and backing paper, ready for the colourful examples of students' work to be put up, and made a lot of new year's resolutions that by half-term had usually fallen by the wayside.

This time, however, she just couldn't get into the spirit of things. Knowing she was going to be leaving her classes, and the school, and the home she'd shared with Alex for the past few years, meant that she didn't feel quite as invested. She still tried her best, and made sure that, when the time came to hand things over to the person who was coming back to school, everything would be in place and easy to pick up, but in her mind, she was already back in Roseford, settling into the gatehouse and starting her combination of new jobs.

She'd been gradually sorting out and packing up her things, and although she was going to miss Alex, the prospect of living alone was something she was really excited about. The summer in Roseford had made her realise that she was quite happy with her own company, and although she'd spent a lot of time with Leo, she'd fallen equally in love with the solitude. Being mistress of her own domain felt very appealing, even if it would only be temporary, once more. Stella hadn't indicated how long she could be a tenant in the gatehouse, but she'd also said that she and Chris would be flexible, and as soon as Rory was more financially secure, she was sure they could work something out. After all, the retreat was on a very stable financial footing now, and Stella could afford to be generous.

The weeks flew by, until it was time to pack up her car and head back to Somerset. Alex had agreed to keep hold of some of Rory's bigger things until she was more settled, but still Rory's Vauxhall was rammed to the gills with her accumulated possessions. She drove carefully and reached the gatehouse at just gone two o'clock on the first Saturday of the October half-term. At least she'd have a week or so to unpack and catch her breath before her first classes at the Halstead House retreat started the week after that.

Halstead House looked beautiful in the late October sunlight. Somerset had been experiencing a run of unseasonably warm weather, resulting in a golden glow that gilded the turning leaves of the trees in the woodland directly behind the house. The gatehouse, a shortbread-coloured stone construction, stood sentry on the left-hand side of the driveway, and as Rory pulled into the parking bay off to the rear of the building, she felt a thrill of excitement. She couldn't quite believe that this was going to be her home. She knew it was only temporary, but she couldn't help imagining what it would be like to stay here longer. She could already anticipate the joy of making it her own.

'Welcome back!' Stella was hurrying down the driveway to meet her as she got out of the car. 'It's so lovely to see you again.'

The two women hugged and Stella handed Rory

the keys, explaining each one on the ring. 'But if you have any problems, just give me a call, or come and find me. I'm about most days, either teaching or planning the next retreat. Chris isn't around a lot at the moment as he's working on another renovation project just the other side of Yeovil, but if you get any urgent issues with the house, give me a shout and we'll get them sorted.'

'It looks wonderful,' Rory breathed as they made their way to the front door. 'I can't wait to get settled in.'

Stella smiled at her. 'I was really happy here when I first came to Roseford,' she said softly. 'I hope, even despite all of the stuff with Leo, that you'll be the same.'

Rory's heart sped up a little at the mention of Leo's name, but she tried not to let it show on her face. He wasn't in Roseford any more, so there was no need to worry about bumping into him. 'I think I will,' she said to Stella. 'I really do think I will.'

Stella said goodbye and they agreed to meet on Monday morning to go through the notes for the course Rory would be running, and to agree when she'd be tutoring Gabe for his English GCSEs. Everything felt as though it was falling into place, and although Rory still wondered what it would have been like if Leo was also living in Roseford, she found herself taken up with starting this next phase. There was too much else to think about without brooding about the loss of Leo McKendrick. She'd spent a lot of time in her teens doing just that, and she was damned if she was going to do it as an adult. Leo had his life, and she had hers, she told herself, not for the first time. But if that was really the case, why did her thoughts keep returning to him? And as she carefully unpacked her car and got ready to begin this new start, why did she keep thinking about how much lovelier it would have been if Leo had still been around?

45

Leo stared in irritated frustration at the laptop screen in front of him. It had been eight weeks since he'd started his new job at Palmer, Dennis and Wright but it felt like eight decades. Aunt Vi and Uncle Bryan had waved him off at Taunton station, but even as the train had pulled out, he'd been second-guessing his decision to continue upon his pre-plotted trajectory. The job offer would have been difficult to walk away from, but he could have done it: could have cited ill health as a reason not to take it. Goodness knows he had enough medical grounds to absolve him of any guilt and responsibility. But he hadn't had the nerve. He just hadn't been brave enough. And now here he was, back in the corporate world, a world he knew so well, trying to adapt again into what he knew best.

The trouble was, after the first few days (if he was honest, the first few hours), he realised he'd made a terrible mistake. No, he thought. Not just one: a lot of terrible mistakes. Taking the job in the first place, turning down Uncle Bryan and Aunt Vi's offer to sell him Roseford Villas when he'd loved running it so much, and, most heart-breaking of all, walking away from Rory for the second time in his life, having re-alised too late that he'd blamed her manuscript for the break-up because he was just too frightened to admit how he really felt about her. This time he was a grown adult and leaving her had been totally his de-cision. He couldn't blame his parents, or anyone else.

Christ, he should have fought harder. He should levelled with her while he had the chance. Instead, he'd let her leave Roseford thinking that he hated her for writing about them, what they'd once been to each other. The truth was, by the time he'd left for London, he didn't care what she chose to write: he only knew that he loved her, and he'd do anything to get her back.

Sighing, he shut the laptop and pushed himself up from his office chair. He didn't have any meetings booked for the rest of the day, which was just as well;

his concentration levels were shot. His back gave a warning twinge, which had been happening more and more since his move to London. He'd put it down to the terrible bed in the rented flat that the law firm had allocated for him while he was trying to find somewhere permanent to live, but he felt as though even sleeping on the best bed in the world would have brought him little comfort. He hadn't slept properly since he'd left Roseford, and deep down he knew he wasn't likely to for as long as he couldn't get Rory out of his head.

Absently, he checked his phone, hoping for a text, or a WhatsApp, or something from her. But unsurprisingly there was nothing. Why would there be? There was nothing left to say. He chucked his phone onto the desk in frustration. What a mess he'd made of his life. She'd avoided him for weeks when they'd both been in Roseford. It was unlikely she'd contact him now they were far away from each other. How they'd managed to keep that distance, he still wasn't sure: but he'd respected the boundary of the chalet, and had made sure he'd given her the space. He kept wondering, now, if he should have done.

'Everything OK?' Andrew Palmer, one of the partners in the law firm, poked his head around Leo's office door. 'I was heading out to lunch if you fancied a bite to eat.'

'Thanks, but I'll grab something later.' Leo forced a smile at his new boss. 'I've not got much of an appetite at the moment.'

Andrew, who was only a few years older than Leo, gave him a reassuring smile. 'Still nervous about being the new boy? I wouldn't worry. You'll be making partner before you know it, with your track record.'

Leo knew that Andrew had intended to reassure him, but his words had exactly the opposite effect. He felt his stomach clenching at the prospect of another long, stultifying stint behind a desk, looking at contracts until dusk fell every evening, taking paperwork home at the weekends and spending day after day locked into the corporate world. The vision made him want to scream. He knew so many people would have given their back teeth to have this opportunity, so why did he feel as if the prison doors were clanging shut behind him, with no chance of parole? He tried to give his best, most confident smile.

'Oh, you know,' he said quickly, 'it's just taking a little while to get back into the job after the time out over the summer. I guess I'm missing the fresh air!'

'Well, call me a dyed-in-the-wool city lad, but too

much greenery brings me out in hives!' Andrew laughed. 'I mean, the wife and I spent three weeks in the Loire Valley last summer and by the end of it I couldn't wait to clap eyes on Canary Wharf again. You can have too much of a good thing, you know.'

Leo wasn't so sure he would ever have had too much of the good things he'd had over the summer, whether it was fresh air, green grass or the opportunity to fall back in love with Rory, but he kept that to himself. 'I'm sure I'll get used to the City again,' he said, picking his phone up from the desk. 'Maybe I will come with you for a sandwich after all.'

'Oh, I think we can do better than that,' Andrew replied. 'I know this great place a couple of streets away that serves a brilliant plat du jour. We'll call it a "welcome back to your spiritual and professional home" treat, shall we? You've been in the wilderness long enough.' Andrew clapped a hand on Leo's shoulder as they left the office, and Leo tried to summon the will to get enthusiastic about the prospect of a smart lunch. Really, he thought, all he wanted was a sandwich, the scent of freshly cut grass and Rory.

46

Another week passed, and Leo's mind hadn't changed. The traffic going past the window of his flat kept him awake, the long hours encased in the modern glass building that was the pride of Palmer, Dennis and Wright felt stifling, and he missed the freedom of the far more casual work attire of shorts and polo shirts he'd donned during his summer as custodian of Roseford Villas. Contract law, the thing that had fired him up in the early years of his career, just wasn't doing it for him any more. He was bored rigid.

Every evening when he returned to the tiny studio flat in North Greenwich, he looked around the four walls and felt claustrophobic. He'd taken to going on long walks, just to get out of the place, but as the evenings grew chillier and the rain started to fall, he realised that, along with the encroaching darkness, this wasn't a solution he could sustain. At least walking for an hour or two guaranteed he was mostly exhausted by the time he fell into bed, but then he'd wake consistently with the early-morning traffic and toss and turn until it was time to get up again. The green space of Greenwich Park gave him the comforting illusion of the countryside, but it didn't feel enough.

Nine weeks had passed since he'd started his new job, and he knew it had to end. Sighing, on the short commute to work, he thought about WhatsApping Andrew Palmer, who'd become a mate in the weeks Leo had been working at the firm, to suggest a meeting. If he didn't make a move soon, he'd be going sick anyway, he feared. Something definitely had to give. If he didn't take charge now, Leo was worried that something was going to be him. But was that really a wise decision? Shaking his head slightly, he closed WhatsApp again. Perhaps he was being too hasty.

As he was checking his work emails, he couldn't resist opening his web browser and looking up Roseford Villas on Rightmove. His aunt and uncle had put the place on the market some weeks ago, but the last time he'd checked with them, no one had shown any interest. It was a tricky time to be in the hospitality trade, even with Roseford's British Heritage Fund connections. They'd been warned by the estate agent that the market was sluggish, but they desperately needed to sign off on the place in Spain, and so were going ahead with the sale. They'd dropped the price within a month, but when he'd phoned Aunt Vi to check in with her last week, there hadn't been any movement. With a jolt, however, as Leo perused the listings for Roseford, he realised that Roseford Villas had disappeared again. Changing his options slightly, he selected 'include properties under offer and SSTC' and searched again. And there it was. Roseford Villas had a flag on it saying, 'Under Offer'.

Leo's heart gave a huge thump. Even though he'd discussed buying the business with Aunt Vi and Uncle Bryan, it still felt strange to think that someone else had shown interest. But, perhaps, it also signalled an ending of that particular line of thought for him. He'd lain awake a lot over the past few weeks, wondering if he had made the right decision in turning them down. Now, it seemed, it was out of his hands. Someone else had rushed in where he'd feared to tread.

Leaning back in his seat on the train, Leo tried to

reconcile the very different emotions that kept fighting for dominance in his brain. On the one hand, it meant that the dream he'd had in the small hours of a London night of upping sticks back to Roseford and taking over the B&B was truly over, which had to be a good thing. It had been a daft plan, anyway. He couldn't be sure he'd have got the mortgage, and even with a decent deposit, it was still a huge financial risk. Putting down roots in Roseford might have seemed appealing when he was between jobs, but did he really want the commitment of running a B&B? What, apart from a couple of months' experience, could he possibly bring to the project in the long term, anyway?

On the other hand, he'd adored being in Roseford. As much as he'd loved his time with Rory, it was the village of Roseford that had stolen his heart as much as she had. Roseford felt like the promise of home, of a new beginning, of something deeper than pushing around the small print of a thousand businesses that weren't his. It felt *real*. Roseford Villas had been his, for a short time, and he'd savoured every minute of it.

In frustration, Leo shrugged himself off the seat as the train got to his stop. It was no use, anyway. Aunt Vi and Uncle Bryan deserved to start the next chapter of their lives, and a firm offer on the table was what was needed for them to do so. A pipe dream from their nephew was about as far from that certainty as it was possible to be. Slouching along the platform to the office, Leo tried to put it all out of his mind. The dream, such as it was, needed to end.

All the same, he might just call Aunt Vi after work. He was curious to see who'd made the offer on Roseford Villas, and what Vi's feelings were about it. Maybe it was the last, final flare of hope in his chest, but he needed to be sure Bryan and Vi were doing the right thing in accepting the offer. As he waved his security pass at the barriers that led to the lift that would take him to yet another day in the glass box inside the building that had become his prison, he tried to tell himself that he wouldn't start googling small business mortgages in his lunch hour. There was no point, unless a miracle happened.

47

Rory didn't take long to unpack her carful of possessions. In the end, she'd been very selective about what she'd chosen to keep. It had felt rather cleansing, sorting everything out that had constituted her life in the flat share with Alex, and as she knew the gatehouse had a fully equipped kitchen, she'd opted not to split the pots and pans. She had brought her Bodum cafetière with her, though, and as she sipped a cup of strong coffee and toyed with the arrangement of her books on one of the many floor-to-ceiling bookcases in the small lounge of the gate-house, Rory felt a sense of contentment washing over her.

As she'd driven through the centre of Roseford,

she'd looked at the shortbread-coloured stone buildings, and the pops of colour outside them from the
winter pansies in hanging baskets and flower tubs,
and felt the reassuring sensation of having made the
right decision. She'd explored the village a great deal
when she'd been living here in the summer, but she
was looking forward to taking more time, now that
she was a proper resident. She'd even bought herself
a new pair of walking boots, so she could get out and
about as the winter set in properly.

Arranging her workspace enhanced this feeling
of rightness. She'd written most of her novel in the
chalet but sitting at the antique mahogany desk in
the small study that would just about have served as
a second bedroom on the first floor of the gatehouse
really made her feel like a writer.

The first week flew by, and at the end of it, Rory
was itching to get started on the workshop she was
teaching at Halstead House. She'd taken the materials that Stella had used for a few of her courses and
adapted them to something she felt more confident
delivering. Stella was a renowned journalist and had
developed her reputation as a writer of excellent literary non-fiction over the years during her long col-
laboration with Roseford Hall, but her teaching style
and her areas of expertise were quite different to

Rory's. Using Stella's notes as a template, Rory had spent a blissful week overhauling them to suit her own methods, and, when she'd presented her ideas, Stella had been over the moon with the results. Stella had advertised the course at the beginning of September, and it had sold out swiftly: if Rory hadn't stepped in to run it, Stella would have done it herself, but she was pleased to hand over the reins to her friend. Stella's trust in her made Rory feel a whole lot more confident about what she was going to be teaching. And, to add icing to the proverbial cake, Stella had set up an extra-special guest to address the course attendees on their last day. Rory knew, if she was being totally honest with herself, that the 'special guest' was probably the reason most people had booked onto the course, but everyone had to start somewhere. She'd begun submitting her novel to literary agents, and although none had as yet asked to read the whole thing, she lived in hope.

As dawn broke on day one of 'Writing the perfect romance novel: a course by Rory Dean, romance writer', Rory awoke feeling a combination of excitement and terror. Had she and Stella over-egged the pudding by creating this course? Would no one turn up for the first couple of days, and suddenly there'd be a crowd for the special guest on the third? No. She couldn't think that way: it would all be fine. If she could teach *Macbeth* to a thirty-strong class of bored, bolshy teenagers on a rainy Thursday afternoon in a damp classroom in York, she could teach an excited group of adults with literary aspirations how to write a novel!

A couple of hours into the course, she was feeling a lot less sanguine. All of them, it appeared, had much more experience of the ups and downs of writing novels than she, with her one, mostly finished book, had. The six guests, all of whom showed remarkable knowledge of the traumas of the novel-submission process, had reacted with polite but sceptical responses to her first morning's seminar, titled 'Bringing your romance to life: drawing on real emotions to tell fictional stories'. Although they hadn't said as much, Rory couldn't have felt more out of her depth if someone had rubber stamped 'IMPOSTER' on her forehead.

'It's no good, Stella,' Rory moaned as she had a cup of coffee in Stella's private living room during the break session. 'They're looking at me as if I'm the biggest fraud this side of Robert Maxwell! I don't think I can pull this off for another two days.'

'Oh, don't be so daft!' Stella replied stoutly. 'What this group needs most of all is time to write. You've been teaching grumpy teenagers to do that for over a decade. I know you might be lacking the commercial success at the moment, but you've got expertise in spades. You have to believe in yourself, Rory, because no one else is going to unless you do first.'

Rory smiled. Stella always knew what to say to put things into perspective, and while she still felt odd about calling herself a fully-fledged writer, there was no arguing with her years of classroom experience. 'Thanks for the pep talk, boss!' she said, draining her coffee cup. 'I'd better get back to it.'

'You've got this, Rory Dean!' Stella replied. 'Get back out there and teach your heart out.'

With this encouragement ringing in her ears, Rory raised her head and plastered on a self-assured smile. Half of conquering the classroom was the illusion of confidence: something told her that teaching at Halstead House needed exactly the same thing.

48

It was no good. Leo couldn't stop thinking about that blasted offer on Roseford Villas. He had enough self-awareness to know that he'd always been the kind of person who wanted something the moment it became unobtainable, but this time he was sure it was more than that. He looked impatiently at the clock in the office, willing the hands to move faster so that he could give his aunt and uncle a call. He'd decided he couldn't wait until the evening to speak to them, and he was itching to get off the Microsoft Teams call he was tied up in and just phone them. He was finding it increasingly difficult to keep his mind on the job. Words onscreen blurred before his eyes, and more than once he'd drifted off during the meeting, only coming back to the virtual room when Andrew Palmer called his name, the second time with more than a trace of impatience.

'Er, sorry, Andy,' Leo replied quickly. 'I was just looking through Section 4a again – thought I'd double-check a possible discrepancy.'

'And is there one?' Andrew had asked, the irritation in his voice still evident.

'One what?'

'A discrepancy?'

Leo's face felt hot with the lie. 'Er, no. No, there isn't.'

Andrew Palmer's sigh was almost imperceptible over the Wi-Fi. 'Well then. Can we proceed?'

Leo nodded, and then, gratefully, put his microphone on 'Mute'. He tried to keep his expression carefully neutral, but the sight of his own, still slightly flushed face staring back at him from a corner of the screen filled him with even more embarrassment. He hated virtual meetings, and the fact that the company had taken to scheduling them more and more was yet another reason why he knew he was very definitely in the wrong place.

Somehow, he managed to get through the rest of it without disgracing himself further, and as he hung up the call, he leaned back in his chair. He still had a truckload of work to move off his desk before he could escape for a coffee, which he felt like he needed more than ever, but he wasn't getting far with it.

It came as no surprise when there was a knock at his door just before eleven o'clock. Not waiting to be called in, Andrew strode through, and sat on the other side of Leo's desk.

'Have you got a minute, Leo?'

Sitting up a little straighter, Leo heard Andrew's tone of voice and his heart began to race. 'I'm sorry about zoning out in the meeting earlier, Andy. I've not had much sleep for the past couple of days. It won't happen again.'

To Leo's surprise, Andrew's expression softened. 'Don't worry,' he said gently. 'I haven't come to carpet you. These things happen, and even the client knows the minutiae of contract law is enough to send anyone to sleep, sometimes.'

Leo's back relaxed a little. But he'd been in the corporate world long enough to know that a quiet voice didn't always mean a pleasant outcome. He waited for the bomb to drop.

'You've been working here just over two months now, Leo,' Andrew continued. 'That's pretty much your probationary period, isn't it?'

'Yeah,' Leo replied. 'End of this week, and I'm through.'

Andrew nodded. 'And in that time, you've not taken a day's leave. Given your, er, medical circumstances, I'd say that was very admirable.'

'I try to take care of myself,' Leo replied. 'There's no reason why I should suffer any ill effects so long as I'm aware of my own limitations.'

'And yet...' Andrew paused. 'Forgive me if I'm overstepping the bounds here, Leo, but you don't seem awfully happy.' He held up a hand as Leo started to interrupt. 'Don't get me wrong – your work, dozing off in this morning's meeting notwithstanding, has been superb. Everything we'd been led to expect from your references, in fact. But here at Palmer, Dennis and Wright, we have a keen eye for the welfare of our colleagues. You stay late, you get in early, you keep a tidy desk... but how is your life, Leo, away from here? What's there for you to make you stay? How are you, *really*?'

Leo's eyes burned at the unexpected intimacy of the question. He and Andrew had become friendly over the time he'd been working at the company, and although Leo couldn't forget that Andrew was his boss, he'd felt a connection between them that had made his transition back into the legal world easier.

Drinks had been shared, and camaraderie had developed. Leo knew Andrew was a details man, and here he was, sitting opposite him, letting him know in the gentlest terms that he saw behind Leo's carefully created façade.

Realising he hadn't answered the question, Leo swallowed hard and met Andrew's gaze with the most determined stare he could. 'I'm fine,' he said firmly. 'It took a while to find my feet here, but I'm glad to be part of the team.' Friend or not, Leo didn't feel as though he could confide how he was feeling to Andrew right now.

Andrew looked back at him, and Leo knew the other man was assessing what he saw. The man was no fool: you didn't get to be a partner in a firm such as this by ignoring the little things, but Leo was determined not to give anything away.

'You know, if there are things on your mind, you can always come to me. If I can't help, I'm sure I can point you in the direction of someone who can.'

Leo swallowed harder this time. He couldn't handle kindness at the moment, not with the thoughts that were turning around and around in his head. He was still so uncertain of things, and didn't really know how to articulate his fears to Andrew.

'I appreciate that, Andrew,' he said quietly. 'I guess it's just taking me a while to feel settled again.'

Andrew smiled at him, and then stood back up. 'We're here if you need us,' he said. 'You're not alone, Leo. You're part of a team, and we look after each other here.'

'Thank you,' Leo said. He watched as Andrew paused for a fraction, and then turned and left his office, closing the door behind him. Leo let his head drop into his hands. He felt the overwhelm encroaching behind his skull again, making his heart race and his skin prickly with adrenaline. Forcing himself to breathe a little more deeply, but not so heavily he would hyperventilate, he tried to push back the feelings of panic that he could feel rising in his chest. Over two months without a break were beginning to take their toll, and he still couldn't get the idea of Roseford Villas being sold out of his head. Focusing on the steady in-out-in-out of his breathing for another sixty seconds or so, he raised his head and, with trembling fingers, drafted an email.

49

Rory tidied up after a successful morning's work, on day three of the romance writing course, and let out a long breath. Two-and-a-bit days of teaching, reading, giving feedback and working on some of her own plot lines had been happily exhausting. This afternoon the group would play host to a very special visitor, in the form of Shona Simmonds, and Rory was very much looking forward to seeing her again. It was Shona who'd advised her to go for it with her own writing, and she was excited to show her how far she'd come since their last encounter.

Shona had stayed the night at Margaret Treloar's home on the outskirts of Roseford Hall, and Simon was bringing her over to Halstead House after lunch for an intimate session with the budding romantic novelists. Rory was buzzing with excitement as much as her small group of students was.

After a light lunch, the group reassembled in the writing space on the first floor of Halstead House, to await their illustrious guest. Rory felt the butterflies returning as she heard Shona's dulcet tones emanating from the hallway. She'd been gradually conquering her nerves during the past forty-eight hours, but now, faced with Shona Simmonds, who was undoubtedly the real deal, she felt like an imposter again.

She needn't have worried. Shona's all-encompassing smile took in the assembled writers sitting around the conference table, one end of which had been laid with tea and cake, and everyone felt the warmth. And when Shona's eyes alighted on Rory, they gave a twinkle of recognition.

'Our special guest this afternoon needs absolutely no introduction...' Rory began, and then proceeded to do just that. Shona settled herself in a comfy chair, just as she had at her gig at RoseFest, and the afternoon was away. With a brief stop for cake, by the end of the afternoon, all of the course attendees felt it had been worth every penny.

As Shona began to wind up, Stella appeared at

the doorway, ready to escort her back to Simon, who had been chatting with Stella and Chris.

'Rory, can you just come down to the kitchen with me?' Stella asked as Rory began to clear away the tea things.

'Sure,' Rory replied. She walked across the room with Shona, who was slightly slower on her feet. When Rory reached Stella, her friend whispered, 'Thought you might like a breather, and a couple of minutes alone with Shona, since you've been flat out all day.'

'Thanks.' Rory smiled. She waited for Shona to catch up, and then, as they walked down the stairs, asked Shona how she'd found the afternoon.

'Oh, very lovely,' Shona replied. 'Of course, I can't do too many of these things, these days, but it's always nice when I do.'

Rory was well aware that Shona's health wasn't great, which made this visit all the more special. She made a mental note to repeat her thanks to Simon for facilitating it.

'I remember when we first met at Roseford Hall,' Shona said. 'When you were so full of hope and enthusiasm, and you asked me for my best piece of advice for a new writer. You were with that good-looking fella. How did that all work out?'

Rory sighed. 'The book? Pretty well. I finished it, and it's on submission now. The fella... not so well.'

'Oh?' Shona raised an eyebrow. 'Shame. He seemed to think very highly of you.'

'In the end, it wasn't enough,' Rory replied. 'Too much water under the bridge for it to work. We weren't who we thought we were.'

'Such wonderful clichés,' Shona observed dryly. 'I do hope your book is better written than that.' She paused on the stairs and regarded Rory with a shrewd eye. 'I've usually got an instinct for these things. Comes of years of writing about love. You learn to recognise it in the real world, too.'

'If only that were the case,' Rory said. 'I feel absolutely deaf, dumb and blind in that regard. Leo... Leo tends to do that to me. He makes me suspend my better judgement.'

'Or maybe he encourages you to take risks with your heart,' Shona said.

'Now who's speaking in clichés,' Rory replied, smiling briefly.

'I'm allowed to. I'm old and far past caring. You, on the other hand...'

'He made his choice to move on. Who am I to argue?' Rory's voice trembled a little. 'It would never have worked between us.'

'Are you quite sure about that?' Shona asked.

Rory shook her head. 'He made it pretty clear the last time we spoke that he didn't want anything else from me. And after it fizzled out, and I left...'

'So, you parted without saying a proper goodbye? Good heavens, the plot thickens!' Shona's eyes twinkled, but there was a shrewdness behind that gaze that Rory didn't misinterpret.

'It's not really a plot if it's real life, Shona,' Rory replied, trying to inject a little lightness into her tone. 'Just bad timing.'

'I do wonder, though...' Shona paused tantalisingly.

'What do you wonder?'

'Whether, if you're brave enough to put your novel out to the wider world, would it be so big a risk to, I don't know what the common mode of communication would be, to "Snap" Leo, and find out how he is? He was a very good-looking chap, and he seemed rather decent.'

Rory burst out laughing. 'I'm not fifteen years old. Snapchat isn't really my thing. But I take your point.'

Shona smiled. 'I'm sorry – I've obviously been listening to my grandchildren too much. But it just seems a shame to throw away something so promising, at least from what I saw.'

Privately, Rory wondered if Stella had been talking about her and Leo's rather precipitously ended romance, but she decided to let it go.

'I'm not brave enough to take the risk that he still feels the same way as he did when we ended things. I can't put myself through that,' Rory said gently. 'I lost him once. I can't lose him again.'

'And who says that you'd lose him?' Shona asked. 'Isn't love worth taking the risk?'

Rory shook her head. 'Not this time. I just don't have it in me.'

For a long moment, Shona scrutinised Rory. 'Are you quite sure about that?'

As they reached the kitchen, and Simon rose from his seat by the table to acknowledge their presence, Rory knew, despite her protestations to the contrary, that she wasn't sure at all.

'What's love about, if it's not about taking risks?' Shona observed. 'I've had five husbands, and, my God, if that hasn't been a mantra for my life, then I don't know what has.'

'But I'm not you, Shona,' Rory chuckled, despite herself. 'I could never be that brave.'

'It's not bravery, you silly goose!' Shona replied. 'It's blazing, impetuous stupidity. But without it, I'd never have experienced all that I have. Isn't that worth being a little bit stupid for?'

'My life is not a romantic novel,' Rory replied. 'And I'm not sure I'm cut out for loving Leo. There's too much history there.'

'Well, I can't tell you what to do, of course,' Shona said, 'but wouldn't it be a shame if you got to my age and the biggest question you were still asking your-self is *what if*?'

Rory shook her head. 'You're incorrigible, Shona.'

'But you also know I'm right.'

Rory didn't grace that with a response. She needed time to think, and come to terms with what life without Leo really meant. She'd been offered a taste of something over the summer, and it was some-thing she'd been devastated to walk away from. The question was, was she willing to fight to get it back? And who was she fighting, anyway? She had the feeling it was no one other than herself.

Much later that evening, Rory kept thinking back to that conversation. Was Shona right, or was she just laying herself open to another heartbreak? For all she knew, Leo was settled in London, and might even have met someone else by now; some glamorous lawyer with whom he could have great fun moving on. Well, she thought, there was only one way to find out. Taking a deep breath, she picked up her phone.

50

After yet another sleepless night, Leo rolled over in
bed and huffed out his frustration. He was still no
closer to finding an answer to the creeping sense of
unease that had dogged him since he'd found out
that an offer had gone in on Roseford Villas. Infuriat-
ingly, his aunt and uncle hadn't picked up the phone
when he'd tried to call them yesterday, and even
when he'd tried several more times, in increasing
desperation through the day, they still hadn't. At least,
he thought, he was going to have some breathing
space next week. He'd emailed Andrew after their
impromptu meeting in his office and requested a few
days' leave, a bit of R&R, he'd said. Andrew, off the

back of their earlier conversation, had approved. One more day at the office, and then he'd have five days to rest and sort out his head.

The trouble was, now he'd committed to it, he had absolutely no idea what to do with the time he'd booked. Staring at the four walls of his small flat was out: he'd be better off at work. He'd hoped to get back to Roseford, having made contact with his aunt and uncle to ensure they'd have room for an impromptu guest, but it seemed a bit risky just to turn up, not having asked them if it was all right first. He didn't want to put them on the spot.

It occurred to Leo that, apart from work, there was nothing, absolutely nothing, in his life any more. His family were still in Melbourne, he didn't have a wife and he didn't have a permanent base. His friends were all busy with families of their own, and there was no one in this country apart from Aunt Vi and Uncle Bryan, of course.

Which left him with a lot of time next week and nothing much to do with it. Perhaps he'd just cancel the leave and go back to work. *God, how tragic*, he thought. Andrew wouldn't be happy, either, having made it clear that he thought Leo needed a break. Glancing at the clock, and with a sigh, he decided to get up. It was a bit early, but at least he'd miss the usual crush on the train if he left soon.

On the way to work, and with a seat on the train for once, he couldn't resist checking Rightmove again. To his surprise, the 'Under Offer' banner had disappeared from the listing again. Refreshing his screen, he blinked and tried to suppress the surge of excitement he felt as he swiped the photos of Rose-ford Villas. Nope. It was back on the market, and as he looked at the price, he saw that it had dropped by twenty grand.

No. It was impossible. He tried to shut down that train of thought. He had a job here, and he had only a few months of experience of running a B&B. It was a stupid, irrational pipe dream. And yet... something about Roseford was calling to him, through the pages of that listing on Rightmove. Ever since he'd left, he'd felt as though he'd walked away from the bright colours of the summer into some grey, urban future, and, even though he'd put everything he could into his new job, deep down he knew it couldn't last. The idea of Roseford had taken hold of him, and the se-ductive possibility of 'What if...' was running inces-santly through his mind. He tried messaging Aunt Vi again, but, frustratingly, the was no signal on the Underground. It would have to wait until he was back street side. He shifted impatiently in his seat and couldn't wait to get off the train when it finally arrived at his stop.

By lunchtime, Leo was pacing his office in agitation. He couldn't concentrate on anything he wanted to. His head was too full of possibilities. He tried Aunt Vi's mobile again, but it went directly to voicemail. The landline had rung and rung when he'd phoned it this morning, too. In one last-ditch attempt, he punched out the landline again, and waited.

And waited.

And waited.

And then, just as he was about to end the call, and chuck his mobile out of the window, there was a click, and Aunt Vi's familiar voice, Yorkshire with its trace of a West Country burr, came down the line.

'Good morning, Roseford Villas. Violet Crosbie speaking, how can I help?'

'Aunt Vi?' Leo was surprised at the tremble in his voice, now that he'd finally got through.

'Leo, my lovely, is that you? How wonderful to hear from you. How are you? How's the new job?'

Leo opened his mouth to speak, but suddenly

found that he couldn't. Drawing a deep breath, fighting back the flood of relief that he'd finally got through to her, but not quite knowing what to tell her about what was on his mind, he blurted out, 'Can I come and stay with you? There's something I really need to talk to you about...'

51

Leo raced back to Somerset on the first train he could get. All he knew was that he had to get to Roseford as soon as he could. Something was calling him back there, and he couldn't fight it. As the miles clocked up, he felt his sense of relief growing in proportion to his sense of nervousness. The further away he got from London, the lighter he felt. He knew it wasn't rational: Aunt Vi had told him, practically ordered him not to rush, that his room would be ready for him whenever he arrived that evening, but Leo knew he just had to go. He'd returned to his flat and chucked as much in a bag as he'd the wherewithal to pack, grabbed a bottle of water and then locked up, wanting to put as much distance between himself and his current circumstances as he could. With his favourite Spotify playlist blaring from his AirPods, he eagerly looked out of the train's window at the changing scenery, hungry for the first glimpse of the West Country.

The traffic gods were with the taxi driver who brought him from Taunton to Roseford, and thankfully there were no major hold-ups on route. Leo felt more than a frisson of excitement that he'd soon be back in Roseford. As he drew closer to the village, he wondered how he could ever have decided to leave.

'Leo!' Aunt Vi met him at the front door with a smile and the warmest of hugs. 'It's so lovely to see you again, and so soon.' Leo hugged her back, realising that this was the first physical contact he'd had, apart from handshakes, since he'd left Roseford. God, he'd missed being part of a family. As she led him through the door and into the hallway, he felt his throat constricting. He was home, he knew it.

'Uncle Bryan's in the living room,' Vi said as they walked through. 'Go and sit down and I'll bring you a cuppa. Have you had tea?'

'No, but I'm not hungry,' Leo said. 'I, er, just wanted to get here.'

Vi leaned forward and gave his arm a squeeze. 'You silly boy,' she chided, 'rushing all this way. Did you think we'd have sold the place in the time it took you to get from London?' She smiled again. 'I'll get you a sarnie to go with that cuppa.'

As Vi bustled off to the kitchen, Leo took a deep breath and pushed open the door to his aunt and uncle's private living room. He assumed they didn't have any guests in tonight, as the main part of the ground floor, with the residents' lounge, the dining room and the small bar area, was in darkness.

'Hello, Uncle Bryan,' Leo said, clocking his uncle ensconced on the sofa, a mug in one hand and the TV remote in the other. Bryan pressed 'Pause', and the coverage of the England Men's Football Euro qualifiers stopped, with Harry Kane in mid-pass.

'All right, Leo,' Bryan said, putting the remote down. 'Good journey?'

'Not bad.' Leo took a seat in the armchair that was at a right angle to the sofa. 'Trains ran on time. That helped.'

'Your aunt getting you a cup of tea?'

'Yeah.'

Leo tried to relax, but it was difficult after such a long journey. Bryan was a lovely man, but he wasn't a talker, so instead of battling with small talk, which they both weren't keen on, Leo asked about the football game.

'They're not doing badly tonight,' Bryan replied. 'A lot of them are graduates from Will Sutherland's Under-19 team. Good lads. He taught them well when he was in charge.'

For a little while they discussed the merits of the current team, Bryan chipping in with some details about the former coach, Will Sutherland, whom Leo hadn't met when he was in Roseford back in the summer, but whom he knew lived in Parson's Grange, the modern mansion on the other side of the village. Will, ex-football manager turned pundit, was, by all accounts, a decent chap, and frequented the local pub often.

'You might meet him—' Uncle Bryan raised a speculative eyebrow '—if you decide that taking this place on is what you actually want to do.'

Leo's heart sped up a little. 'I hope so,' he replied, which seemed to suffice as an answer to both remarks. He knew that Uncle Bryan was the more pragmatic of the two, and that, having turned them down once, Leo would need to give a lot of assurances that taking on Roseford Villas was something he was really serious about, and that he could actually afford to do. Bryan would take no prisoners in that regard, no matter how much he wanted to sell to Leo.

Aunt Vi came back into the room with a mug of

tea and a ham sandwich. She passed both to Leo, and Bryan resumed the football game while Leo tucked in. As soon as Leo had taken his last mouthful, however, the pause button was pressed once more.

'So, lad, you've decided you actually do want to take this place off our hands, then? Better late than never.'

Leo gave his uncle a nervous smile. 'I know it took me a while to get my head straight about it, but the longer I've been in London, the more I've realised how much I love it here. When I saw you had a buyer, I can't describe the panic I felt.' He shook his head. 'I thought that was that, it was all over, so when the listing appeared again on Rightmove... well, it made me get my act together.'

'The buyer wasn't serious,' Bryan said, frowning. 'Put an offer in, but then pulled out when another place came up on the coast. The estate agents were a bit previous when they changed the listing.' Bryan shifted in his seat. 'Although they did advise us to drop the price, since our seller in Spain wants things tied up by Christmas. Are you in a position to make that happen, son?'

Leo swallowed. Glancing at Aunt Vi, who had taken a back seat during this conversation, he looked back at Bryan. 'I should be. I've been transferred my share of the sale of the house in Melbourne, which is a fair deposit, but I need to talk to a mortgage broker on Monday to see if they think I'm good for the finance. It might not be easy, since I've only been back in the country for a few months, but hopefully I'll be able to convince them I'm a decent proposition.'

'Well, we'll vouch for you, love,' Violet said. 'I don't know if that'll make a difference, but...'

Bryan shot her a warning glance. 'I think we'll wait and see what the broker says. But listen, lad, we can't afford to hang around. The house in Spain won't be there forever, and while family is family, business is most definitely business.'

Leo nodded, not surprised by the sombre tone of Bryan's voice. While Vi had always been the public face of Roseford Villas, Bryan had been there in the background, managing the finances, keeping the logistics moving. Leo knew that his uncle wouldn't hesitate to pull the plug if Leo wasn't in a position to make good on his offer to buy, but this knowledge merely acted as a motivator rather than a deterrent.

'I completely understand, Uncle Bryan,' Leo said. 'And I won't mess you about. If I can't make it work financially, then I won't keep you waiting. But if there's any way I can buy Roseford Villas, then, believe me, I will try.' He glanced around the living room before continuing, to gather his thoughts. 'I didn't realise how much I loved being here until I left. And now, all I want to do is come back, and make it mine.'

Vi smiled at him, and he felt grateful as she reached out and squeezed his hand. 'And we'd like nothing more than to sell it to you, my love. Keeping it in the family would be the best thing we could do.'

'But if it's not possible...' Bryan's voice trailed off, but his message was loud and clear. It just renewed Leo's determination.

'I'll phone the mortgage broker first thing on Monday morning,' Leo assured him. 'And then, at least, we'll know, one way or the other.'

With that, suddenly feeling exhausted from the journey, Leo excused himself to his room. He had a lot to think about, and a lot to organise if Roseford Villas was truly going to be his. But for the moment, all he wanted to do was sleep. As he drifted off that night, his thoughts returned to Rory. He often caught himself wondering about her just before he fell asleep, remembering her smile, and what it had been like to feel her in his arms. Would it be too weird if he sent her a 'how are you?' text in the morning, he wondered.

52

Rory woke up the morning after the writing retreat had ended with feelings that alternated between relief and despondency. She'd really enjoyed teaching the course, and in the end, she felt as though she'd won over the attendees. Her chat with Shona had also given her a lot to think about, both in terms of her novel and the way things had ended with Leo. She wondered, as she tended to do when she woke up in the morning, what he was doing right now. It was a chilly autumn Saturday in November, a far cry from the warm summer days they'd spent together, and Rory wondered whether the rain was falling in London, or if the sun was peeking through the cloud cover as it was here. She couldn't help it: things still felt unfinished between them. Pondering her phone, she shook her head. What good would it do to text him? He was miles away, and even if he did reply, it might not be with words she wanted to hear.

She swung herself out of bed and into the shower. She had a tutoring session with Gabe this afternoon, her first one, and she needed to mug up on the key themes and ideas from the poetry anthology he was studying for his exams. Gabe, who was a sweet boy but probably wouldn't be best pleased at having to devote an hour of his Saturday to the study of poetry when he could be out with his mates, deserved the best she could give him.

As she looked over the anthology Gabe had been assigned for his exams, she munched absently on a piece of toast and sipped her coffee. She was starting a part-time supply teaching post at the local secondary school at the end of next week, so she'd better get her head around that too. The piecemeal nature of her employment and income was worrying her slightly, but Stella had already booked her for a repeat of the romance writing course to run in January, which would boost things a little, even if most of that would be in lieu of rent. She was in a better position than she could have been, she kept reminding herself.

The morning rushed by, and as she spent a productive hour with Gabe, who was initially reluctant, but at least seemed to appreciate the time by the end, Rory was keen to get out and stretch her legs. She'd take a walk to the village and blow away the cobwebs. She didn't have much in for dinner, either, so she thought she might as well grab something from Southgate's Stores. Wrapping up against the chill in the air with her warm winter coat and a bright blue scarf, she set out from the gatehouse, enjoying the autumn sunshine, which never failed to lift her spirits.

Grabbing a couple of things, she tucked them into the wicker shopping basket she'd brought with her, that Stella had laughingly given her as a 'moving in' present (complete with wine, bread, a pint of milk and a jar of coffee – all of the writerly essentials, Stella had grinned), and then mooched back out onto the main street. She had no desire to head straight back to the gatehouse, as she knew she'd spend time fretting about starting at a new school instead of doing anything productive, so she headed down the road a bit to Roseford Reloved, the second-hand and vintage clothes shop. She wasn't really in the market for anything, but she liked to browse.

A few minutes later, she was dithering about

whether or not she had the funds for a cosy grey cashmere-wool blend jumper, which would be perfect for the chilly nights in the cottage, and chatting to the shop's owner, Polly Parrott.

'It's certainly getting colder,' Polly said. 'The ceiling fell in almost a year ago, but thankfully the place is weatherproof now. It used to be arctic in here in the winter!'

'I bet.' Rory smiled. She'd heard the story about Polly's ceiling from Stella, who'd also told her that Polly's partner Will Sutherland had been right under the ceiling when it had collapsed. Thankfully, this hadn't put too much of a dampener on their relationship as they were now living together in Will's house on the outskirts of the village.

'So, shall I put that jumper aside for you?' Polly asked. 'The colour suits you.'

Rory blushed. 'I'm on a bit of a budget,' she confessed. 'I'm not sure I can stretch to it.' Regretfully she put it back on the rail. 'But if it's still here next week...'

Polly smiled. 'Here,' she said, and handed Rory a voucher for 20 per cent off. 'If this helps to change your mind, it's my festive season discount. I shouldn't really do it until the start of December, but I always try to help my customers bag a bargain!'

Rory took the leaflet. 'That's really kind,' she said. But she shook her head. 'I'll leave it for now, I think.' Giving the jumper a last, longing glance, she said goodbye to Polly and wandered back out onto the street. She really should get back to the gatehouse now. The fire needed lighting, if the place wasn't going to get too cold. The bright sun overhead was deceptive: the evening would soon be drawing in, and, much as she was enjoying living alone, she couldn't help missing Alex's company. The two of them had looked out for each other in the time they'd shared the flat, and Rory missed the reassurance of having someone under the same roof, even though she'd enjoyed living alone since she'd moved back to Roseford. She knew Stella was only a stone's throw away, but it wasn't the same. Besides, Stella was busy with her own life and family: Rory didn't want to impose.

For a fleeting few steps of her walk home, she wondered what it would have been like had she still got the anticipation and excitement of seeing Leo again. Even if they'd had to do the long-distance thing for a while, the tantalising possibility of being with him, however infrequently, would have given them both something to keep them warm on chilly winter nights. Once more, her fingers swiped her phone to where his number was still stored. Maybe she should just send him a text, see what his response was, rather than spend any more time agonising. The worst that could happen was that he'd just ignore it. He wasn't the type to send back a bitchy, horrible response, she was sure of that. She'd bottled out last night, after composing several versions of the same thing. Maybe, emboldened after a glass of the wine she still had from Stella's welcome basket, she'd just do it.

53

Monday morning came, and Leo was up before it got light. He didn't want to keep his aunt and uncle waiting, and he needed to speak to the mortgage broker immediately they opened. With trembling hands, he dialled the number he'd located of a local firm, and within moments he was speaking to an adviser.

It soon became clear that, as Leo hadn't been back in the country for very long, his application for a business mortgage was going to be rather more complex than he'd hoped. Of course, he'd realised that there might be issues, but as the adviser went through the finer points with him, his heart sank. No matter that he had a hefty chunk of deposit, there just wasn't sufficient proof of income and residence to back up his application. As he ended the call, he let out a long sigh.

'Shit...' he muttered. What was he going to tell Aunt Vi and Uncle Bryan now? The dream, it seemed, was over. They'd wanted to keep the business in the family, but he couldn't make it happen, for himself or for them. Time just wasn't on his side. They couldn't wait another six months, and he couldn't not.

Disillusioned, he shambled downstairs to the kitchen, where Aunt Vi was preparing breakfast and sorting out the jobs that needed doing before the new guests arrived later that day. They had four rooms occupied tonight, and although Leo knew they were shipshape, he also knew that Vi would insist on doing one last hoover and check to make sure they were perfect. It was her attention to detail that made this place such a winner. But not for much longer. Soon it would be in someone else's hands.

'Everything all right, love?' Vi asked as he entered the kitchen.

Leo forced a smile. 'Not really. I've just spoken to the mortgage broker. They, er, they don't think a loan of the size I'd need is a goer, I'm afraid.' He plonked himself down at the large table in the centre of the kitchen. 'I'm so sorry, Aunt Vi. I should have looked into this before I came hooning down here, raising your hopes.'

'Oh, love.' Vi was obviously trying to hide her disappointment, which made Leo feel even worse. 'So that's it, then?'

Leo nodded. 'I'm afraid so.'

The ensuing silence lasted until it was broken by Uncle Bryan coming in from the garden, where he'd been vacuuming up the fallen leaves that had littered the lawn overnight. Leo glanced up, and just before Bryan closed the door, he caught sight of the chalet, looking cold and unloved at the bottom of the sweep of neatly cut grass that shouldn't need another mow until the spring, now. His heart ached to think that, by the time the warmer weather came, someone else would be in charge here.

'No luck then, I presume?' Bryan asked gruffly. 'Well, it was a bit of a pie in the sky idea, really, wasn't it, lad? You didn't really think it through. No sense in dwelling on it.'

The reproach in his uncle's voice cut through Leo's despondent mood, and he felt a flare of irritation. 'It wasn't pie in the sky!' he said shortly. 'I really wanted to take Roseford Villas on.' He found he was glaring at his uncle, and rapidly tried to adjust his expression. 'I know you probably think I was just playing about this summer, but I used to love it here as a kid, and I really wanted to be the one who could continue its future. I'm gutted, genuinely, that it doesn't seem possible, at least according to the mortgage broker it's not, anyway.'

Leo, ignoring a warning twinge from his back, thrust himself up from the wooden kitchen chair. 'I'm sorry I've disappointed you, Uncle Bryan.'

Bryan's gaze stilled Leo's impulse to walk out of the kitchen. 'Are you finished, lad?'

Leo nodded, suddenly ashamed of himself for his childish outburst. More than once, in his childhood, he'd run foul of being called a spoiled brat: now he was just proving that point.

'Sit back down, then.' It wasn't a request. Leo sat.

There was a pause while Bryan poured himself, Vi and Leo a cup of tea, and then brought Leo's mug over to the table.

'So, what did they say?' Bryan asked.

'I haven't got enough recent employment history in the UK,' Leo replied. 'They won't lend me the amount I'd need for the mortgage, despite the healthy deposit I've got. In this current market: it's too much of a risk for them.'

Bryan sat back in his chair. 'So that's it, then.' His gaze was on Leo. 'Shame, really, you seemed to take to living here. Would have liked it to have gone to you, rather than someone we don't know.' He took a long sip of his tea. 'Oh, well, Vi, best ring the estate agent, see if there are any nibbles at their end.'

Leo's irritation, that his uncle could be so offhand with him, fought his careful attempts to stay calm. 'I more than took to it, Uncle Bryan,' he said. 'I bloody loved being here. And I made a good job of running it. I have so many ideas, good ideas, that could take Roseford Villas forward into a long future. I'm sorry that I can't be the one to do that.'

'You'll find something else,' Bryan replied. 'You've still got a job to go back to, haven't you?'

The thought of going back to his glass box in the City of London filled Leo with a panic he couldn't swallow down. 'Yes,' he said weakly. 'I suppose there's that.'

'Well, I can't sit here gassing all day,' Bryan said. 'I've got work to do.' He rose from the table, tea in hand. Just as Bryan was about to walk out of the door, Leo clocked the pleading gaze from his aunt to his uncle.

'Don't you think you've put him through enough, Bryan? Why don't you just tell him?'

Leo's pulse quickened. 'Tell me what?'

Bryan sighed. 'All right.' He took another swallow

of his tea. 'I wanted to be sure that you really were serious about taking a business like this on. It's not a thing you can play at, Leo. It's hard work, and long work, and you're busy when everyone else is on holiday. It's long nights, and early mornings, and very physical at times. But you proved yourself over the summer, and I'd like to think, given the chance, you'd be able to prove yourself in the long term.'

'That's not going to happen now, though, is it?' Leo muttered. He felt like the teenager he once was, when he'd come to spend some time here.

'Not necessarily.' Bryan glanced again at his wife, and even in his current state of agitation, Leo noticed the look.

'What do you mean?' he asked.

'Look, lad, if it were up to your Aunt Vi, she'd hand you the keys right now and have done with it, and to hell with the costs. She's always had a soft spot for you, and, if I'm being honest, so have I.'

'Thank you.' Leo smiled slightly. He'd always liked and respected Uncle Bryan, but this bluff Yorkshireman had perpetually played his emotions close to his chest. He'd never once made an admission like that. It felt like a victory, despite the disappointment of the morning.

'But we have to be realistic here,' Bryan continued, silencing Leo again with a look. 'We're going to Spain, and we will sell Roseford Villas as soon as possible to fund that, come hell or high water. That plan is non-negotiable.'

'I get that,' Leo replied, baffled as to why Bryan was insisting on repeating the details they'd been through.

'Good.' Bryan paused again. 'But we can help you to take over this place, if you're sure that's what you really, really want.'

Leo's 'What?' shot out of his mouth before he could stop it. 'I'm sorry, Uncle Bryan, but what do you mean?'

Bryan gave a brief smile. 'I've been doing some research of my own, and your aunt and I can act as guarantors for you. If you're absolutely sure that you are the right fit for a business like this?'

Leo's mouth dropped open in astonishment. 'You'd do that for me?' he asked, eventually.

'We would. And when you're solvent enough, and the mortgage company are agreeable, we can quietly remove ourselves from the agreement, and Roseford Villas will be entirely yours. What do you reckon?'

Leo's knees gave a dangerous wobble, and he had to grab the table for support. 'Are you quite, quite sure, Uncle Bryan? I mean, it's a hell of a commitment.'

'Why?' Bryan shot back. 'Are you planning on running out on us? I thought you were up for the challenge.'

'Oh, I am, I am,' Leo said quickly, trying to get his head around just what was happening in this kitchen. 'It's just... why would you take the risk?'

Bryan looked at him for a long moment. 'We never had kids of our own,' he said, rather gruffly. 'And you and your sister and brother staying here in the summer when you were younger... well, it kind of gave us the experience of having our own children, without the years of financial agony.' He smiled briefly. 'We want to do this for you, Leo, and if you can keep a room for us on the odd occasion when we might like to come and visit, then that's all to the good.'

'I will,' Leo said, swallowing hard to fight down the lump in his own throat. 'Shall I, er, shall I ring the broker back? See what they say?'

'I would, lad,' Bryan replied. 'Before I change my mind. Not that your Aunt Vi would let me now, of course!'

'A Yorkshireman's word is his bond,' Aunt Vi

teased, smiling. 'Now, get that phone call made, Leo, let's make it official.'

Leo looked at his aunt and uncle, and before Uncle Bryan could scuttle back out of the kitchen door, Leo had reached out and given him a hug. 'Thank you,' he said quietly. 'Thank you both, so much.'

'Ah, get on with you, you soppy sod!' Bryan replied, but he clapped Leo on the back before he released him. 'Now, get on that phone.'

54

After that, things seemed to move very quickly. Over the next week or so, Leo's application for a business mortgage went in, with Bryan and Vi as guarantors. The purchase of their property in Spain, along with the sale of Roseford Villas, left them in a good financial position to act, and Leo was amazed, even with his background in contract law, how quickly the wheels started turning. He went back to London at the end of the week feeling so much lighter, and as if he'd finally started the rest of his life.

Of course, there was still the job in London to think about. He wasn't quite sure when the purchase of Roseford Villas would be complete, and in the meantime he had to keep working, as well as working out when to hand in his notice. Fortunately, the fact that he now had a credible exit from London life boosted his mood, and he put in a lot of hours, ensuring that whoever took over from him would find the job in good order.

By mid-December, the exchange and completion dates had been set. Aunt Vi and Uncle Bryan were staying on until early spring, as their place in Spain wouldn't be ready before then, and Leo was glad: they'd be able to show him how to do the things he hadn't experienced during the quieter months, such as the accounts, and liaising with suppliers, ready for him to take over when they left.

'Well, we're sorry to see you go,' Andrew Palmer said, as he took Leo out for a goodbye drink. 'But I could see your heart was never really in it. Better to get out now than be signed off with stress further down the line.'

Leo raised his pint in acknowledgement of Andrew's words. 'I appreciate your magnanimity, under the circumstances,' he replied. 'I mean, I never intended to walk out after three months. I really thought I'd be here for the long haul when I took the job, you know.'

Andrew looked at him sympathetically. 'I know you did. You've never seemed the type to take a job just because you had to. Maybe I'll break my die-hard vow to avoid the countryside and bring the wife down to this B&B of yours once you're fully up and running. I'd like to see the place that's managed to drag you away from a decent career!'

'I'd like to see you there.' Leo grinned. 'And I'll make sure there's a bottle or two of good wine in, so you don't feel you're too far into the social badlands!'

They shook hands at the end of the night, and as Leo wended his way back to the flat, he felt an enormous sense of relief. It hadn't worked here in London, and although he'd known that from the start, he still couldn't quite believe how things *had* sorted themselves out. Corinne had once teased him that he'd led a charmed life, and, until the past couple of years, he'd been inclined to agree. Perhaps things were finally getting back on track for him.

The next morning, he packed up his flat for the last time and handed the keys back to the letting agent. He'd rented a car to drive back to Somerset, and this time he intended to stay there.

The traffic was heavy that night, and by the time Leo had made it to the motorway junction nearest Roseford, he felt knackered. At least this was the last time he'd be making this trip for a long while. As he pulled into the drive of Roseford Villas, and grabbed his overnight bag out of the boot, he decided the rest of his stuff could wait until morning. He'd been living out of holdalls and suitcases for so long that one more night wouldn't matter.

Aunt Vi greeted him on the doorstep, but, eschewing any dinner, he decided just to head up to bed. The relief at being here, as he pushed the door open to the room he'd called his own since the first time he'd moved here, was almost tangible in the air.

As Leo was wearily unpacking his bag, there was a quiet knock at the door.

'Come in,' he called.

Aunt Vi pushed the door open and smiled. 'I'm so glad you're here, Leo. I worried about you doing that long drive. I can now let your mum know you made it OK, since I doubt you've texted her.'

'She'll be at work, Aunt Vi,' Leo replied. 'But don't worry, I'll call her later. Well, when I can get my head around what time it is in Melbourne, anyway.'

'You know, it all seems to be falling into place rather well, given the confusion at the start,' Vi said. She placed the cup of Horlicks she was carrying down on a coaster on the chest of drawers by the bedroom door. 'I know you said you weren't hungry, but I thought some of this would do you good. Bryan calls it Yorkshire Laudanum, you know. Knock you out in a minute if you drink it before bed.'

Leo smiled. 'What would I do without you, Aunt Vi?'

Vi smiled back. 'Get on with you. Now, is there anything else you need before I leave you alone?'

'I'll be right, thanks,' Leo replied. 'I'm just glad to be back.'

'We're glad you're here, too,' Vi said. 'I know your Uncle Bryan won't say it in so many words, but he's right proud you're taking over.'

'You've done more than I ever could have hoped,' Leo said softly. 'You've put your trust in me to run this place, and I can never repay you for that.'

'You might think differently once we've handed over the reins entirely,' Vi replied dryly. 'Looking after it for the summer was one thing, but forever? I hope you know what you're taking on.'

'I'll have great teachers,' Leo said, smiling at his aunt.

'Oh,' Vi said, furrowing her brow, 'that reminds me. I know what I meant to tell you. I was talking to Stella Simpson, who runs the retreat at the other end of the village, the other day. She said that girl who rented the chalet last summer has moved back to the village. You know, the one you got, er, friendly with? What was her name?'

'Rory,' Leo said. He sat down onto the bed with a jarring thump to the base of his spine. 'Aunt Vi, are you sure?'

'Well, Stella told me, so I'd be surprised if she was mistaken. She's doing some supply teaching in one of the local schools, apparently.'

'Did Stella say where she was living?' Leo asked, cursing the excited tremble in his voice.

'No,' Vi replied. 'I didn't really think to ask. Sorry, love. I was a bit too concerned with getting something for Uncle Bryan's headache. We'd run out of painkillers, you see, and the cost of paracetamol at that village shop! Honestly, you could buy ten packets in the supermarket for less...'

Leo didn't take in the finer details of the cost of over-the-counter analgesics at this point, he was too shaken up by the revelation that Rory was back in Roseford. She was really, really back! And now, as of tonight, so was he. Once Aunt Vi had wished him goodnight and closed the bedroom door, Leo pulled out his phone. With trembling hands, he swiped to her number. For the next half an hour, he dithered over the precise wording of the text he wanted to send. What should he say? Eventually, after typing and deleting what felt like dozens of variants of the same thing, he settled on a message:

Hi Rory. Hope you're well. I hear you're back in Roseford. Can we talk?

Taking a deep breath, he pressed 'Send'.

He then spent the next half an hour waiting to see if she'd read it. By the time he'd got ready for bed, downed the rapidly cooling Horlicks and switched off the light, he was still waiting.

55

After a stomach-churningly sweaty, nervous and sleepless night, caused by the combination of the realisation that he was now taking over Roseford Villas *for real*, and that Rory still hadn't read his text, Leo pulled himself out of bed to a cold, crisp, frosty day. After showering and chucking on some clothes, he went down to the kitchen to find Aunt Vi already in full flow with the breakfast service for the residents.

'Shouldn't I be doing that?' Leo asked as she glanced up from the eggs she was scrambling and smiled briefly at him before returning her attention to the pan.

'Thought you'd like a day or so to settle in before we start the actual training,' Aunt Vi replied, with a brief smile over her shoulder. 'Although I'm sure you're already familiar with a lot of it from when you were here before.'

'Just like riding a bike,' Leo said, smiling back despite his tiredness. Aunt Vi always did know how to make him feel better. He grabbed the toast rack, already loaded up with white and brown. 'Which table is this for?'

'The couple by the window,' Vi replied. 'Thanks, love.'

Leo helped out with the breakfast service and tried valiantly to put what he'd learned about Rory's whereabouts to the back of his mind. If she wanted to, she'd reply to him. If she didn't... well, he'd have to accept that.

After clearing down the breakfast things, he asked if Vi minded if he went out to the village.

'Of course not, love. As I said, you can be a guest for a couple of days, before we really get going with the handover. But while you're down there, would you be able to collect a frock that Polly's altering for me? She owns the dress shop in the village, Roseford Reloved. I know I shouldn't be shopping for Spain yet, but I saw something on her sale rail that I just had to have, and when it was a bit big, she said she'd take it in. I tried it on the other day, but didn't have my purse with me, so left it there. I'll settle up with you when I get back.'

'No worries,' Leo replied. 'I won't be long.'

Chucking on a soft, navy-blue jumper, and his dark brown leather jacket that was hanging up on the coat rack in the hall, Leo felt the bite of the cold as he left the house. He sped up a little, and soon the pace warmed him. He'd have to get used to the colder winters now he was a permanent resident, not just of the UK but of Roseford. The West Country tended to get cold and damp rather than snowy, but all the same, it wouldn't do any harm to invest in some warmer clothing.

As he approached the main street, he could see that the tourists, though fewer than in the summer, were already starting to arrive. Ducking into Roseford Reloved, he spotted a couple of people already perusing the rails.

'Hi there,' the proprietor greeted him as he approached the counter. This must be Polly, Leo thought. 'How can I help?'

'I've come to pick up a dress for my aunt, Violet Crosbie,' Leo replied. 'She said you'd been altering it for her?'

'Ah, yes, just give me a sec.' Polly vanished into the back room, and Leo cast his eyes around the shop. It was mostly womenswear, but he noticed a small rack of gents' clothing off to the left. Nothing that caught his eye, particularly, but Polly had a nice selection. The shop had a pleasant atmosphere, and Polly's eye for colour meant that the rails and stands of clothing on their wooden hangers looked attractive, and invited customers to browse. She'd put together a window display of autumnal colours, deep reds, oranges and dark browns, that was orchestrated to catch the eye of passing tourists and locals alike.

'Here we go.' Polly was back promptly. 'That'll be thirty-five pounds, please.'

Leo handed over his card and the transaction was completed promptly.

'So, a little bird tells me that you're going to be taking over Roseford Villas soon,' Polly said as she carefully wrapped the dress in tissue paper. 'Congratulations.'

'Thank you,' Leo replied. He remembered how fast news travelled in the village, and he wasn't surprised that the word was already out about the change of ownership. 'I really enjoyed looking after it in the summer, so it seemed like the next logical step.'

'Well, I wish you the best of luck,' Polly replied, handing over the dress, which she'd slipped into a pretty paper bag with the store's logo on it. 'Having a small business is a heck of a learning curve, but it's worth every minute.'

'I'll remember to come to you if I have any questions.' Leo smiled.

'Do,' Polly replied. 'As I'm sure you noticed when you were here over the summer, we're a real network here, and I'm know that anyone on the high street would be happy to help, if you need us. Lizzie Warner, who owns the florist a couple of doors down, is a good friend, and she was in marketing before she took on the flower shop, so she's always got great ideas about how to drum up trade. We've got an informal local business group going, if you fancy coming along to that when you get settled.'

Leo smiled again. He was touched by her concern and offer of help, and although his aunt and uncle would be on hand for a few more months, he was glad to know that there would be people around who he could call upon for advice if he needed it.

'Thanks,' he said, as he put his card back in his wallet. 'That all sounds really helpful, and it would be great to make some connections and do some networking, see how we can all help each other out.' But as he spoke, he noticed that Polly's gaze had shifted as the bell above the shop's front door tinkled, signalling the entrance of another customer.

'Ah, so you're back again, then?' Polly replied, a teasing note in her voice directed at the new customer. 'Can't keep away from the place now?'

Leo automatically glanced around to see the new arrival, and as he did so, he nearly dropped the carrier bag he was holding. There, standing in the doorway, a look of shock and surprise written all over her face, was Rory.

56

Rory, who found herself at a loose end, had decided to have a wander into the village for a coffee and a browse at Roseford Reloved. Since she'd spotted the cashmere jumper a few weeks back, she'd been popping back in, buying smaller things, but not quite taking the plunge on the item that had attracted her in the first place. Perhaps today was the day. She had been feeling the cold lately, and the thought of a cosy new jumper to keep out the chill was a comforting one. And a little luxury wasn't a bad thing, especially when she'd been working so hard at her new school, on her novel and on preparing revisions to the romance course she was going to be leading once again in the new year. As she pushed open the door and heard the cheery ping of the bell above her head, she looked to the counter, and her smile of greeting for Polly froze on her face. What the heck was Leo doing here?

'Um, yeah,' she managed, as she realised she hadn't answered Polly's cheerful question about her return. 'I, er, thought I'd finally come back for the jumper, the grey one I spotted a few weeks back, if you've still got it?'

Polly gave her a quizzical look, before she nodded. 'I popped it out in the stock room,' she said as she dug it out. 'I thought you'd be back for it eventually. I have an instinct for these things. I won't be a tick...' She went to go out the back again.

'Actually, never mind,' Rory replied hastily. 'I'll, er, I'll come back some other time. I'm, er, in a bit of a rush...' She couldn't do this right now. She wasn't prepared for seeing Leo again. She might have composed all manner of texts to him that she still hadn't sent, but now she felt completely robbed of the ability to form a coherent sentence. Leo looked utterly gorgeous in that navy jumper and jacket, with his hair, a little longer than it had been back in the summer, tumbling carelessly over his brow. She'd forgotten just how attractive he was, and how he had the ability to turn her knees to the consistency of custard whenever he looked at her that way.

'All right,' Polly replied, a look of concern crossing her face. 'Well, I can keep it back for you for a little bit longer. Just let me know, yeah?'

'I will.' Rory turned quickly, and before she could hesitate, she rushed back out of the shop.

How could he be here? How could she not have known? She was so torn. On the one hand, she wanted to linger, to talk to him, but on the other, the memory of that last, mortifying encounter between them still felt as though it had happened yesterday.

'Rory!' His voice calling out to her stayed her rapid progress down the main street. 'Rory, wait, please.'

It was the 'please' that finally made her stop. He sounded so desperate, and she never could resist him when he pleaded. With a deep breath, she turned around.

'Leo? What are you doing here?' As she finally slowed down, her knees started to tremble. 'I thought you were in London.' She gripped hold of the wicker shopping basket she'd brought out with her for dear life, watching the leaves of the potted basil plant she'd bought from Southgate's Stores shaking as much as she was. She felt mortified that he could still have this effect on her.

'I was,' Leo said, giving her a nervous, tentative smile. 'Look, can we talk? I texted you yesterday, when Aunt Vi told me she'd heard you were back, but...'

Rory shook her head. 'I left my phone up at Roseford Hall last night, in the archive room. I was so bushed after spending all day up there that I didn't realise until I looked for it this morning. I was going to pop and get it when I'd finished my shopping.' She was sure she didn't imagine the look of relief that flitted over Leo's face as she said that.

'Do you mind if I walk up with you?' Leo asked. 'I'd, er, I'd really like to talk to you about how things ended between us.'

Rory tried a nonchalant shrug, but merely succeeded in upending the pot of basil in her shopping basket. 'Bugger,' she muttered, as she righted it. Smiling briefly at Leo, she conceded. 'Sure.'

They fell into step with each other along Roseford's historic main street, dodging the tourists that were ambling at their own pace.

'So, are you, er, in Roseford for long?' Rory asked. It felt like an echo of the conversation they'd had back in the summer when they'd first been reunited.

Leo paused before he replied, and Rory noticed that he suddenly looked even more nervous. 'I hope so,' he said softly. 'It depends.'

'On what?'

Leo smiled, and Rory had to clench her hands even harder on the handle of the basket.

'Well, mainly on how successful Roseford Villas is, now that I'm taking it over,' he said. 'I mean, I've only really had a summer's experience at running the place, so it's going to be a pretty steep learning curve, but I'm hopeful, with a little hard work, that I'll do Uncle Bryan and Auntie Vi proud.'

'You... you're taking it over?' Rory paused in her steps and hopped out of the road just in time as a car came around the corner. 'Since when?'

'Eventually!' Leo gave a quick laugh. 'I mean, Aunt Vi and Uncle Bryan are still in situ for the time being, as their place in Spain won't be ready for them until early spring, and they're showing me the ropes, but it's all been signed over to me, and contracts were exchanged last week. Completion is in a couple of days' time, but since we're all family, it's been quite straightforward.'

'But what about your career? Won't you miss law?'

Leo shook his head. 'Not really. I kind of knew the London job was just a stop-gap. What I didn't realise was that I needed to spend some time doing it to know that it wasn't what I wanted any more. Being here in Roseford was what I wanted.'

Rory was shocked at how happy and at peace Leo seemed with these life-changing decisions, until she realised she'd pretty much done the same thing over the past few months. Fair enough, she hadn't taken the plunge and bought a B&B, but the move to the West Country and the change in her working situation were radical enough.

'Well, I'm glad you found what you wanted,' Rory said, trying to keep things light. 'It's good to see you again.'

Leo looked momentarily confused, but she could see he was working his way up to something else.

'But what made you come back here?' Leo's brow was furrowed. 'I thought you were just here for the summer.' He smiled at her again. 'Did you, er, finish the novel you were writing?'

Rory paused, unsure about what to say. On the one hand, she felt relieved that Leo had clearly made the decision to return to Roseford because he wanted to, not because he'd heard she'd moved back here. That would have been more pressure and expectation than she could take. On the other, the fact that he knew she was living in Roseford, too, at least for the foreseeable future, meant a whole new set of pressures anyway. She had no desire to make him feel as though he had to take an interest in her again. After all, he'd made it pretty clear when they'd had their last exchange exactly how he felt about her novel, and, by extension, her, for having written it.

'Oh, it's going fine,' Rory said, deciding to tackle the last of the questions first. 'I've been busy at school, but I've been sending it out to agents and publishers.'

'That's great!' Leo smiled broadly. 'I'm so pleased you managed to get it finished. I always knew you had it in you.'

Rory couldn't help the raised eyebrow of surprise at the positivity in his tone. After all, their last conversation about her novel had hardly been a positive one. 'I'm glad you're so pleased,' she said guardedly. Her reticence wasn't lost on him, she could see from the expression on his face.

'Well,' Leo said, and for the first time since they'd bumped into each other, he looked shy. 'If you, er, wanted to catch up over a drink sometime while you're here, just text me, when you get your phone back. I'd love to see you again.'

Rory nodded, although she wasn't entirely sure if she could face another stilted exchange with Leo, even if alcohol was involved. 'Thanks, I will,' she said briefly. 'I'll, er, see you around.'

'See you,' Leo said. Rory hurried off before he could try to prolong the conversation. Her thoughts were whirling wildly in her head, and she needed some time to process them. Leo was back in Roseford! And it seemed as though he'd got over his concerns about what she was writing, although he hadn't said it in so many words. What did that mean for them both, now they were going to be in the same place at the same time, and in Leo's case, permanently? He had seemed delighted to bump into her, and she had noticed how genuinely pleased he was to see her. She collected her phone from Roseford Hall and then hurried back to the gatehouse, where she sorted out the basil plant. Later that afternoon, as she absently poured hot water on some leaves from her herb box on the windowsill, it wasn't until she sniffed the pungent aroma she realised she'd picked those same leaves and put them in her cup instead of mint. She was obviously more jolted than she'd thought.

57

Well, that went great! Leo's inner monologue was relentless as he trudged back up the street. He'd been so flummoxed by seeing Rory in Roseford Reloved that he'd totally lost the plot about what was most important to say to her. He'd imagined, when he'd sent her the text the previous night, that their first exchange would have been a lot easier than that, but the fact she'd seemed as shell-shocked as he'd been when they'd clapped eyes on each other hadn't helped. She'd clearly not wanted to prolong the conversation. It was like a morning after exchange, without having had the fun of the night before!

Pausing for a moment outside Roseford Reloved, Leo wondered what he could do to mend things. The first thing he'd intended to do had been to apologise: the second, to find out where she was living. He'd done neither of those things, and while the reason she hadn't responded to his text had seemed legitimate, there was no guarantee she would actually choose to answer it when she had got her phone back. What if she just didn't bother? Then it came to him. Pushing open the door of the shop, he walked back through.

'Hi again!' Polly exclaimed as she caught sight of him. 'Is there something else I can help you with?'

Leo smiled at her. 'Yes,' he said, pulling out his wallet again. 'I think there is...'

Some time later, he was walking briskly back up the hill towards Roseford Villas and although he wasn't quite sure, yet, what his plan was, at least the first step seemed a decent one. Now he just had to get his act together and carry out the second one.

'Thanks, love,' Aunt Vi said when he handed over the dress in its bag to her. 'What do I owe you?'

'Oh, don't worry,' Leo said fondly. 'It's the least I can do, as your freeloading guest for a couple more days. But there is something you can help me with, if that's OK?'

'Of course,' Vi said. 'What can I do?'

'Do you have anyone in the chalet at the

moment?'

'No,' Vi replied. 'We don't book it out in the off season as it takes a lot to heat. It's mothballed until April. Why?'

Leo paused, then took a deep breath. 'I, er, do you think I could use it for an evening? I've got something in mind, and the chalet is kind of central to it.'

'Of course,' Vi replied. 'Technically, it's yours now, anyway. But wouldn't you be warmer in the dining room?'

Leo blushed. 'I want to recreate something, for someone I really need to make an effort for.'

'This wouldn't be the young lady who was in the chalet over the summer, would it?' Vi's eyes twinkled.

'Possibly.' Leo grinned. 'The only problem is, I'm not sure she'll want to hear from me, on the evidence of the conversation we've just had, but I'm going to give it my best shot!'

'I'm sure she'll hear you out, love,' Vi replied. 'And it sounds like you've nothing to lose, anyway.'

'I hope you're right, Aunt Vi,' Leo replied. He put the other package to one side and began the agonising process of composing a text.

Text sent, to keep his mind off the possibility of a negative reply, Leo began sorting out the chalet. If Rory refused his invitation, he'd lock himself in there and have a good cry, so the effort wouldn't go to waste. It took a while to get it feeling warm in there, but after a couple of hours, it had reached a half-decent temperature, and he'd given the place a bit of a freshen up, airing it out and ensuring everything was in place. He'd borrowed some candles and decent wine glasses from the dining room of Roseford Villas, as well as a tablecloth. As far as dinner was concerned, he was cheating a bit and planned to use the kitchen in the main house, but having filled Aunt Vi in on his plan, she'd offered to whip him up something lovely. A bottle of wine on the table, and his preparations were complete.

A ping from his phone made his heart start to race. Grabbing it from where he'd been charging it up on the counter of the chalet, it raced faster as he saw the name. The signal from the Wi-Fi wasn't great this far down the garden, and his data wasn't marvellous either, so the message hadn't previewed on his Home Screen. Swiping quickly, the few seconds before the message appeared felt agonising.

Yes, that's fine. I'm at home this afternoon. Pop over when you're ready.

It was a start, Leo thought. Now, all he had to do

was get through the next few hours without losing his mind with nerves.

Sometime later, everything was ready. With a shaking hand, he sealed the envelope and then picked up the package he'd be taking with him. Locking the door of the chalet, but keeping the heating on, he headed back down the hill towards his destination.

'I really appreciate this, Stella,' Leo said as he was invited through into the impressive hallway of Halstead House. 'I'm sorry to put you in the middle but hopefully things will work out.'

Stella regarded him carefully. 'I hope so, Leo. But she was very hurt about the way things ended between you. Try not to mess it up this time.'

'I'm going to do my best,' Leo laughed nervously. 'And, as I said, I'm really thankful that you've agreed to do this.' He handed over the tissue paper-wrapped package and the envelope. It had taken him a long time to think about the precise wording of what was inside, but he really hoped what he'd written would at least persuade Rory to come to the chalet.

'Are you sure it wouldn't just be easier to go over and deliver these yourself?' Stella asked. 'I mean, you've literally just walked past her front door...'

'Have I?' Leo's heart leapt.

'Yep.' Stella smiled at him. 'She's my tenant in the gatehouse.'

Leo's hands started to shake. With a supreme effort of will, he shook his head, gathering his thoughts as he did so. 'I want to give her the option to do what she feels is right for her. If I just rock up there on the doorstep, it's crossing a boundary. I was angry with her for what I perceived to be a similar thing back in the summer – I don't want to put her in the same position.'

'For what it's worth,' Stella said, 'I've read the current draft of Rory's novel, and I don't think you need to worry. She's a great writer, and she's done justice to what you used to have.'

'I know, and I feel like such an idiot for reacting in the way I did.' Leo felt the urge to level with Stella about the thinking he'd been doing over the past few months but decided that it was Rory who needed to know first, if he got that opportunity.

'Good luck,' Stella said as Leo turned to leave. 'I hope it works out for you, Leo.'

'Thank you,' Leo replied. 'Me too.'

As he headed back to Roseford Villas, he tried to breathe away the nerves. His fate was in Rory's hands now. All he could do was hope she'd give him a chance to explain.

58

The chime of the doorbell cut into Rory's thoughts, and she jumped. She'd been so deeply into extending the first draft of her next novel that she'd lost track of everything else around her. She leapt up from her desk chair and hurried to the door.

When she got there, she smiled to see it was Stella on the other side.

'Hey,' she said. 'Have you come to serve me notice?' It had become a standing joke between the friends, and Stella grinned.

'Not today, but if you could learn to type a little more quietly, the neighbours would appreciate it!'

'Got time for a cuppa?' Rory asked.

Stella shook her head. 'Not right now, but I've got a delivery for you.'

'Amazon drive straight past my house on the way to yours!' Rory said, mildly exasperated. 'I really need to add a note to the delivery instructions, to stop them disturbing you with my stuff.'

'It's not from Amazon.' Stella's voice was gentle. 'It's from someone a little closer to home.'

Rory started, and as Stella passed her the package, with a letter on top, she nearly dropped it. 'What is this, Stella?'

Stella smiled. 'It's from someone who misses you very much. He asked me to give it to you, so you weren't put on the spot.'

'Oh...' Rory turned and wandered through the small hallway of the gatehouse and to the kitchen.

'Will you be all right?' Stella asked, still on the doorstep.

'Yeah,' Rory replied, glancing back at Stella. Realising she'd been too flummoxed by the package, she smiled at her friend. 'Sorry. Thank you for bringing this over. I'll be fine.'

'OK,' Stella said, a note of concern in her voice. 'If you're sure...'

'I'm sure. Can we talk later?'

'Of course.' Stella closed the front door behind

her, leaving Rory staring at the envelope and the parcel in her hands.

In all the time since she and Leo had called a halt to their relationship, she'd gone round and round in circles, thinking about what might have happened between them, if things had ended differently. In the end, she'd come to the decision that she'd wasted enough hours on the 'what ifs' when they'd been teenagers: there wasn't any point in going back there again. With time and space, she'd realised that as far as she was concerned, with herself and Leo it would be all, or it would be nothing.

Pondering all this, she meandered over to the kitchen table and sat down. She picked up the envelope and turned it over and over in her hands. It seemed a delightful call-back to their past, when Airmail missives on blue, almost transparent paper had flown their way across the world to her. She knew the medium of communication would have been a deliberate nod to that time in their lives, and that Leo would have considered it carefully. The lawyer in him would have weighed up every pro and con, before settling on a plan. Even the request for Stella to be the messenger had been a carefully considered move, meant to give Rory the space to make an informed decision.

She couldn't stare at the envelope all afternoon. Sliding a finger under the flap, she pulled out a perfectly folded sheet of writing paper. As she flipped it open, she noticed his penmanship hadn't changed, either. She'd loved his handwriting, full of loops and flourishes and hinting at the loving man underneath that slightly aloof demeanour. The words he'd written were no less passionate than his handwriting.

Dearest Rory,

I am so sorry, for everything. Through my own hubris and self-absorption, and a desire to keep the broken pieces of myself protected at all costs, I made a huge mistake. I've been trying to think of the words to communicate all of this, but every time I'm face to face with you I just can't summon them up. That's why you're holding this in your hands, now.

When we were so far apart, all those years ago, it was always easier to write down my feelings, put them in an envelope and send them winging their way to you. I never was any good at speaking about my emotions: the written word came to me so much more easily. The liberation of being able to send those feelings to you, to be read in your own time, was something for which I was always grateful, in some odd way, no matter how much I wished we were together in the same place.

So, I've decided to write everything down, in the vain hope that you'll understand why I reacted the way I did when I read your first draft. You see, reading what you'd been inspired to write, the things about our relationship that I'd buried for so long, was a revelation I just wasn't ready to face, and the thought of those words getting out there, for others to read, made me remember those feelings that I hadn't considered for over twenty years. I felt jealous of the pages you'd written on, and jealous of the readers who were, eventually, going to read what felt so personal, and while you reassured me that ideas and manuscripts change, it still felt like a violation.

However, time and distance, as we both well know, can change a lot of things. I now realise how wrong I was not to trust you. You weren't just a witness to our relationship: you were one half of it, and at times, I'd say, the better half at that. I always trusted you, and I trust you now. And so, I want to say I'm sorry, and I hope you can forgive me for throwing away what could have been a wonderful second opportunity for us. It wasn't just reading your novel. It was the knowledge that we'd still have a lot to face, and the acknowledgement that I still had a lot of decisions to make for myself, before I could let anyone else into my life, even you.

Time and distance have worked though. And if serendipity, Fate or whatever has seen fit to put us both in the same place at the same time, I desperately want to know if you'd consider giving us, the grown-up, sensible us, a second (third?) chance. If you feel as though we can at least talk about this, then I'd love it if you would join me at the chalet at seven o'clock tonight. But whatever you decide, the gift is yours. You always said I had an eye for the details: well, this is one detail I wanted to act upon. If I can't be the one to keep you warm on these cold winter's nights, then perhaps it will.

Yours, in hope,
Leo

Rory's hands were trembling so badly as she finished reading the letter that she tore the tissue paper that wrapped the gift it came with. As she did, a heat rushed through her. There, inside the paper, was the grey cashmere jumper she'd been resisting for weeks. And if that wasn't a sign, then she wasn't sure if she'd ever get a better one.

59

Checking her reflection for the last time in the mirror in the hallway, at five to seven Rory left the gatehouse. She decided to drive up to Roseford Villas. If things went sideways with Leo, she could make a quick exit, and if they didn't... well, she could always walk home later. Taking a deep breath, she closed the front door and drove the short distance to the B&B.

Rory could see the lights from the chalet as she parked in the driveway and hurried down the garden path. The chalet itself had been hung with miniature fairy lights, and there were already candles lit on the table she'd spent the summer eating and writing on. Warm memories of a holiday well spent washed over her. Although things hadn't ended well with Leo that

time around, she instantly realised that, by inviting
her back here for the evening, he was trying to recap-
ture some of the early, heady emotions they'd both
felt. And, much as she was trying to resist and keep
her rational head on, she realised it was working.

She reached the door of the chalet, and there,
looking deceptively relaxed on the bench seat, was
Leo. As he caught sight of her on the other side of the
door, he jumped to his feet and, betraying the nerves
that were obviously hovering beneath that apparently calm exterior, nearly overturned the candle-be-
decked table. Rory couldn't help but smile as he
righted them hastily before hurrying to open the
door.

'Hi,' she said, still smiling. 'I hope you're not
going to burn the place down before we even get the
chance to have dinner!'

Leo smiled back, and Rory's heart began to melt.
Stop it, she thought. It couldn't be that easy. Could it?

'I've copped out on cooking dinner, I'm afraid,'
Leo admitted. 'Aunt Vi rustled us up a Beef
Wellington that I'm keeping warm in the oven here!'

'Well, at least we won't starve!' Rory laughed nervously. She stepped over the threshold and noticed
Leo looking at her appreciatively. 'So, you got the
jumper, then?' he asked.

Rory glanced down at herself. 'I did. Thank you. It's beautiful.'

'You're beautiful in it,' Leo replied, then blushed.

Rory shook her head. 'You're such a dork.'

Leo gestured to the wine, and when Rory nodded, he poured her a large glass.

'And you, er, got the letter, too?' he asked her as he passed her a glass.

'Yup.' Rory was tempted to elaborate, but some part of her wanted to make Leo do a little more of the running. Just because she knew what she wanted, didn't mean he got to have this all his own way.

'So... what did you think?'

'Well, you know I've always loved your handwriting!' Rory quipped. 'And I think it kind of evens the score a bit. You read something of mine, and now I've read something of yours.'

Leo's look of exasperation made her relent. She put her glass down on the table, and, reaching out, took one of his hands in hers. 'I appreciate the apology, Leo, and, if I'm being honest, I know why you were so upset. I think that, if I'd been through what you had over the past couple of years, I'd be feeling pretty broken, too, and even if my rough draft was just a catalyst, it's probably a good thing that we've both had time to think things over. We're not kids any more, and we can't just walk away as if nothing ever happened, especially now we're both living in the same place.'

Leo squeezed her hand. 'So, what are you saying, Rory?'

Rory paused, gathering her own thoughts for a blessed few seconds longer. She'd been through all of this in her own mind, over and over again that afternoon, but now she was having to say it, she wanted to get it right. Leo had expressed himself on paper, but she, the writer, was now going to have to speak the contents of her own mind out loud. She knew when she did, things were going to change forever.

'What I'm saying, Leo, is that, as a sensible grown-up, with all of my heart, and everything I know to be true, yes, I would very much like to give things between us another chance. I know it won't be easy, and I know we have a lot to work through, but something about this, this time, feels right. For once in my life, I'm going to take a risk. I'd like us to try again, and I really, really want to be with you.' She looked up at him, and to her relief, his eyes were tender with love.

'Can I tell you something, Aurora Henderson?'

Rory shook her head. 'No, but you can tell Rory Dean if you like.'

Leo smiled. 'OK. Rory Dean, I'm in love with you.

Completely, outrageously and ridiculously in love with you. I've missed you so much, not just since the summer, but since always. I love you so much that I don't even care if that first draft I read is the one you go on to publish. I just know that I don't ever want to be without you, ever again. I know I messed up, but if this life in Roseford is my new start, then I want to think that maybe it might be a new start with you in it.'

Rory waited for him to finish, and then carefully leaned up on tiptoe to kiss him. It was a kiss that made them both forget the slight chill that still hung in the air in the chalet.

'So, where do we go from here?' Leo asked, as they broke apart again.

'Well, I'm starving,' Rory replied. 'Is that Beef Wellington still warm?'

'Absolutely.' Leo smiled. 'Coming right up.'

'Wonderful.'

They sat at the small table, in the chalet where everything had started, and as the stars came out in the clear skies over the village of Roseford, both re-alised that they had, at long last, come home.

EPILOGUE

ONE YEAR LATER

'Have I told you how proud I am of you?' Leo asked as he brought in the large cardboard box to the living room of the gatehouse.

'Yes.' Rory grinned up at him as he set it down in front of her. 'Many times, and in many ways. But I love that you are.' She felt a real sense of exhilaration as she reached for the kitchen knife she'd rushed out to get, and cut the tape on top of the box. Before she lifted the flaps, though, she paused.

'What is it?' Leo asked, looking speculatively at her.

Rory laughed nervously. 'I can't quite believe I'm doing this! After all this time, and all those rejections, in a minute I'm going to be holding my very own novel in my hands.'

'Well, get on with it then!' Leo said, grinning at her. 'Some of us have got guests to get back to...'

'All right, all right,' Rory replied. Taking a deep breath, she opened the box, and there, lying securely under a layer of packing paper, was a pile of the most gorgeous-looking books she'd ever seen. This was her story, contained within the pages, and it was finally going out into the world. Carefully, as if she was holding a newborn baby, she lifted one out of the box and turned it over in her hands.

'Can I see?' Leo moved behind her, and wrapped his arms around her, so that his hands covered hers. 'They really have done a great job, haven't they? I think Edmund and Frederick would be proud.'

'And it was good of Shona Simmonds to give me that cover quote,' Rory continued. 'I mean, her quotes are like gold dust... it means a lot that she liked it enough to quote for it.'

'Probably wanted to hitch her wagon to a rising star,' Leo said lightly. 'She's not daft, you know.'

Rory laughed. 'Well, whatever it was, I still can't believe her name's on the same cover as mine!'

'Another reason to be proud,' Leo said, nuzzling

her neck. She felt herself starting to turn to jelly, as she always did when he touched her.

'And are you proud?' Rory murmured, turning to face him.

'Always,' Leo replied, kissing her. 'Congratulations, Rory Dean, romance writer.'

At that moment, his phone pinged.

'Sorry,' he said, extricating himself from her arms. 'That's the new booking alert. I'd better check it and see when they're arriving.' He kissed her again. 'Will I see you later?'

Rory smiled. 'Yes, absolutely.'

As Leo hurried out of the gatehouse and back to Roseford Villas, Rory watched his progress down the driveway fondly. In the year since that evening at the chalet, they'd grown closer, and while Leo had been very busy with the B&B, and Rory had been working all hours at school, or on her novel, they'd found time to get to know each other again. Rory was still living at the gatehouse, as it suited her to have the headspace of living alone while she was writing, but eventually she and Leo were hoping to take the next step and move in together. Tonight, they'd celebrate the arrival of her new book, and then she'd put the finishing touches on the next novel, which she'd been contracted to write soon after a publisher had accepted the first. While she wouldn't be drawing on her own romantic life for the next book, she was definitely looking forward to starting a brand-new chapter for real.

As she held the novel in her hands, she carefully opened the cover, and read the dedication. She'd agonised more over the wording of that short sentence than any other part of the novel. But in the end, the words had come to her. Smiling, she traced a finger over the words, murmuring them to herself. 'For Edmund and Frederick, who provided much of the inspiration, and Leo, whom I hope will go on to provide even more.'

She hoped Edmund and Frederick would have been pleased with her efforts. Their story hadn't had a happy ending, but there had been happiness in their lives before they'd been parted. The exhibition at Roseford Hall had opened a few months back, and Rory and Stella had been delighted to have been publicly credited with the discovery. The letters and photographs they'd found had pride of place, and had been carefully enlarged to form a central part of the exhibition. Something about the heartbreakingly happy faces of Edmund and Frederick, looking carefree and in love, still made Rory's throat ache, even though she'd looked at the photo a hundred times since she'd found it. The contrast with Edmund's portrait in the Long Gallery was poignant, but in a way it completed his story.

For herself and Leo, the recent months together in Roseford had been a wonderful beginning. After a twenty-year pause, they were discovering each other again, and it had been a year that neither would ever forget. As she held the book in her hands that had been the inspiration for her to come to Roseford, Rory smiled. The past had brought her and Leo back together, and the future would be their happily ever after.

ACKNOWLEDGEMENTS

As ever, I'm so grateful to my wonderful editor Sarah Ritherdon and the endlessly enthusiastic and committed team at Boldwood, and especially Alice Moore, who has made this whole series look so wonderful with her beautiful covers. Bringing these stories to readers is such a thrill, and one I couldn't do without their help, support and vision. In addition, many, many thanks to my agent Sara Keane for her help and assistance over the years. More thanks go to Harriett Hare, audio narrator extraordinaire, who brings such life to my stories. Further thanks to Cecily Blench and Sandra Ferguson for eagle eyes and gentle suggestions to make things even better.

Thanks, also, to Nick, Flora and Roseanna, who endure having a writer in the house with good grace and humour, and to the other family and friends who put up with my creative tunnel vision at times. I couldn't do this without you, and I appreciate every last one of you. A special shout out this time to Backwell School English Department, who have seen more of me of late than usual, and still managed to cope with me when I'm in the depths of writing a novel as well as teaching teenagers. You're the very best at what you do, and it's an honour to work with you – you truly are the 'workfam'!

ABOUT THE AUTHOR

Fay Keenan is the author of the bestselling *Little Somerby* series of novels. She has led writing workshops with Bristol University and has been a visiting speaker in schools. She is a full-time teacher and lives in Somerset.

Sign up to Fay Keenan's mailing list for news, competitions and updates on future books.

Visit Fay's website: https://faykeenan.com/

Follow Fay on social media here:

x.com/faykeenan

instagram.com/faykeenanauthor

bookbub.com/authors/fay-keenan

facebook.com/faykeenanauthor

ALSO BY FAY KEENAN

Willowbury Series

A Place to Call Home

Snowflakes Over Bay Tree Terrace

Just for the Summer

Roseford Series

New Beginnings at Roseford Hall

Winter Kisses at Roseford Café

Finding Love at Roseford Blooms

Winter Wishes at Roseford Reloved

Coming Home to Roseford Villas

LOVE NOTES

LOVE IN EVERY CHAPTER

WHERE ALL YOUR ROMANCE
DREAMS COME TRUE!

THE HOME OF BESTSELLING
ROMANCE AND WOMEN'S
FICTION

WARNING:
MAY CONTAIN SPICE

SIGN UP TO OUR
NEWSLETTER

https://bit.ly/Lovenotesnews

Boldwood

Boldwood Books is an award-winning fiction publishing company seeking out the best stories from around the world.

Find out more at www.boldwoodbooks.com

Join our reader community for brilliant books, competitions and offers!

Follow us
@BoldwoodBooks
@TheBoldBookClub

Sign up to our weekly deals newsletter

https://bit.ly/BoldwoodBNewsletter